## "Would you like to dance?"

Ace hesitated for a moment, then placed her hand in Shane's. "I'd love to."

They moved to the center of the room, the world around them fading as they swayed to the music.

Shane's hand rested on Ace's waist, sending a shiver down his spine. They moved in perfect sync, the tension between them palpable.

"You know," Ace said softly, looking up at him, "it's nice to see you outside of the hotel for a change."

"Yeah," Shane agreed, his voice barely above a whisper. "It's nice to just enjoy the moment."

As they danced, Shane's thoughts raced. He couldn't deny the attraction he felt for Ace, the way she made him feel alive and grounded at the same time. But he also knew that this wasn't the right time for romance. His focus had to be the hotel.

Yet with Ace in his arms, Shane wanted to hold on to this feeling. It was intoxicating, and he found himself getting lost in her eyes...

Dear Reader,

I'm excited to share Shane Worthington and Alison "Ace" Martin's journey in *His Carolina Redemption*, a romance that blends some of my favorite tropes—opposites attract, homecoming, enemies to lovers and workplace romance—all set on a beautiful island off the coast of South Carolina.

After his father's death, Shane returns to Polk Island, torn over whether to sell the family's beloved Polk Island Hotel. This forces him to confront old wounds. Ace, the head of security, fiercely guards both her career and her heart. Though she dreams of motherhood, her painful past has made her wary of marriage.

Working together ignites tension as they clash over the hotel's future—Shane sees it as a burden, while Ace is determined to save it in honor of his father. As they face professional conflicts, a mystery involving a stolen heirloom and suspicious employees tests Ace's skills and breaks through Shane's emotional walls.

At its core, *His Carolina Redemption* is a story of second chances—for love and for preserving a legacy. I hope you enjoy following Shane and Ace as they heal old scars and discover an unexpected love.

Warmly,

*Jacquelin Thomas*

# HIS CAROLINA REDEMPTION

## JACQUELIN THOMAS

HEARTWARMING

**Harlequin®**
**HEARTWARMING™**

ISBN-13: 978-1-335-05159-2

His Carolina Redemption

Recycling programs for this product may not exist in your area.

Harlequin Enterprises ULC
22 Adelaide St. West, 41st Floor
Toronto, Ontario M5H 4E3, Canada
www.Harlequin.com

**Printed in U.S.A.**

**Jacquelin Thomas** is an award-winning, bestselling author with more than fifty-five books in print. When not writing, she is busy catching up on her reading, attending sporting events and spoiling her grandchildren. Jacquelin and her family live in North Carolina.

### Books by Jacquelin Thomas

### Harlequin Heartwarming

#### *Polk Island*

*A Family for the Firefighter*
*Her Hometown Hero*
*Her Marine Hero*
*His Partnership Proposal*
*Twins for the Holidays*

### Love Inspired Suspense

*Sorority Cold Case*

### Love Inspired Cold Case

*Evidence Uncovered*
*Cold Case Deceit*

### Love Inspired The Protectors

*Vigilante Justice*

Visit the Author Profile page
at Harlequin.com for more titles.

To my beloved daughter Lauren, and my son, Jonathan—
your unwavering support and love inspire me every day.
And to my late daughter, Bevin—your memory shines
brightly in my heart and in everything I create.
This book is for all of you, with all my love.

# CHAPTER ONE

THE SHARP CRY of seagulls pierced the air as Shane Worthington's shoes touched the rough boards of Polk Island's old dock. As he did, six years' worth of absence dissipated like the morning fog. Each step was a reluctant reunion with the past, echoing through the silent whispers of what once was. The salty breeze danced around him, a familiar embrace carrying fragments of lost memories from childhood. He watched as common loons took nosedives into the ocean, then soared upward as if it was a game.

As his father's death called him back to this place of beauty, with its crystal-blue waters and sun-kissed shores, Shane found himself standing on the precipice of his past, caught between duty and the desire to escape once again. He clenched his jaw, steeling himself for what was to come.

As he gazed at the distant grandeur of the Polk Island Hotel, Shane thought he could almost hear his father's voice floating on the wind, reminding him of his promise.

Memories flooded his mind—the thrill of exploring every nook and cranny of the hotel growing up, family dinners filled with laughter and love. But a bitter truth tainted those memories—his father's infidelity had shattered his idyllic world, prompting him to leave the island and home he loved so much.

Despite being thrilled to be back in the familiar comfort of home, Shane wasn't quite ready to face anyone…or the task waiting for him. He needed a moment to clear his mind and collect himself. That was why he'd asked the taxi driver to drop him off at North Beach, a place that always brought him a sense of peace and serenity.

"I knew I'd find you here."

With a small smile, Shane turned to face his mother.

Madelyn Worthington's vibrant brown eyes were dull with grief. Her hair, once long and flowing, was cropped into a short style that framed her face in soft curls. His gaze strayed to the silver-gray strands in the front. They weren't there when his parents had visited him in Los Angeles two years ago.

Against the backdrop of the bright May sunshine, Madelyn stood out in her simple black linen dress with elbow-length sleeves, an appropriate choice for the season and the occasion.

Shane stepped into her welcoming arms, feeling the weight of her sorrow and his own guilt.

"I'm so sorry, Mom," he murmured, his voice thick with emotion. "I should've come sooner." But he couldn't bear to see his father's life slipping away before his eyes. So instead of returning while his dad was sick, he'd stayed away until the funeral, which brought him home now.

Madelyn held him tightly, her hand gently smoothing over his back to comfort him, though her eyes revealed the sadness that lingered between them. "You're here now, son, that's what matters."

Shane nodded, but regret washed over him once again. He knew deep down that he should have come back home sooner, but the memory of catching his father with another woman still caused him pain and feelings of betrayal. It was the final straw that had driven him to accept a job offer with the Alexander-DePaul Hotel chain—he'd run away from his feelings and the man he used to admire. Now, with his father gone, it was Shane's duty to take over running the family hotel. Despite his conflicted feelings around his father, he didn't want to let Angus Jr. down. He didn't want to let any of his family down…but he didn't know how he could live up to expectations with what he'd learned recently about the state of the hotel.

Madelyn leaned back, her hands tightly gripping his shoulders as she searched his face. "Shane, listen to me," she said, her voice firm. "Everyone is gathering at the hotel. We'll attend this dinner for friends, family and staff, then go home and grieve in private. But for now, we must show strength to the world."

"Dad used to say that all the time," Shane remarked.

She smiled faintly. "And where do you think he got it from?"

He chuckled.

Arm in arm, they made their way toward the hotel courtesy car.

"How are you really holding up?" Shane asked with concern when they were inside the vehicle.

"I feel numb," Madelyn admitted while backing out of the parking space. "Losing my husband… the love of my life… Son, I can't lie. It's hard to process. I'm sad and angry, but also relieved. Your dad was in so much pain. It broke my heart every time he groaned… He's not suffering anymore, but I'm going to miss him so much." She gave a sad shake of her head. "That man was so good to me."

Shane was torn between honoring his mother's unwavering loyalty toward his father and the resentment he still felt over his father's affair. Madelyn never liked secrets—a fact that made him want to reveal the truth—yet a part of him couldn't bear to hurt his mother. It was hard to look Madelyn in the eye, knowing he was keeping something of this magnitude from her.

She merged onto Main Street, the grand presence of the Polk Island Hotel growing larger with every mile.

The hotel's exterior was a sight to behold; its white columns and wraparound porch exuded Southern charm and grace. Inside, he'd find intricate tapestries and antique furniture passed down through the generations, including a gallery displaying artwork and artifacts collected throughout the hotel's history.

Madelyn parked the car, and they got out. As they approached the hotel, a tidal wave of feelings overcame him—regrets, sadness, but also joy. He opened the door for his mother and stepped in after her.

In the breathtaking lobby, gold accents and plush furnishings spoke of elegance, while the large windows allowed natural light to flood in, showcasing the photographs that lined the walls, which captured special moments from the hotel's past and his family's history. A sweeping staircase led up to the second floor, where the banquet rooms were located.

On his way to the second floor, Shane was met with familiar faces. Mrs. Higgins, the head of housekeeping known for her stern attitude, and Mr. Patel, the cheerful chef at their renowned restaurant North Winds. His older brother, Kenyon, was the executive chef of the seafood-focused sister restaurant, South Winds.

The housekeeper took his left hand in her own. "I'm sorry for your loss. I was so happy when your mother told me you were coming home."

Shane gave the woman a small smile. "Thank you for your kind words, Mrs. Higgins."

"I surely hope you're back home to stay." She pushed away a gray strand of hair from her face. "We need you."

Before he could respond, Raj Patel interjected, "Shane, it is so good to see you. We are all so very sad that your father is no longer here. We will miss him greatly. He was a good man."

Shane nodded stiffly, then quickened his pace to catch up with his mother.

Several of their relatives had already arrived. Madelyn had informed him that his brother Aiden wouldn't arrive until tomorrow.

He was most looking forward to seeing his siblings. Shane strode into the Willow Ballroom, found family members seated near the front of the room and joined them.

"The prodigal son has finally returned," Kenyon exclaimed. "I keep telling you that home is where you belong, bro."

Shane's sister London, who was five years younger and a middle child like Aiden, said, "You missed so much while you were gone."

He looked down at her growing belly momentarily, then replied, "I can see that now." Since when was London pregnant?

She stood up, hugged him tightly and said, "I'm glad you're home. Especially now." Lowering her voice, she added, "I asked them not to say anything to you. I wanted to be the one to tell you about the baby… It's taken me a minute to process the fact that I'm going to be somebody's mother."

Shane had questions, but now wasn't the time to seek answers. He and his sister would have their moment. His youngest sister, Cia, joined London's embrace. "I missed you, too," she said.

He then offered his hand to his youngest brother, Micah, in a silent greeting before settling down beside him.

As Shane's eyes moved around the room, he took in all the guests who had come to offer support during this difficult period for his family.

His gaze settled on the woman having a conversation with his mother.

She was wearing black trousers and a matching blazer with the hotel's logo displayed prominently on the left side. He knew most of the hotel staff—so many of them had been working here for decades. But he didn't recognize her. Her hair, a blend of warm caramel and honey hues, was styled into thin, intricate braids that were carefully arranged into a neat bun at the nape of her neck, revealing the graceful curve of her jawline and the elegant slope of her shoulders. The ombré effect of her hair added depth and dimension, making it seem as if strands of gold were woven throughout. Her posture was confident, and her sharp eyes seemed to be scanning the room intently.

"Who's that woman with Mom?" he asked no one in particular.

"That's Alison Martin, the head of security," Micah answered. "She prefers to be called Ace."

"She's the head of security *here at the hotel*?"

"Why do you sound so surprised?" London asked. "Ace used to be a police officer. She also teaches self-defense classes to women at a YMCA in Charleston."

Holding his hands up, Shane said, "I didn't mean anything by it. I was just wondering what happened to George."

Kenyon took a sip of water. "He retired about five years ago, I think."

Ace met his gaze, and Shane felt a sudden surge of connection that cut through the heaviness of his grief. She was beautiful—stunning, even.

She gave him a silent nod before returning her attention to Madelyn. All of her movements seemed so self-assured, causing Shane to question whether it was her confidence or her attractiveness that had influenced his father's decision to hire her.

He averted his gaze… He'd been staring. That wouldn't do. Shane had learned early on not to mix work with pleasure. He'd seen colleagues destroy their own career potential by allowing emotions to cloud their judgment, leading to messy relationships and strained team dynamics. He'd worked tirelessly to establish a strong reputation within the Alexander-DePaul Hotel chain and refused to jeopardize it for personal attachments. He valued professionalism and clear boundaries—getting involved romantically, especially at work, only complicated things, and he couldn't afford that risk.

He was here to help his family organize a funeral, then see to the business of running the hotel. Both tasks weighed on him, overwhelmed him. As much as he wanted to be home, he couldn't help but wonder when he could leave again.

ACE MARTIN STOOD at her post by the ballroom entrance keeping a sharp and vigilant watch on the incoming guests and relatives of the Worthington family. It was her duty to ensure safety and order even under these sad circumstances, a responsibility she took with utmost seriousness.

She was filled with a sense of unease today. The hotel had been abuzz with rumors since the passing of Angus Elijah Worthington Jr., and now that his estranged son had returned to take over, they worried about this shift in leadership and what it meant for the hotel. Although Ace knew this is what Angus Jr. wanted—had even asked Ace to support Shane before he'd passed—she still felt conflicted about Shane's presence. But she needed to put that aside and remain compassionate and professional.

She smiled as Leon Rothchild and his wife, Misty, approached, their arms linked.

"Hey, you two!" Ace exclaimed with genuine

warmth. She and Misty shared a hug, while Leon shook hands with her. Leon and Misty Rothchild were close friends, and Ace had grown fond of their three children, often spending time with them as if they were family.

"How's everyone holding up?" he asked. "I can hardly believe Mr. Angus is gone."

She couldn't believe it, either. Her boss had been a mentor for her since he'd hired her on at the hotel. "As well as can be expected," she replied. "Madelyn has been incredibly strong through this difficult and heartbreaking time."

Leon's nod showed that he understood all too well—after all, he had been a widower before meeting Misty. He could empathize with the pain Madelyn was going through.

The Rothchild family—whose ancestors, like the Worthingtons', were among the first settlers on the island—grew in number, their heritage deeply rooted in Polk Island's history. As descendants of Polk Rothchild, the island's first settler and namesake, their presence carried both history and influence. Leon's brother Trey and his wife, Gia, walked hand in hand toward the exclusive dining room, his cane tapping rhythmically against the hardwood floor. Rusty and Eleanor, Trey and Leon's aunt and uncle, arrived shortly after, their cheerful conversation echoing through the room, bringing with them an unmistakable vitality. Each family member, in their own way, reflected the enduring spirit of their ancestor, shaping the island's future while honoring its past.

Numerous Worthington family members arrived, including Louella Jameson, a cousin who lived on that island, and her fiancé, Noah. They were escorted over to Madelyn to pay their respects. While many had ties to the island, it was Louella's father who shared a particularly deep connection to its rich history, their roots entwined in its tapestry.

Ace welcomed each person warmly, taking care to acknowledge them individually. All the while, she kept tabs on Shane Worthington as he made his way about the room. He was handsome, she'd give him that. But how would he oversee things in his father's stead? On the one hand, she wondered what changes he would bring to the hotel. But on the other hand, she couldn't shake off her suspicions about his intentions—especially given his connection to the Alexander-DePaul hotel chain in Beverly Hills. Malcolm Alexander, the CEO, had a well-known reputation for buying boutique hotels and converting them into luxury spa resorts.

Was Shane planning to sell the hotel? The thought gnawed at her. After all, he'd been absent from Polk Island for so long, and now the control of his father's legacy rested in his hands. Ace could only hope that her late employer had known what he was doing when he left Shane in charge.

The Willow Ballroom doors swung open with a

soft creak, drawing Ace's attention. She straight-ened imperceptibly, focusing on the lone figure dressed in black jeans and a crisp black and white shirt.

He glanced at her, smiling. "Hi. I'm here to pay my respects and support my family."

She nodded, still unable to place him. "You are…?"

"Oliver," he responded smoothly. "Oliver Worthington."

She relaxed her stance when Madelyn stood up and gestured for him to join her.

Ace turned her attention back to Shane. He was taller than she had imagined, his posture exuding a quiet strength. From head to toe, his appearance was polished, and his dark brown eyes seemed to hold a world of secrets. Not only was he handsome, but he also seemed to command attention without uttering a word, his expression guarded yet betray-ing a hint of vulnerability.

A fleeting moment of attraction sent a shiver down Ace's spine when their eyes met briefly. In that instant, she saw something in Shane's gaze—a weight of responsibility, a burden of unresolved emotions that mirrored her own struggles. But she quickly pushed aside the feeling, knowing better than to let her guard down.

Ace had learned hard lessons about trust and vulnerability years ago, lessons forged in the pain of her first marriage, which ended in a traumatic divorce. That chapter of her life had left deep scars, making her wary of relationships, especially in the wake of what came next. After being shot in the line of duty as a police officer, her world had shifted once again when doctors diagnosed her with polycystic ovary syndrome. The news had hit her harder than the bullet ever could have. She was told that if she wanted to become a mother, she should act sooner rather than later. The decision hung over her, just as Shane's next choices seemed to weigh on him.

Shane suddenly got up from the table and walked toward Raj Patel with purposeful strides. They talked briefly before Raj headed back to the kitchen and Shane returned to his seat.

With a heavy sigh, Ace returned her focus to her duties, her mind buzzing with unanswered questions and the unsettling presence of Shane Worthington lingering in the air. As a former member of law enforcement and now the head of security, Ace was accustomed to facing threats head-on. But the greatest danger may be the unexpected arrival of this man, who would now hold her professional fate in his hands.

STEPPING OUT ONTO the hotel's grand balcony, Shane immersed himself in the cool night air, a soothing balm for his turbulent thoughts. The rhythmic crash of waves against the shore failed to silence the storm raging within him.

Shane had felt a mix of pride and nostalgia as

he'd wandered through the property earlier, mingling with relatives and hotel staff. The hotel had been his family's legacy for generations. His three times great-grandfather, Asa Worthington, had arrived on the island in 1872 at the insistence of brothers Polk and Hoss Rothchild. A skilled carpenter, he'd built a small house for his family. Quickly noting that there were just a few houses that rented rooms to people needing a place to stay, Asa decided the island needed a hotel. By 1880, he had expanded his house to include twenty rooms and a large dining area.

In 1893, the island was hit by a fierce tropical cyclone that caused damage to the hotel. Asa made the decision to not only repair, but also expand the property upward four levels. He died in 1910. Under the management of his daughter Agnes and her younger brother, Joshua, the hotel continued to grow and prosper. Joshua oversaw the addition of twenty more guest rooms, bringing the total number to forty, and added a large ballroom.

Following Joshua's death in 1940, the property was passed down to his son, Angus Elijah Worthington, Sr. Shane's grandfather. He took over as the owner and manager until his own passing in 1975. During his time at the helm, the hotel underwent a significant expansion that included the addition of a swimming pool, gallery space, and twenty new guest rooms, five of which were luxurious suites. He also oversaw the renovation of the second-floor ballroom, divided it into two smaller rooms and a storage area, while retaining a large portion as the Grand Ballroom.

Yet today, the hotel faced financial ruin. That was a fact his father had shared only with Shane. The last time the hotel saw a decline in guests was due to World War II. However, the hotel served as temporary housing for military personnel. Postwar, tourism boomed once more.

Through hard times, the hotel had always managed to survive. And now, under Shane's leadership, it might not. He'd studied all the numbers and discovered that the best way to save it was to sell it.

Lost in his contemplations, Shane was startled by someone's approach. Ace stood beside him, her perfume mingling with the salty breeze.

"Hi, I'm Ace, the head of security for the hotel," she introduced herself formally, her voice carrying genuine concern. "Rough evening?" Her eyes reflected compassion.

His smile was strained as he nodded, trying to hide the turmoil within. "You could say that. I'm Shane, by the way."

Ace's expression darkened in understanding. "I can only imagine how difficult this must be for you and your family. My team and I will be close by in case any of you need assistance getting away from here."

Feeling torn between gratitude for Ace's support and frustration at his family's situation, Shane struggled to find the right words. "Thank you, Ace."

Standing together, they gazed out at the vast ocean under the moonlight, each apparently lost in their own thoughts. Laughter and chatter from inside blended with the gentle melody of the waves, creating serenity.

Shane confessed, "The weight of the past collides with uncertainty about the future in moments like these." He gazed at the distant horizon, as if he could find answers in the fading light.

For so long, Shane had kept his emotions locked away, hidden beneath the surface. But in this quiet moment, in kind Ace's understanding, he found himself lowering the walls he'd built, allowing a sliver of vulnerability to show.

Ace turned to him, her gaze a blend of compassion and insight. "Sometimes we're torn between honoring our roots and embracing what lies ahead."

Shane nodded in agreement. "Exactly. I want to honor my family legacy but I question the sacrifices required."

"It's never an easy choice," she responded. "Angus Jr. said he trusted that you would do what's best for this hotel. I choose to believe him…" After a brief pause, she added, "I'd better get back inside."

"When my mother asks, let her know that I'll be inside shortly." He knew that Madelyn sent Ace to check on him.

"Will do," she responded. And then she disappeared through the door.

STEPPING BACK INTO the embrace of the Willow Ballroom, Ace savored the welcoming chill of air-conditioning, a sweet surrender from the oppressive heat outside. Soft laughter and lively banter floated around her, contrasting sharply with Shane's melancholy, which she'd left on the balcony. His sorrow over his father's passing seemed as thick as a dense fog.

Now, with the sounds of joy enveloping her, Ace couldn't shake the impression Shane had left behind. He was different from what she had initially thought. Instead of the cold, detached figure she'd anticipated, he'd revealed a vulnerability that surprised her. In their brief conversation, Shane had peeled back layers of his stoic exterior, exposing a rawness that she hadn't expected.

Ace considered his words, reflecting on all he carried. This was a man wrestling with his emotions, not just someone focused on profits and legacy. She had assumed he would be self-absorbed, caught up in the pressures of his position and indifferent to the people around him. But instead, she found a kindred spirit grappling with loss and longing—a man who felt deeply, even if he struggled to show it.

Ace couldn't help but feel a flicker of empathy for him. Perhaps there was more to Shane than met the eye. In that brief exchange on the balcony, she'd glimpsed a man searching for connection amid his burdens, and it made her reconsider everything she thought she knew about him.

She treaded toward the quieter end of the ballroom to clear her head over a fresh glass of water. Her gaze traveled the room, landing on Trey and Gia, then Leon and Misty. They all looked happy and in love.

Her ex-husband's ruthlessness was etched deeply in her mind, punctuating her ability to trust anew. Instead of the cozy family gatherings and baby giggles she had once dreamed for herself, images of a tormenting past filled her years.

Leaning against the balustrade, Ace took a glass of water from a nearby server, feeling suddenly parched.

"Thank you for checking on my son." Madelyn's voice broke through her reverie.

"He knew that you'd sent me," she responded.

"Shane has always been perceptive," Madelyn replied. "He has a way of seeing through things."

Ace nodded, and after a short conversation with Madelyn, she took her leave for the evening. Her obligations here satisfactorily fulfilled, she had somewhere else to be, another concern to take care of. The party would continue for another couple of hours, and Ace would leave things in the capable hands of her team. Leaving the painful memories entwined in the cobwebs right where they belonged, she stepped out of the ballroom and exited the hotel.

# CHAPTER TWO

SHANE WAS FILLED with joy as he reunited with his siblings once again when he returned to the ballroom after getting some air. He found them all gathered around the same table.

Kenyon sat on his right while Micah occupied the seat on his left. Cia sat directly across from him. Meanwhile, Trey and Gia were engaged in conversation with London. The familiar bond and companionship brought back a sense of warmth and belonging that Shane had greatly missed during his time away.

Kenyon approached him. "Hey, Shane. I wanted to talk to you about something."

Shane tilted his head, waiting. "Sure. What's up?"

Kenyon hesitated, looking down at his hands. "I think…you should be the one to speak for the family at the funeral."

Shane's brows furrowed. "Me? Kenyon, you're the oldest. It should be you up there."

Kenyon let out a small laugh, shaking his head. "Look, you know I'm not one for public speaking.

Never have been. I'm not sure I could get through it without…getting overly emotional." He paused, giving Shane a knowing look. "I've always liked staying out of the spotlight."

"But—"

"I shine in the kitchen, Shane. That's where I'm comfortable, where I know I belong." Kenyon shrugged, gesturing around as if to emphasize the busy, bustling world outside the kitchen that wasn't for him. "Public speaking? That was never my thing. And honestly, it was never Dad's thing either, but he learned to thrive in it because he had to."

Shane's expression softened as he listened, filled with understanding.

Kenyon laid a hand on his shoulder. "You're the one most like Dad in that way. You're good in front of people…it's like you feed off it. You've got his presence—the kind that fills a room and makes people feel something. I think… I think he'd want you to speak for us."

After a long pause, Shane nodded slowly, accepting the responsibility. "All right. I'll do it if the rest of the family agrees." He gripped his brother's shoulder. "But just know, if I have to get up there, having you beside me, even if you don't say a word, would mean a lot."

Kenyon's smile softened, a hint of relief in his eyes. "You got it. I'll be right there." His gaze traveled toward the entrance. "Look who just arrived..." His voice dripped with disdain.

Shane quickly glanced over his shoulder, his eyes narrowing as he spotted his cousin. "What is he doing here?"

Micah gritted out, "I'd like to know that, too."

London sat down at the table, her expression becoming somber. "Why is Oliver here? After everything he's done, I never thought he'd show his face again on the island."

Shane was taken aback by his cousin's boldness in coming here. Oliver had caused pain and betrayal to their family over the years. There was the incident where he attempted to sue Angus Jr., accusing him of withholding profits as a shareholder. Then, there was the time he claimed to have found their grandfather's original will, which supposedly stated that the hotel should have gone to Oliver instead. Although it proved to be a forgery, these actions created a divide that still lingered.

Madelyn escorted Oliver to their table, and the atmosphere shifted with tension. The siblings exchanged uneasy looks, each likely wondering why he'd suddenly returned out of nowhere. They braced themselves for the impending confrontation, each of them holding their breath, waiting to see what Oliver had to say. The bitterness between Shane and his cousin was unmistakable as they stared each other down.

"Hey, fam..." Oliver greeted.

Silence.

"Tonight, we are a family," Madelyn stated. "Let's act like it. Oliver is here to show support."

"I doubt that," London uttered. "More like he came here looking to start trouble as usual."

"I'll have none of that," her mother cautioned in a tone that brooked no argument. "We are Worthingtons. That name means something—has meant something for generations—and we will not allow it to be tarnished. Have I made myself clear?"

Shane assessed Oliver, who responded, "I hear you, Aunt Maddie. Despite everything that's happened, I loved my uncle. I looked up to him. I have to say that I'm really going to miss him."

"Why didn't you bring Aunt Alice with you?" Micah asked.

Madelyn sent a sharp glare in his direction before saying, "Alice and I spoke earlier. She's not feeling well, but she wanted to be here with us. I told her to stay home and recuperate. She had a mini stroke a week ago," she stated. "Oliver, take this seat right here. You'll sit beside me."

He sat down, a smug expression on his face. "So, Shane…what's it like working with the great Malcolm Alexander?"

Clenching his jaw, he eyed Oliver while trying to contain the anger simmering within him. "Malcolm's a seasoned businessman. I've learned a lot from him."

Oliver flashed a self-satisfied grin, clearly enjoying Shane's discomfort. "I bet you've become quite the city slicker, rubbing elbows with fancy hotel magnates in Los Angeles. Must be a far cry from this little island life, huh?"

Shane shifted the conversation. "Let's just focus on why we're here tonight. To honor my father and support each other in this difficult time. This is the reason why you came, right? Although I don't believe it."

Madelyn interjected, her voice firm. "This is the last time I'm going to say this. We're *family*, and family stands together."

She glanced pointedly at Shane, and then Oliver, who seemed to bristle at her words, but wisely he held his tongue.

As the evening wore on, Shane observed Oliver closely, trying to decipher his true motives for being present at the family gathering. His complexion, the color of milk chocolate, contrasted with his dark hair, which lay in subtle waves atop his head. His face was clean-shaven, and his sharp features gave him an air of quiet intensity.

When the time came to raise a toast to his father's memory, Shane noticed his cousin's hand tightening around his glass, a shadow of a smirk playing on his lips, barely noticeable to anyone but Shane. It was in that moment that he knew without a doubt that Oliver's intentions were far from benign.

ACE FOUND SOLACE in the short drive from Polk Island to Charleston. The day's work had been long and taxing, filled with the usual security details and ensuring the Worthington family's privacy during this difficult time.

As she'd left the family gathering, the sunset cast a warm, golden hue across the hotel's manicured lawns and flower beds, a stark contrast to the turmoil in Ace's heart. The sun dipped lower, painting the sky with streaks of pink and orange as she crossed the bridge from the island to the mainland. Ace parked in her usual spot outside the YMCA.

Charleston was a charming place, with its historic buildings and cobblestone streets. The vibrancy of the city was a perfect backdrop for Ace's dual life. By day, she was the head of security; by evening, she transformed into a mentor and protector, teaching women how to defend themselves.

Ace headed inside, the familiar scent of the gym—a mix of sweat, rubber mats, and cleaning supplies—filling her senses. The cheerful buzz of voices was a welcome contrast to the somber atmosphere she'd left behind.

The reception staff greeted her warmly as she made her way to the locker room.

Inside, Ace quickly changed into her workout gear: black leggings, a fitted tank top, and sturdy athletic shoes. She pulled her long braids into a high ponytail, the ombré strands swaying as she moved.

A glance in the mirror revealed her determined expression, her medium brown eyes reflecting the strength and resilience that had defined her life.

As she entered the gym, the clatter of weights and the rhythmic thudding of feet on treadmills created a symphony of activity. The self-defense class was held in a large studio room with mirrored walls and padded floors.

A group of women had already gathered and were chatting animatedly and stretching in preparation for tonight's class.

"Good evening, everyone," Ace called out, her voice strong and steady. "Let's get started."

The women formed a circle around her, and Ace began the class with warm-up exercises, guiding them through a series of stretches and aerobic movements to get their blood pumping.

As they moved, she shared advice and encouragement, her voice steady to keep them focused. "Remember, self-defense isn't just about physical strength," Ace said, her tone firm but encouraging. "It's about awareness, confidence, and using your mind as much as your body."

She demonstrated various techniques, from basic stances to more advanced maneuvers, breaking down each movement with precision and clarity.

The women followed her lead, their eyes glued to her every move. Ace corrected their form gently but firmly, offering tips and adjustments to ensure they could perform the techniques effectively.

As the class progressed, the room filled with the sound of focused effort—heavy breathing, the pounding of feet on mats, and the occasional grunt of exertion. However, despite the peaceful atmosphere, Ace couldn't shake off the lingering fear and trauma from childhood abuse—emotional abuse in her marriage, being ambushed and shot during a routine wellness check. She pushed through it, however, determined not to let it affect her ability to help these women find strength and empowerment in themselves.

Ace moved among her students, offering personalized guidance and encouragement. She loved seeing the transformation in these women, watching their confidence grow with each session.

During a break, one of the women approached her, a hesitant smile on her face. "Ace, I just wanted to thank you. I've been taking this class for a few weeks now, and it's made such a difference in my life. I feel so much more confident and capable."

Ace smiled warmly, placing a reassuring hand on the woman's shoulder. "That's what this is all about. Empowering ourselves and each other. You're doing great. Keep it up."

The class ended with a cool-down session, as Ace led her students through gentle stretches and breathing exercises to relax their muscles and calm their minds. Then the class wrapped up and the women slowly left the gym.

Alone in the studio, Ace took a moment to

breathe deeply, the satisfaction of a job well done filling her heart. She looked at her reflection in the mirror, seeing not just the strong, capable woman she had become, but also the scared girl she once was—the girl who had vowed never to be a victim again.

Growing up in a home filled with abuse, she had been physically attacked by her stepfather while trying to protect her mother, an experience that left deep scars but also ignited a fierce determination within her. It was one of the reasons she'd became a police officer—to reclaim her power and protect others from the kind of suffering she had endured growing up.

Ace, having served on the force for five years, had been shot while conducting a welfare check on a woman who had been physically assaulted by her boyfriend. She'd been ready to leave behind that life, the role of protector, when Angus Jr., an acquaintance of her ex-husband, offered her a second chance. He said he'd seen her strength, resilience, and unwavering sense of justice—qualities that mirrored his own values. He believed she deserved a fresh start and trusted her to lead his security team at the hotel, knowing she had the grit and integrity to protect what mattered most. She'd tried every day on the job to be worthy of that fresh start. After losing her husband and experiencing a career change, the hotel had become like a home to her, and the staff was like a family.

The drive back to Polk Island was quiet. Ace's thoughts drifted to Shane Worthington. She needed to suppress the attraction that his presence stirred within her, to remind herself of the pain and heartache she'd endured in the past.

She pulled into her driveway thirty minutes later and stepped out of the car, feeling both grateful for her strength and accomplishments, but also vulnerable and victimized by her past. Ace looked forward to taking a relaxing bath and trying to find some peace before facing whatever challenges tomorrow would bring.

OLIVER WORTHINGTON WAS FILLED with nostalgia as he scanned the opulent Willow Ballroom, remembering the times he'd come here as a child. But at the same time, his chest tightened since he knew that the reason for this trip was not a happy reunion.

He could sense the tension radiating off his cousins, who had always held a grudge against him. Despite the animosity that existed between their fathers, Jacob and Angus Jr., the family had come together to support Oliver and his mother when his father died. He'd do the same for his cousins now. However, there was another reason why he had returned to the island—to claim what was rightfully his. The Polk Island Hotel was a part of his inheritance and seeing his cousin Shane, who'd left to work for a competitor, sitting at the table only fueled Oliver's frustration.

His eyes were drawn to the ornate chandelier above, its crystal droplets casting rainbows on the walls.

Their grandfather, Angus Sr., had seen a similar one in the home of a doctor in Charleston. Elijah had searched until he found the one hanging above, massive but elegant. The family story, passed down like an heirloom, resonated with Oliver. It was his turn now to uphold that legacy, perhaps even to add his own mark to it.

He glanced upward to the chandelier once more. Each crystal refracted light in a way that seemed almost alive, echoing the resilience of the Worthington name and the duty to preserve the island's heritage. To Oliver, the chandelier was more than just a fixture; it was a reminder of the family's commitment to the past and its promise for the future. Standing beneath it, he felt the depth of that promise, a responsibility he couldn't ignore, even after so many years away.

During the meal, Oliver's mind wandered back to the childhood memories shared with Shane and his other cousins. They'd once gotten along well, playing together for hours on end. They used to sneak into the hotel's Grand Ballroom after hours, imagining themselves as royalty dancing under the shimmering lights. But those carefree days had long passed, replaced by bitter rivalries and unresolved conflicts.

The tension in the room thickened with every passing moment, suffocating Oliver as he grappled with conflicting emotions. The memories of their shared past tugged at his heartstrings, and he yearned for the simplicity of childhood camaraderie. However, the stark reality of his strained relationship with his cousins loomed, casting a shadow over any semblance of true reconciliation.

Oliver wasn't here for reconciliation, anyway. He had hatched a plan to undermine Shane and discredit him in the eyes of their family. He had contacts within the Alexander-DePaul conglomerate and had heard rumors that Shane was considering selling the hotel to Malcolm—a move that would betray their grandfather's legacy.

As the meal ended, Oliver made a silent vow to himself. The Polk Island Hotel was not just a building to him—it was a symbol of his birthright, a history intertwined with his very identity. He refused to stand idly by while Shane, with his allegiance to Malcolm, was left to dictate the hotel's fate. He'd do whatever was necessary to protect this place.

As the family rose from the table to circulate the room and thank their guests, Oliver felt a hand on his arm.

Turning, he met Cia's gaze.

"I just want you to know that I'm watching you,"

she stated. "I won't stand by and allow you to tear our family apart."

Her eyes sparked with defiance. He could sense the protective shield she had erected around her siblings and the hotel. The warning settled on his shoulders, a clear indication that his plans would not be easily executed.

He raised an eyebrow. "Good to see you, too," he responded.

"I mean it," Cia uttered. "Don't come with the shenanigans…"

"*I heard you*. And I'll say this one more time… I came to say goodbye to my uncle." He kept his gaze steady, letting her see the truth of his words. Oliver grieved for his uncle, a man who'd treated him with kindness and respect over the years. Angus Jr. deserved his respect—and his farewell.

Oliver's love for his uncle didn't erase the injustice that had been done to his father years ago, the way his father had been overlooked, cast aside for decisions that weren't his own. There was a debt still unsettled, a wrong he couldn't let stand.

Oliver took a breath, keeping his expression impassive. No, paying his respects wouldn't stop him from setting things right. He'd come home not just to mourn, but to restore balance, even if it meant confronting the very family members he'd once revered.

Shane approached him next. The tension crackled

between them, unspoken words hanging heavy in the air. "Oliver, I know why you're here," he began.

His accusation cut through the air like a knife, his words laced with defiance.

Oliver met his cousin's gaze head-on, and he refused to back down in the face of Shane's scrutiny. His jaw tightened, his resolve hardening. "Do you?"

"It's not going to happen. You will never be the minority owner and general manager of this hotel. My father and his attorney made sure of it."

"Hey, did Uncle know that you intend to sell the hotel to Malcolm Alexander?" Oliver retorted, the tension between them intense.

Shane's eyes widened in shock, a mixture of anger and disbelief washing over his face. "You don't know what you're talking about, Oliver. Why would you care? You've made it clear you're not part of this family anymore."

Oliver shrugged, smirking. "Just curious. I mean, given Malcolm's reputation, it wouldn't surprise me if you're willing to sell him your soul along with the hotel. He's known for buying properties like this and turning them into cash cows, after all."

"Malcolm's a businessman, not a monster," Shane shot back defensively. "It doesn't have anything to do with you, so I suggest you stay out of it."

Oliver scoffed with bitterness. "I'm still very

much a Worthington. That means that I'm entitled to know *everything* that's going on with the hotel."

Shane sighed. "I've spent the last six years in Los Angeles, working with Malcolm in hotels that don't hold a candle to what we have here, as far as I'm concerned. But times are changing, Oliver. We need to adapt or risk losing everything."

Oliver's gaze remained unwavering, his steely resolve matching Shane's intensity. "Adapt by selling out? You're willing to erase our history for the promise of a few more dollars in the bank? When Grandpa added air-conditioning, color TVs in the early seventies, business nearly doubled. A couple years later, he added a second restaurant and swimming pool."

Shane took a step closer, the space between them crackling. "This isn't just about money. It's about *survival*. The hotel is struggling, and the truth is that there might not be anything left to salvage."

Oliver narrowed his eyes and squared his shoulders. "Survival? Is that what you call it? Selling our birthright, Shane? I won't stand by and watch you dismantle everything our ancestors built just because you're too afraid to fight for it."

Shane's expression turned to one of frustration mixed with guilt at Oliver's words. He knew his cousin's attachment to the hotel ran just as deep as his own. But what were his intentions with the place?

"This isn't about fear. It's about making a tough

choice for the future of our family," he replied. "I'm trying to do what's best for all of us."

Oliver shook his head, disbelief filling him. "This isn't just about you, your brothers and sisters. I haven't forgotten that my father was robbed of his inheritance and mine."

"Grandpa put my dad in charge before he died. Uncle Jacob was upset over the decision. He chose to walk away from the hotel, leave the island and never look back. That was the choice that *he* made."

"We were treated like outsiders," Oliver snapped in response. "What could my father do but leave and make a name for himself elsewhere? Grandpa hadn't left room for him in the hotel's future."

"That's not true," Shane stated. "It may have been your perception, but that isn't the reality. My father and I had several conversations before he died about what's best for this family. Trust that I already have his blessing on whatever is decided. He trusted me and I'm asking you to do the same."

"Trust has to be earned," Oliver responded, then walked away. He was done with this conversation.

He took the elevator downstairs to the lobby.

Oliver approached Guest Services, admiring the sleek design with accents of gold and polished marble. Two women stood behind the desk, and the one with blond hair exuded an air of aloofness as she glanced up at him with a practiced smile.

"I'm Oliver Worthington," he confidently announced, his name rolling off his tongue smoothly.

"I'll be staying in one of the family suites during my visit on the island."

The woman's demeanor changed immediately as she typed in his information, her fingers dancing across the keyboard.

He noted her name on the badge she wore.

Caroline.

Oliver noticed the other employee standing a few feet away, watching him with slight recognition in her hazel eyes. She fingered one of the thin locs that fell almost to her waist.

"I just need your driver's license, Mr. Worthington," Caroline said, gesturing toward a small scanner on the desk.

Oliver handed over his license and caught the gaze of the other woman as she gave him a quick wink. Despite the familiarity in her eyes, they both wore expressions of casual indifference, pretending not to know each other.

He didn't have to read her name tag to know that her name was Emma.

She was part of his plan to take down his family, a crucial ally in a game that required careful maneuvering to expose Shane's dealings with the Alexander-DePaul conglomerate. He and Emma had spent countless hours trying to hack into Shane's email and had been rewarded for their diligence a few days ago.

The air was thick with unacknowledged tension

as they exchanged brief glances, silently agreeing to keep their relationship under wraps for now.

Oliver had instructed Emma to anonymously leak Shane's emails with Malcolm to his aunt Madelyn and his cousins after his uncle's memorial. He experienced a twinge of guilt for betraying his cousin. But he knew that this was necessary to protect their family legacy from falling into the wrong hands.

He glanced at Emma again, his hands trembling slightly as he thought of the repercussions that could emerge from his betrayal. But, in his heart, he knew he was fighting for the greater good.

As Caroline finished checking him in and returned his license with a polite smile, Oliver accepted it with practiced grace.

Before heading toward the private elevators that led to the family suites, he couldn't resist sharing a brief, knowing glance with Emma. The look was subtle, almost imperceptible to anyone else, but it carried the weight of their secret and the plans they had set in motion.

Located on the top floor of Polk Island Hotel, the Worthington Suites I and II were accessible only by private elevator. These luxurious suites boasted breathtaking views of the island through large windows and had been designed with plush furnishings and elegant decorations. Each suite had its own unique layout, with a grand living room and a well-appointed bedroom. Paintings adorned the walls, and soft carpets covered the floors, with the hotel's logo emblazoned on various pieces of furniture and artwork, adding to the sense of exclusivity. His grandmother had overseen the interior design and added her own personal touches to each suite in 1990.

After getting settled, Oliver stood on the balcony that overlooked the ocean. The sun had set hours ago, and he listened to the waves in the night, dimly lit by the lights spilling from the hotel grounds.

As the only son of Angus Sr.'s eldest son, Oliver believed the hotel was his birthright. From the days of his three-times-great-grandfather, Asa Worthington, it had always passed to the firstborn son or daughter—until his grandfather had broken tradition, giving the hotel to Oliver's uncle instead of his father.

His plan had begun and now he just needed to bide his time. He'd expose Shane's true intentions and create discord within the family, while positioning himself as the rightful heir to the hotel. Oliver was determined to seize his destiny, no matter the cost.

# *CHAPTER THREE*

THE WORTHINGTONS WAITED until everyone left the ballroom before exiting the hotel.

Shane made his way to the back seat of Kenyon's dark blue SUV as their mother took a seat in the front. He was grateful that Oliver had decided not to join them. Shane had had his fill of the man's unwelcome company.

The familiar drive brought him back to the home that held a lifetime of memories, a magnificent Charleston-style two-story residence framed by elegant peach-colored roses. The delicate ruffled petals reached out toward him as if welcoming him home with open arms, their sweet scent filling the evening air and wrapping him in a warm hug.

Shane's eyes were drawn to the stunning sight of large vases overflowing with the same lovely flowers adorning the balcony. Even in the moonlight, they seemed to dance in the gentle breeze, against the white pillars and windows of the house.

These roses held a special place in Shane's heart, as they were his mother's pride and joy. She'd told him they were called Free Spirit, and they truly embodied her wild and free-spirited nature. He remembered how Madelyn would tend to the blooms with such love and care, just like she did with her family.

His father had handpicked these vibrant roses for his mother's wedding bouquet, been captivated by their bold hue and unique raspberry-tinted guard petals. And even after all these years, her love for these flowers never wavered. She continued to grow them in her garden, a symbol of their enduring love since the day they said, "I do."

Stepping out of the car, Shane took a deep breath, savoring the familiar fragrance that filled his lungs. These roses were more than just flowers; they were a reminder of where he came from and the strong bond of family that he cherished above all else.

He walked up the stone pathway leading to the front door. The sound of his footsteps seemed to harmonize with the rustling of the leaves in the old oak tree that stood tall in the yard, its branches swaying like outstretched arms welcoming him back.

As he reached the door, a tidal wave of emotions flooded over Shane. The memories came rushing back—the last time he had stood on this doorstep, his father had begged him to stay.

At that time, Shane never thought he would return, but now he was back, facing the ghosts of his past. His parents and siblings had visited him in Los Angeles two years ago. Despite their brief reunion, there'd still been tension between Shane and Angus Jr.

But everything changed when his father was diagnosed with stage 4 metastatic pancreatic cancer. A devastating blow that shook Shane's world to its core, bringing forth a whirlwind of emotions that he couldn't easily contain.

He pushed the door open, revealing the familiar hallway adorned with pictures of happier times. Shane's gaze fell upon a photograph of his parents on their wedding day, his mother radiant in her white wedding dress holding a bouquet of Free Spirit roses, his father beaming beside her with pride and joy etched into every line on his face.

Shane felt a lump form in his throat as he touched the frame gently, a wave of grief crashing over him like a sudden storm.

Taking a deep breath, he moved farther into the house, the floorboards creaking beneath his feet as if whispering secrets of the past. The familiar scent of his mother's favorite peach-scented candles lingered in the air, wrapping around him like a comforting blanket.

As he wandered through the rooms, memories flooded back to him in vivid flashes—birthday celebrations in the cozy kitchen, lazy Sunday mornings spent watching cartoons in the living room, whispered conversations shared late at night in the dim glow of a bedside lamp.

Shane felt a pang of regret for all the moments he had taken for granted, all the times he had brushed off his mother's attempts to get him to come home for a visit. He wished he could turn back time, relive those precious moments, and savor them like drops of rain in a parched land.

Lost in his thoughts, Shane found himself standing in front of the door to his childhood bedroom.

Hesitating for a moment, he slowly turned the handle and pushed it open, revealing a room frozen in time. The walls were still adorned with posters of his favorite bands and the desk was cluttered with notes and sketches from his college years.

But what caught Shane's eye was the old wooden chest at the foot of his bed—a treasure trove of memories that he had long forgotten.

With trembling hands, he lifted the lid and was greeted by an avalanche of nostalgia—old concert tickets, letters from friends, and a worn-out journal filled with his innermost thoughts.

As Shane flipped through the pages of the journal, his heart ached with a bittersweet longing. The words written in his own hand, the ink slightly faded with time, transported him back to a younger version of himself, full of dreams, hopes, and fears that seemed worlds away from the man he had become.

Each page turned was like peeling back layers of his past, revealing vulnerabilities he had long since buried beneath responsibility and duty.

The young man in those pages had ambitions

that soared high above the worries that now clouded his mind. There were sketches of superheroes, alternate universes, and doodles that captured moments of whimsy and freedom.

Tears welled up in his eyes as he read an entry from the day that he left for Los Angeles to pursue his career in hotel management. The excitement and trepidation intertwined in his words mirrored the conflicted emotions swirling inside him now.

Shane realized that in his pursuit of a future, he had unwittingly left behind a part of himself—the part that believed in endless possibilities and dared to dream without reservations.

As the last page of the journal fluttered under his touch, Shane's gaze was drawn to a faded photograph tucked between the worn pages.

It was a picture of him and Angus Jr., laughing under the warm glow of a sunset on Polk Island. Shane's heart clenched at the sight of his father's contagious smile, a smile that had once lit up his world with its brightness.

In that moment, amid the waves of nostalgia and regret crashing over him, Shane realized that he missed his father terribly. His world would never be the same.

THE NEXT DAY passed in a blur of arrangements and preparations for the upcoming memorial service and private burial to take place in four days. Shane found himself immersed in the chaos of schedules and guest lists, as he coordinated with the florist, discussed menu options with Kenyon, and ensured that the memorial was arranged to his mother's precise specifications.

Each sibling took on their designated tasks with a sense of duty and purpose, their movements orchestrated by a lifetime of shared history and unspoken bonds.But every detail required Shane's attention, every decision a reminder of the gravity of the upcoming event. He moved from one task to the next with a sense of urgency, yet a part of him felt numb, as he went through the motions without fully processing the significance of each action.

Kenyon was equally busy making sure the banquet staff prepared the menu for the repast according to his mother's wishes, while Cia handled the influx of calls from friends and relatives offering condolences and support. Micah was managing the guest list and coordinating travel arrangements for out-of-town relatives. He had an innate ability to keep things organized and running smoothly, a talent that was invaluable during times like this. He was an invaluable member of the hotel staff as well, working the front desk and Guest Services with what seemed like practiced ease.

Although six months pregnant, London tried her best to help despite everyone insisting that she take it easy. The family was on edge, worried about the strain all this was putting on her.

Their brother Aiden had arrived from Charlotte,

North Carolina, half an hour ago. He immediately jumped in to help, his presence a comforting addition to the family dynamic. Despite living away from the island, Aiden's connection to the family remained strong, and his support during this time was deeply appreciated.

Even his cousin Luella had come over to help, replacing London. She stayed for a couple hours before having to leave.

Madelyn, despite her grief, remained a pillar of strength, gently guiding everyone through their duties and offering comfort where it was needed.

Shane found himself lingering in the living room with his mother that evening while they waited for the others to join them for dinner.

She placed a hand on his arm. "I know it's tough, but we'll get through this."

Shane embraced his mother, feeling the warmth and comfort of her unwavering support. "We will, Mom," he said determinedly.

Having been given twenty percent of the total shares of the hotel as part of his inheritance, Shane was now the minority owner of the Polk Island Hotel. His mother would receive a third of the remaining shares with the rest divided between his siblings and Oliver.

He couldn't shake off the feeling of mistrust toward his cousin. He knew that Oliver would never be satisfied with just a portion of the shares, and that made him uneasy.

Lost in thought, Shane was brought back to reality by a knock on the front door. "I'll get it," Cia yelled from somewhere in the house.

Shane walked to the foyer just as Ace entered, carrying two large bags.

Their eyes met, and her direct gaze caught him completely off guard. There was something magnetic about the way she moved—gracefully, confidently, yet unassuming—that stirred something deep inside him. His pulse quickened, heart thumping in rhythm with her steps.

"Chef Patel made dinner," Ace announced with a warm, easy smile that sent a shiver down Shane's spine. Her voice was smooth, effortless, and suddenly, the room felt smaller, as though the space between them had shrunk.

Before he could even process a response, Cia swooped in to take the bags. "I'll take those to the kitchen. I hope you'll join us for dinner, Ace," Cia called over her shoulder.

Ace hesitated, her gaze flickering toward Shane. "I don't want to impose—"

"You're not imposing at all," he cut in, his voice firmer than he'd intended. His eyes locked onto hers, feeling that pull that seemed impossible to ignore. "Looks like Raj sent over plenty of food. There's more than enough."

She shook her head, politely declining. "Thanks, but I have plans. I'll leave you to your family dinner." He didn't know why he felt so disappointed in her response. Shane's gaze never wavered. He didn't want her to leave.

Shane's voice trembled with sincerity as he thanked Ace for all she had done for his family, especially his father. He'd heard that Ace and his father worked well together, as Angus Jr. did with all the heads of hotel departments.

Ace's expression changed briefly, a hint of something unreadable crossing her features before softening. "It was my duty," she replied simply.

Curious, Shane asked, "What was it like to work for him?" He watched her closely, eager to gain insight into who she was and what the hotel meant to her. He could sense that it held a special place in her heart beyond just being a job.

After considering for a moment, Ace spoke with warmth creeping into her tone. "Your father was demanding, but he truly believed in this place. He expected the same level of dedication from everyone around him." She paused, looking at him intensely. "He taught me more than just about the hotel. He taught me about loyalty to something greater than myself."

Shane nodded, feeling his perspective on Ace shift slightly. "I hope we can work together as well as you did with my father," he offered tentatively.

Ace studied him for a long moment, her gaze sharp and assessing. It felt as if she could see straight through the walls he had built around his heart. "That depends," she finally said, "on whether you plan to run the hotel in the same way your father did."

Her words lingered in the air, sparking questions in Shane's mind. Had his father's approach to running the hotel left a deeper impact on Ace—and perhaps even on the hotel itself—than he'd realized? For the first time, he began to question whether his vision for the future of the hotel aligned with his father's legacy or if it needed to evolve.

# CHAPTER FOUR

THE TRANSFORMATION OF the Grand Ballroom into a memorial setting was both an act of reverence and a testament to Angus Jr.'s legacy. The spacious room had been meticulously arranged to reflect the solemnity of the occasion. The walls, adorned with soft drapes in muted tones, created an intimate atmosphere. A large portrait of Angus Jr. stood at the front of the room, surrounded by an array of white lilies and Free Spirit roses from Madelyn's own gardens.

Rows of chairs faced the podium, each seat draped with a small black ribbon. The grand piano, usually reserved for joyous celebrations, now filled the room with the melancholic strains of a classical requiem. The soft lighting cast a gentle glow, adding a touch of warmth to the somber setting. Pictures of Angus Jr. throughout different stages of his life were displayed on easels around the room, capturing his larger-than-life personality and charm. Cia and her special-events team had done a great job with the decor.

The Worthington family had attended a private graveside service for Angus Jr. before the memorial. Now Shane sat in his seat, trying to keep his emotions in check as he listened to family and friends speak about his father.

Each story highlighted a different facet of the man who had been both a beacon of wisdom and a source of conflict in Shane's life. While they praised his father's charisma and leadership, Shane couldn't help but feel a wave of mixed emotions. He remembered the good times, the laughter, and the lessons, but also the painful moments of their tumultuous relationship. He resented his father for leaving him with so much baggage to unpack.

His eyes shifted to his mother, who sat two seats away. Her composed demeanor masked the deep pain in her eyes, but Shane could see the toll the loss had taken on her.

She had been the family's rock, but now the cracks were beginning to show. The weight of responsibility loomed heavily over him as he thought about the future of the Polk Island Hotel. It was now up to him and his siblings to uphold their father's reputation while forging their own path.

Taking a deep breath, Shane rose from his seat and walked slowly up to the podium to give the eulogy with Kenyon by his side. The room fell silent, all eyes on him. He felt the collective grief of those gathered, mingling with his own sorrow and uncertainty.

"Thank you all for being here," he began, his voice steady despite the turmoil within. He glanced over at his brother who encouraged him with a nod.

"Today, we gather not just to mourn the loss of my father, but to celebrate his life and the impact he had on each of us. As a father, he always had high standards for my siblings and me. He pushed us to be our best."

Shane paused, taking a deep breath before continuing. "But we also had our moments of disagreement," he admitted, glancing down at his notes briefly. "They seemed never-ending at times, but looking back now, I see how they helped shape us into the adults we are today."

As he spoke, Shane felt a weight lift off his shoulders. He paused, looking out at the faces of friends, family, and colleagues in attendance. "Angus Jr. was a man of many talents and passions. His vision and dedication were unmatched, and his legacy is something we will strive to uphold."

Memories of his father came to him… Angus Jr. teaching him to fish on the island's shores, the stern lectures about responsibility, and the rare moments of vulnerability when his father had shared his dreams for the future. "Angus Jr. was not a perfect man. He had his flaws, as we all do." Suddenly, the image of his dad with another woman gripped him. He took a calming break. "But he taught us the value of hard work, determination, and family. Those lessons will stay with us forever."

He glanced at his siblings—Kenyon, Micah, Cia, Aiden, and London—and drew strength from their presence. "To my family, I want to say that we will get through this together. We will honor Dad's memory by continuing his work and supporting each other, just as he would have wanted."

Shane's eyes met London's. She sat with her hand gently resting on her belly. She gave him a small, encouraging nod, her own pain and resolve mirrored in her expression. "Dad was so excited about becoming a grandfather. He talked about it all the time," he said, his voice softening. After the diagnosis, he'd called home more frequently to check in. He knew his dad couldn't wait for his children to have kids of their own, though Shane didn't realize before seeing London how close that time would come. "We will make sure his grandchild knows the incredible man he was."

As he finished his speech, Shane felt a mixture of sadness and relief. He had spoken the truth, acknowledged the complexities of his relationship with his father, and set a tone of unity and determination for his family.

The audience erupted into applause. He hoped his words resonated with them, and that each person could find a piece of their own story in his heartfelt tribute to his father.

Returning to his seat, Shane felt a comforting hand on his shoulder—his mother's silent support.

As the clapping subsided, an elderly man in the front row stood up slowly, his eyes glistening with tears. "I worked with your father for many, many years," he began, his voice thick with emotion. "And I can say without a doubt that Angus Jr. would be so proud of the man you've become, Shane."

The room was hushed as everyone turned their attention to the old man, hanging on to his every word. "He may have been tough at times, but he had a heart of gold," the man continued, a small smile on his lips. "And I see that same heart in you today."

London reached over, taking Shane's hand in her own. "Everything you said was perfect," she whispered. "I believe Daddy's looking down with a smile."

ACE JOINED SOME of the hotel staff gathered around a table during the repast after the service. She kept her eyes fixed on the plate in front of her, not wanting to engage in conversation or make eye contact with anyone. The chatter and laughter from the other staff members seemed distant and unimportant as she fought to keep her tears at bay. The jovial atmosphere felt like a stark contrast to the heaviness of the reason they were all gathered.

Although Ace knew Angus Jr. didn't want those

left behind to revel in sadness, he hadn't just been her employer—he had also been a friend. She hadn't expected him to call and offer her a job, especially knowing he was acquainted with her ex-husband. Yet, Angus Jr. hadn't let any history or gossip sway his opinion of her. Instead, he respected her courage and her unwavering sense of justice.

When he learned that she was considering leaving the police force, Angus Jr. surprised her with an unexpected offer. He wanted her on his team, saying he recognized the strength and resolve she'd shown both in her work and personal life. His faith in her felt like a lifeline, the beginning of a new chapter she hadn't foreseen. The gesture had meant more to her than she'd let on at the time—it was the validation she needed at a moment when her life felt unsteady.

A lone tear slipped down her cheek, and she quickly swiped it away, her heart heavy with gratitude and loss.

Ace suddenly felt someone staring at her. She looked up and found herself locking gazes with Shane Worthington. Even from across the room, his piercing brown eyes held an intensity that made her heart race for reasons she couldn't quite understand.

Shane held her gaze for a beat too long before he finally looked away. Ace felt a strange mix of annoyance and curiosity at his sudden interest in her. She knew Shane only through the staff grapevine and the memories of him shared by Angus Jr. She couldn't figure out why he was looking at her like that now.

As the repast wore on, Ace found herself stealing glances in Shane's direction whenever she could. There was something about him that drew her in, despite her best efforts to resist. Maybe it was the way he carried himself with an air of mystery, or the quiet confidence in his every move. Whatever it was, Ace couldn't deny the spark of attraction that flared to life whenever their eyes met.

But she quickly pushed aside those thoughts. Ace couldn't afford to be sidetracked by a man who was likely just as arrogant as the rumors said, or as stubborn as his father had declared. More pressing was the matter of the hotel's future. She needed to find the right moment to ask Shane if there was any truth to the rumors about selling the property to Malcolm Alexander. If there was, it would affect everything—and she needed to know where he stood.

Ace focused on her meal, determined not to let Shane's enigmatic presence distract her. She ate in silence, refusing to let her thoughts drift toward him.

However, as the day progressed, fate seemed intent on throwing them together. Shane approached her table as she was talking to Raj and said, "I want to thank all of you." He glanced around at the staff seated at the table. "You were my dad's pride and joy. He would always say that whenever he was away, he had full confidence knowing that everyone would work in excellence."

"Your father was the best boss I've ever had," Luke, the bar manager, stated. "When my mother died, she didn't have no insurance. I didn't know what I was gonna do, but Angus Jr., he gave me the money to bury her. I offered to pay him back in installments…have him take it out of my check each week, but he wouldn't hear of it."

Shane nodded. "That sounds like him."

"I'll say this…" Caroline, one of the front desk clerks, said. "Angus Jr. loved his family. All he talked about were his children. He was so proud of y'all."

Shane cleared his throat, trying to keep his composure. "Yeah, he did love us. More than anything," he said softly, a hint of vulnerability in his voice.

Ace couldn't help but notice how different he seemed in that moment, stripped of the bravado and confidence she'd seen earlier as he made his way about the room.

The conversation continued, with Shane taking a seat as each person at the table shared their own stories and memories of Shane's father.

As the afternoon wore on, Ace found herself feeling a strange mix of emotions—sympathy for the Worthington family's loss, nostalgia for the time she had spent working for Angus Jr., and a growing sense of connection to the man sitting across from her.

THAT EVENING, after his father's memorial, Shane didn't return to his mother's house. Instead, he went down to Guest Services.

"Good evening, Mr. Worthington," a woman with long locs greeted, her voice soft and respectful. "I offer my condolences for your loss."

"Thank you, Emma," Shane replied, reading her name badge and appreciating the sincerity in her tone. "I'm checking into the Worthington I suite."

She nodded and swiftly processed the reservation. "Of course. Micah thought you might, so he made sure it was prepped and ready for you. Here are your keys. If you need anything, please don't hesitate to ask."

"Thanks," Shane said, taking the keys and heading toward the elevators, which he rode to the top floor. While there would always be a place for him at his mother's, Shane preferred to stay at the hotel. His childhood home evoked too many old memories of his father. Plus, this would give Shane a chance to observe the inner workings of the hotel as he stepped into his father's shoes.

Entering the Worthington I suite, Shane was immediately hit by a wave of nostalgia. This particular suite of rooms had always been his father's favorite. Its luxurious yet tasteful decor reflected the pride his family took in their heritage. Shane took a moment to breathe it all in, trying to find some comfort amid the turmoil of the day.

Just as he was beginning to relax, a knock on the door pulled him back to the present.

He opened it to find one of the bellhops, who was a longstanding employee.

"Hey, Chuck…" Shane greeted.

Keeping his voice to a loud whisper, he stated, "I thought you would want to know that Oliver is staying in the Worthington II suite."

Shane's jaw tightened. It didn't surprise him that his cousin would be staying directly across the hall. "Thanks for letting me know."

Closing the door, he tried to push aside thoughts of Oliver to save the hotel.

He sank into the plush armchair by the window and looked out at the twinkling lights of the island below. Shane leaned back and closed his eyes, trying to quiet the storm of thoughts swirling in his mind. He needed to be clear-headed and strong— for his family, for the hotel, and for the future that was now in his hands.

Unable to clear his head, Shane decided to stroll the halls of the hotel, the weight of his family's legacy heavy on his shoulders. At times, the creaking floorboards beneath his feet echoed the turmoil in his mind as he grappled with the decision that lay before him.

Each step he took seemed to reverberate through the walls, a stark reminder of the history and memories woven into the very fabric of the hotel. The dimly lit corridors whispered tales of past triumphs and hardships, reminding Shane of the sacrifices made by those who came before him.

He came to a sudden halt outside the Worthington Gallery, which displayed fragments of his family's past. The gallery housed artwork and artifacts the family had acquired through the years, including a priceless statue that was the crown jewel of the collection. Shane couldn't understand why his father would showcase such a valuable family treasure in public instead of safeguarding it in a vault. The sculpture, created in 1901 by renowned artist Lorne, had been given to Asa Worthington from their illustrious cousin.

The figure, emerging from flowing fabric, symbolized transformation and growth. With elongated limbs, a serene expression, and hands gently outstretched, the statue evoked both inner peace and longing. The artist's use of layered patina created a luminous effect, shifting between greens, blues, and golds. Shane stared at the piece, the decision whether to sell the hotel weighing heavily on his heart. Earlier, when he'd watched his siblings and mother leave for their ancestral home, an inner battle raged within him. He wasn't sure if he could let go of this piece of his identity, but he also knew that holding on to it might prevent him from securing a better future for his loved ones. His father had grappled with the same conflicting emotions.

He left the gallery and continued walking until

he ended up at a window, watching the waves crash against the shore.

Selling the hotel to the Alexander-DePaul chain seemed like the most rational choice, a way to secure a stable future for his loved ones even if it meant severing ties to their past. His father had also wrestled with this decision, ultimately giving his blessing after talking to Malcolm.

Shane returned to his suite and went to bed, still feeling unsettled.

It felt just like yesterday that Angus Jr.'s attorney had reached out to him. Only three short weeks ago, Shane had received the unexpected call and learned that his father wanted him to take over the hotel.

In their Zoom meetings, his father had spoken with a sense of urgency, carefully reviewing all the legal and financial aspects of the hotel. Despite their strained relationship over the years, Angus Jr. had been resolute in his decision to exclude Kenyon, London, and the others from taking over. Kenyon, a skilled chef, had no interest in managing the hotel and was focused on his culinary career. London was heavily invested in her own business, a honeybee farm, and the younger siblings lacked the necessary experience that Shane possessed.

Angus Jr.'s reasoning was clear—Shane was the only one with the expertise to handle the challenge. But more importantly, he didn't want his family to be burdened by the hotel's financial struggles while also dealing with his terminal illness.

Shane had agreed. The decision wasn't easy, but he felt a sense of duty and a hope for reconciliation. Seeing his father weak but still fighting against the inevitable, he couldn't help but feel compassion. Shane was grateful that they'd been able to make peace before Angus Jr. passed away. It was a small comfort, knowing that they had managed to bridge the gap between them, however briefly.

Now, lying in the quiet darkness of his room, Shane couldn't shake the enormity of the responsibility he had taken on. He was the one everyone expected to turn around the dire situation. He knew that saving the hotel wouldn't be easy, but he was determined to honor his father's last request to protect the family.

The path ahead was uncertain.

He closed his eyes, hoping that sleep would come and bring with it some clarity for the days ahead.

# *CHAPTER FIVE*

THE DAYS AFTER the funeral dawned with the same sense of urgency Ace had felt at her late boss's service. The memorial had gone smoothly, though Ace's heart still ached over Angus's death and for his family. When Shane strolled past Guest Services and settled into one of the chairs in the back of the lobby two days later, she saw an opportunity to approach him.

She made her way over and silently handed him a cup of herbal tea before leaning against the bookshelf across from him. Observing him carefully, she remarked, "You seem like you could use this more than I can."

Shane glanced up, clearly surprised by the gesture, and accepted the warm drink with a grateful nod. "Thanks."

Ace could see the conflict swirling in Shane's eyes. She knew that whatever was troubling him was deeply rooted in his connection to this hotel, to his family's legacy. That had been evident at the service, in the way he'd spoken about his father and the hotel.

Ace also felt a duty to the hotel, which was why she didn't want to delay in bringing up a topic she knew was burdening the hotel employees.

"The staff…" she began. "They're worried about their future here at the hotel," she said, not wanting to mince words. "There are rumors swirling… people think you're planning to sell the hotel to Malcolm Alexander."

Shane's jaw clenched at the mention of Malcolm, the tension unmistakable.

After a long pause, he finally spoke, his voice laced with hesitation. "I'm not surprised by the rumors. The truth is, I don't know what to do." He sighed deeply. "My family's split between tradition and practicality. Selling would solve so many problems, but…it feels like I'd be betraying everything my family worked to build."

Ace's heart tugged as she listened, her own feelings for the hotel unexpectedly mingling with her growing awareness of Shane. This job was a part of her, a sanctuary she didn't want to lose. And then, there was Shane himself—the man she didn't want to admit was getting under her skin.

"I can't imagine what you're going through," she responded, "but I do know one thing. Your father believed in you. Whether you decide to sell or not, his legacy lives on through you. But if I'm honest, I'm hoping you won't sell. Everyone here feels the same."

His gaze softened at her words, and for a moment, the tension in the room eased. Shane's eyes flickered with gratitude, and something more—something that made Ace's pulse quicken. He took a deep breath, exhaling slowly as if releasing some of the burden he carried.

"Ace, you've given me a lot to think about," he said quietly. "Please, don't mention this to anyone just yet. When the time comes, I'll meet with the staff."

She nodded. "I won't say a word."

Shane's lips curved into a slight smile. "Thanks for the tea."

Her heart skipped at the warmth in his voice. "Enjoy your day... Mr. Worthington."

His smile deepened. "Just Shane. Mr. Worthington was my grandfather."

He was gorgeous when he smiled. She chuckled, a soft laugh escaping her. "Your dad used to say that."

He grinned again. But even as she watched him go, the tension of the moment lingered, her thoughts still on Shane Worthington—and the spark of attraction she felt for him.

SHANE HEADED OUT to join his family for brunch. The concierge had handed him the keys to one of the hotel's courtesy cars—a sleek black Mercedes that hummed smoothly under his touch.

As he pulled up to his childhood home, a familiar twinge of anxiety tightened in his chest. The house, once a symbol of stability, now felt like a place where decisions hung in the air, unresolved. Shane knew the conversation about selling the hotel was inevitable, and he was certain his family had already considered the possibility. After all, the rumors had already started swirling, if what Ace said was true.

But the truth was what he'd told Ace—he didn't know what to do. He wasn't sure why he'd admitted that to her. Except that her demeanor seemed to put him at ease, and he didn't want to explore too closely why that was.

Selling would ease the financial strain and simplify the future, but it also felt like a betrayal of everything his father had worked for. His mother and siblings probably had concerns of their own, and he wasn't sure if they were ready to hear what he was considering.

Stepping out of the car, Shane took a deep breath and looked at the house again. They'd only laid Angus Jr. to rest two days ago, and the grief was still raw. Was now really the right time to bring up such a monumental decision? So much was still up in the air, so many emotions yet to settle. He rubbed the back of his neck, knowing he couldn't avoid the conversation forever, but maybe—just maybe—it could wait a little longer. Shane's heart raced as he entered the family home, using his old key.

From the foyer, he heard his five siblings chatting in the living room, rehashing details from the memorial service.

They looked up expectantly as he walked in, a mix of hope and apprehension evident in their eyes.

London spoke up first. "What happened to you yesterday? I thought you would've come by the house to check on Mama."

There was a hint of disapproval in her tone, clearly showing that she was not pleased with his decision to stay away from the family. London was five years younger than him. She had just graduated college when Shane decided to leave home. She was now the successful owner of LW's Honey Farm. In fact, she'd recently landed a distribution deal with a chain of supermarkets.

"I called and talked to Mom yesterday. Sorry, but I needed some time to process things on my own," Shane replied, feeling slightly defensive under her skeptical gaze. He'd spent the day hidden away in the Worthington I suite, going over numbers and thinking through a potential sale with Malcom Alexander.

"Give your brother a break," Madelyn stated from the foyer. "Some people need their space from time to time." She placed a gentle hand on Shane's arm, then announced, "Anything that needs to be discussed can wait until after we finish eating."

Shane wrapped his arms around his mother in a tight embrace. He spoke softly, keeping their conversation private. "I'm sorry. Did it bother you that I didn't come by?"

Madelyn shook her head. "Son, I know you...it's fine."

The looks from his siblings spoke of something going on that he was unaware of. Surely, they weren't upset with him for staying at the hotel.

As they walked into the dining room, the doorbell echoed through the house.

"That must be Oliver," Madelyn said, adjusting her apron.

"Why is he here?" Kenyon asked.

"I asked him to come," she replied.

Shane's footsteps creaked on the hardwood floor as he made his way to the door and pulled it open.

"Hey, cousin..." Oliver stood in front of him, his smile artificial and his hands shoved deep into his pockets.

Without a response, Shane stepped aside to let him enter the house. Interactions with his cousin always left a bitter taste in his mouth. Their strained relationship stemmed from childhood rivalries that had never quite dissipated and his past attempts to sue Angus Jr.

Madelyn greeted him warmly, and Oliver sauntered into the foyer, casting a disdainful glance around the familiar surroundings as if he found them distasteful. Seated around the table, Shane and his siblings engaged in light conversations that did little to ease the tension in the room.

It was during one of these lulls that Oliver leaned in ever so slightly, his voice a low murmur clearly meant for Shane's ears only. "You might be able to convince the others to consider selling, but I'll never agree to it."

He met his cousin's gaze head-on, his own resolve unwavering despite the unmistakable hostility emanating from Oliver. "My family and I will decide what is best for *us* and the hotel."

Madelyn's keen eyes darted between Shane and Oliver from her place at the head of the table. She sensed the unresolved conflict hanging thick in the air like a storm about to break. With a gentle but firm tone, she addressed them both, her matriarchal presence demanding attention. "This bickering won't lead us anywhere," she chided, her voice carrying years of wisdom and love for her family.

Shane bowed his head slightly, acknowledging his mother's intervention with respect.

Oliver grumbled under his breath but fell silent, knowing better than to defy Madelyn's authority.

"I agree," Kenyon interjected. He was the eldest of the siblings. He looked none too pleased to see Oliver as well. "Mom and I went through all this trouble to make all our favorites. Let's just shut up and eat. Enjoy the food."

"Are we just going to pretend that we don't know what's really going on?" Oliver asked, a bewildered look coloring his expression. "Am I the only one who received the emails?"

Kenyon sent his cousin a sharp glare while Shane frowned in confusion.

"What are you talking about?" he asked. "What emails?"

"You just don't know when to shut up," London snapped, looking at Oliver. "Didn't Mama just say that we'd talk after we eat?" She reached for a tray piled with turkey sausage. "Don't you get tired of being a troublemaker?"

Fury flashed in Madelyn's eyes. "This discussion is tabled until after we finish eating. Oliver, if what you have to say isn't about the food, weather, or life in general, we don't want to hear from you."

"Understood," he responded while spooning hash-brown potatoes onto his plate.

Madelyn asked Kenyon to bless the food, and he nodded and bowed his head.

After the blessing, they dug into the fluffy scrambled eggs with cheese and spinach, crispy bacon, turkey sausage, and warm, homemade waffles.

Shane topped his waffles with plump strawberries and blueberries and a dollop of whipped butter before drizzling just a touch of syrup on top. He had no idea what had taken place but pushed it aside to enjoy the food on his plate.

The brunch was delicious but the conversation felt awkward and forced throughout the meal. After everyone had eaten their fill, Shane said, "I don't know what's going on here, but I can feel the tension in this room. Can someone enlighten me?"

"We received emails from an anonymous sender," Kenyon replied. "Emails that were exchanged between you and Malcolm Alexander... Looks like you two were negotiating the sale of the hotel."

Shane's chest clenched. He had hoped to keep his conversations with Malcolm Alexander a secret until the right time, but it seemed that the truth was now out in the open. He felt trapped and unsure of how to explain himself. This wasn't how he had anticipated his family finding out about his plans for the hotel.

Madelyn shifted her gaze to Shane, her expression softening with understanding. "I know your heart is torn, my dear. But I have to say that I don't think we're at a point where we need to consider selling." There was a touch of sadness in her eyes.

Shane's throat constricted, and he swallowed hard as his mother's words landed like a sledgehammer on his heart. He lifted his eyes to meet her gaze, revealing the turmoil within. The portraits of his ancestors adorning the dove-gray walls of the dining room seemed to silently pass judgment on him.

He wondered how his personal emails had gotten to his family.

Clearing his throat, Oliver said, "Apparently, we all received the same email and from the way it reads...you've all but signed on the dotted line.

Were any of you aware of his plans?" His cousin glanced around the table. *"Because I wasn't."*

"We need to talk about the hotel's financial situation," Shane said, his voice steady but grave. "As most of you know, Dad and I had several conversations before he passed away. But what you don't know is that the hotel is in trouble. I looked at the financials and the numbers are worse than I expected. Dad made me promise not to say anything to y'all. He wanted me to do what was best even if it meant selling to Malcolm."

The room fell silent as his family processed his words.

Madelyn's face tightened, and London looked down at her hands, worry etched across her features. Kenyon, Cia, and Micah exchanged glances, their expressions unreadable. Aiden reached over, covering their mother's hand with his own.

"What kind of trouble are we talking about?" Kenyon finally asked, breaking the silence.

"We're running at a significant loss," Shane replied. "Bookings are down, maintenance costs are up, and we've got outstanding debts that we can't ignore. If we don't do something soon, we risk losing everything."

Madelyn shook her head slowly. "We've been through tough times before, Shane. We can get through this."

"I understand, Mom. But this is different. The market is changing, and we're not keeping up. We need a substantial injection of capital to turn things around, and I'm not sure where we can get it."

London looked up, her eyes filled with concern. "What are our options?"

Shane hesitated for a moment before continuing. "Malcolm has offered to buy the hotel. Under his proposal, we can continue to manage it and include a clause that allows us to buy it back from him in the future."

Her brow furrowed. "Is selling to Malcolm really our only way out?"

He nodded. "It seems like the best option right now. It would allow us to secure the capital we need immediately. Plus, we'll have a pathway to regain ownership once we stabilize our finances."

The room erupted into a chorus of objections. Madelyn's face turned pale, and she shook her head more emphatically. "No, *absolutely not*. This hotel is our family's legacy. We can't just sell it off."

Kenyon leaned forward, his expression resolute. "I agree with Mom. This place means too much to us. I know you trust Malcolm. He seems like a nice man, but I don't want to sell."

Cia nodded in agreement. "Selling isn't the answer. There must be another way."

Shane held up his hands, trying to calm the room. "I understand how you all feel. Believe me, I don't want to sell, either. But Malcolm's offer is a good one. It's more than fair, and it would solve our financial problems instantly. We're looking at bankruptcy otherwise." Malcom had been a mentor to Shane since he left home—he trusted the man, believed that someday they could buy the hotel back. Though he understood why the others were hesitant to sell.

Micah, who had been quiet until now, spoke up. "But at what cost, Shane? This hotel is more than just bricks and mortar. It's our history, our memories. Selling it would be like selling a part of ourselves. There has to be another option out there."

Shane sighed, feeling the weight of their words. He knew they were right, but he also knew the harsh realities they faced. "I know it's a hard decision. But we need to think about the future. If we lose the hotel because we can't pay our debts, we lose everything, anyway."

Madelyn reached out and took Shane's hand, her grip firm. "Generations of Worthingtons worked too hard to build this place up. We can't let it go now."

"Mom's right. We're not ready to give up," Kenyon declared, his eyes filled with determination as he looked around the table at his family.

"All right," Shane eventually conceded, surveying each person at the table with careful consideration. He wouldn't sell outright against his family's wishes. Especially against his mother's wishes. Though eventually they may come to see this was their best option. "We'll explore other possibilities, no matter how unlikely they may seem. But we must be realistic about the challenges ahead. This won't be easy, and we need to prepare ourselves for some difficult times."

Everyone nodded in agreement. Together, they would fight to keep their hotel in the family. It wouldn't be a simple task, but as long as they stayed united, there might be a chance.

Oliver's piercing gaze disrupted the peace that had settled over the table.

Without breaking eye contact, Shane addressed him directly, his voice strong. "I understand your reservations. But we can't ignore what this hotel means to all of us."

"You were the one pushing to sell it," Oliver huffed. "How do I know you'll do everything in your power to save our legacy?"

"I guess you'll just have to watch from the sidelines."

As his siblings began discussing alternative strategies, Shane's mind wandered back to the many memories they had created within the walls of the Polk Island Hotel. He was determined to do whatever it took to keep that heart beating.

When they decided to relocate to the living room, Cia gravitated toward Shane.

"I—" He hesitated.

She raised her hand gently, silencing him. "Remember when I used to call out your name and fearlessly leap into your arms?"

He smiled warmly, recalling those memories. "You'd jump from anywhere, without hesitation."

Her brow creased. "Do you understand why I did it?"

"Not entirely," Shane admitted. "Maybe just to irritate me. You don't know how many times I worried that I wouldn't catch you."

Her laughter filled the air. "It was because of my unwavering trust in you. I knew with certainty that you would always be there to catch me." Her expression grew serious again. "I still have faith in you. I believe wholeheartedly that you will do what is right for the family and the hotel."

Shane felt a lump form in his throat as he gazed into Cia's eyes, seeing the steadfast trust she held in him. Her words resonated deep within him, stirring the already tumultuous conflict that raged within his heart. "I will find a way to honor our family's legacy and ensure our future, Cia. We'll make decisions about the hotel as a family," he responded.

Cia's eyes sparkled with gratitude. She squeezed his arm gently before offering a soft smile.

His father had kept his mother and siblings away from the financials, but Shane felt differently, and he felt stronger about this after speaking to his siblings. Maybe he didn't have to carry all this alone. They each owned a shareable interest. They had a right to know what was going on. This was only the beginning of Shane's plans to transform how Angus Jr. managed the hotel.

OLIVER HAD FOOLISHLY hoped that his aunt and cousins would take his side in the conflict with Shane. However, he quickly realized that they were still a tight-knit family who always stood by each other's sides. Despite this setback, Oliver refused to give up. He was determined to find a way to expose the chinks in Shane's heroic armor to his mother and siblings.

He glanced down at his watch, then prepared to leave. He was meeting Emma.

Shane followed him outside the house. "I can't prove it, but I'm pretty sure you're behind those emails," he accused, his voice sharp with anger and suspicion. "Somehow you hacked my account."

Oliver turned to face him, keeping his expression blank. "I received the same letter that your mom and siblings got," he responded evenly. "Someone sent them to us. My thought is that it's someone from Alexander-DePaul."

Shane's brow furrowed as he processed this information. "What would be the reason?" he asked, his tone more curious than accusatory now.

Oliver shrugged nonchalantly, trying to appear as if the situation didn't bother him. "I don't know. Maybe they just don't like you. Who knows… I'm glad they sent it. Otherwise, we'd all be in the dark."

Shane's frustration was unmistakable. "I would've told all of you everything once the time was right," he insisted, his voice tinged with defensive desperation.

"This decision isn't yours to make alone, Shane," Oliver retorted. "You might think you're the hero of this story, but the choices that affect the family aren't yours to dictate."

Shane glared at his cousin, not speaking. The family rift was more evident than ever, and Oliver knew that this confrontation was just the beginning.

"I'm going back to the hotel," Oliver announced.

"I hope you're planning to pack up and go back to Atlanta," Shane quipped.

"Sorry to disappoint you, cousin. I intend to hang around a little longer."

"Don't you have a job to go back to?" Shane asked.

"I can work remotely," Oliver responded. "No need to worry about me."

"Fine. Do whatever you want, Oliver. Just stay out of my way."

He smirked, a flash of defiance in his eyes. "I won't stand by and watch you ruin everything our ancestors built just because you think it's the right thing to do. As much as you want to deny it, I'm still a Worthington."

"In name only," Shane growled back. "Family wouldn't do the things you've done."

Oliver unlocked the sleek, black door to his Escalade and eased into the plush leather seat, closing the door on his cousin.

The soft scent of buttery leather enveloped him as he settled in.

His phone vibrated on the sleek console, its screen illuminating with an incoming call.

"Ma, hey…" he greeted his mother, hearing the apprehension and weariness in his own voice. He hadn't spoken to Alice Worthington in almost a month.

"Why did I have to hear from Madelyn that you were on the island? I surely hope you're not there causing trouble." The stern yet concerned voice pierced through the car's quiet ambiance.

He released a short sigh, watching Shane reenter the house in his rearview mirror. "I wanted to say a final goodbye to my uncle," Oliver explained.

"I hope you're telling me true, son." Alice's presence was felt even through the phone.

He could see her in his mind. Her authority was not dimmed by her petite and slender frame. Her delicate features belied the underlying strength and determination that made her a formidable force, especially when she was angered.

"How are you doing?" he asked, trying to steer the conversation in a different direction. "Why didn't you tell me about the stroke?"

"It was a small one and I didn't want you worried. For the most part, I have my good days and bad days. Today is a mix of both, I suppose," Alice replied. "But my faith remains strong. How is Madelyn coping?"

"You and Aunt Maddie are some of the strongest women I know. She seems sad, but she's making sure everyone else is okay."

There was a pause on the line. "I wish I could be there with her."

"You know she would want you to focus on your own well-being," Oliver said gently.

"That's why she insisted I stay home. But she still needs someone to take care of her."

"She has her children," Oliver reminded her. "Trust me, Ma…she's doing fine."

"When are you leaving the island?" Alice asked. "I'd love to see you, son. It's been a while."

"I'm not sure yet. But I'm planning to visit you sometime next week."

They chatted for a few more minutes before ending the call.

Oliver gazed out at the island scenery as he pulled out of the driveway and made the short trip back to the hotel. He wished navigating his family dynamics could be as simple as navigating the streets of his hometown. Unfortunately, a difficult and winding road lay ahead of him.

ON MONDAY OF the following week, Shane made his first formal appearance as minority owner/general manager of the Polk Island Hotel.

He sat down at his father's desk, the glow of his laptop casting a harsh light on his furrowed brow.

The email that had stirred so much turmoil within his family replayed in his mind. He was certain Oliver had sent it, but his cousin's vehement denial—and the revelation that he, too, had received an email about Shane's plans to sell the hotel to Malcolm Alexander—left him questioning everything.

Shane sighed, rubbing his temples. The stakes were high, and the fallout from the email had been immediate and damaging. His mother and siblings had all been adamantly opposed to the idea of selling the hotel, and now tensions were higher than ever. While Cia supported him, he'd been met with aloof distance from his brothers over the past couple days. He shouldn't have kept things from them. After all, Kenyon and Micah worked at the hotel and had a vested interest in what would happen to it.

Still, Shane would've told them at the right time had the news not been leaked. Determined to get to the bottom of it, Shane decided to speak with someone in the IT department. Maybe they could trace the email back to its source. He grabbed his phone and dialed the extension for Nelson, the head of IT.

"Nelson, it's Shane Worthington. I need your help with something urgent," he said as soon as the call connected.

Nelson's voice, steady and professional, was a source of comfort for Shane. "Mr. Worthington, what can I assist you with?"

"Somebody hacked into my email. I need to know how it happened. And I also need help tracing an email that was sent to my family."

"I'll do my best to figure it out."

Shane forwarded the email that his family had

received and said, "Thanks. Please update me once you've found any information."

"Will do, Mr. Worthington. I'll start working on it right away."

"Please just call me Shane," he said, then hung up.

The wait was excruciating. He paced the length of his office, his mind racing with possibilities. If it wasn't Oliver who'd sent it, who could it be? Someone with inside knowledge of his plans and a vested interest in stirring up trouble.

The only person who'd approached him about the sale was Ace…and he'd all but admitted he was considering it. But as head of security, he knew she was more discreet than that. Even when she was direct, she always seemed compassionate. Shane admired that about her, and not for the first time in the last few days, he found himself thinking of her lovely face, curious about her.

Shane's phone buzzed.

"I have some information for you," Nelson said. "The email was sent through a masked IP address, which makes it difficult to trace directly. However, there are a few indicators that can help narrow it down. The email header shows that it passed through a series of servers that are commonly used for anonymizing messages. This suggests it was deliberately obscured."

Shane felt a pang of frustration. "So, it was someone who knew what they were doing?"

"Yes, definitely. But there's more. While the exact sender is still masked, I found a potential lead," Nelson continued. "There are digital fingerprints left behind that suggest the email originated from a network associated with one of our frequent vendors. The email was routed through their servers."

Shane's heart raced. This was the break he needed. "Which vendor?"

"It looks like it's from one of the subcontractors we use for events—Springhill Event Services. They have access to a lot of our internal information because of the work they do here."

Shane frowned. "I see."

"Someone with access to their network could have sent it. It's a bit of a long shot, but it might be worth looking into."

"Thank you, Nelson. You've been a great help. I'll take it from here."

He quickly called Cia, asking her for the contact info for Springhill Event Services. He assured her all was fine when she asked why he needed it.

Shane leaned back in his chair, his thoughts racing. He had always prided himself on his ability to read people and situations, but this was proving to be more complex than he'd anticipated. If someone within Springhill was responsible, it meant the betrayal was even closer than he had realized.

# CHAPTER SIX

SHANE STEPPED INTO the office of the Polk Island Hotel for the second day in a row. The room exuded the old Southern charm that his late father had cherished, from the antique furniture to the lace curtains gently swaying in the afternoon breeze.

He scanned the room, noting the blend of nostalgia and outdated decor, a stark reminder of the generational gap he intended to bridge with modern strategies. But updating the office was low on his list of priorities now.

His first meeting was with Lilly, the assistant general manager, who provided detailed updates on operations to Shane. Compared to previous years, summer bookings were lower than expected, and as much as Shane hated to do it, they'd determined that budget cuts were necessary across all departments. It wasn't ideal, but without an influx of cash and no pending sale, they needed to get ahead of the situation.

They agreed to present this at the weekly staff meeting, which was next on his calendar.

They walked into a room across from Shane's office.

He sat down at the head of a long, polished oak table while Lilly took a seat at the opposite end. She'd seemed unsettled by their previous meeting, but he knew he had her support.

The department heads of the hotel filed in, their chatter dying down as they noticed Shane's serious expression.

He glanced up at the clock—it was time to start. He took a deep breath, steeling himself for the difficult conversation ahead.

"Good morning, everyone," Shane began. "Thank you for coming. I know we're all busy, so I'll get straight to the point."

The room was silent, all eyes on him. Shane could feel the tension building, a sense of unease spreading among the department heads.

"You may not have been aware, but the hotel has been facing some financial challenges," he continued. "After a thorough review of our current situation and projections, it's become clear that we need to make some immediate changes to ensure the sustainability of the hotel."

Shane paused, letting his words sink in. The murmurs started almost immediately, anxious whispers passing between colleagues. Only Cia appeared calm. Micah's and Kenyon's expressions were unreadable.

He held up a hand to quiet the room.

"I'm announcing a series of budget cuts across all departments," Shane said firmly. He and Lilly agreed they'd start with reducing nonessential purchases and reviewing vendor contracts. "These cuts are necessary to keep the hotel afloat during this difficult period. I know this is not what anyone wants to hear, but it's a reality we must face together."

The room erupted into a flurry of protests and concerned voices. Shane expected this reaction, but it still hit him like a punch to the gut. He raised his voice to regain control of the meeting.

"Please, I understand your concerns," he said. "I assure you, these decisions were not made lightly. We've analyzed every possible option, and these cuts are the most viable solution at this time."

"Shane," said Mrs. Higgins, the head of housekeeping, her voice tinged with worry. "How deep are these cuts? What are we looking at?"

Shane nodded, acknowledging her question. "Each department will need to reduce their budget by ten percent," he said. "I know it's significant, but we've tried to make it as equitable as possible. This means tightening operational costs, deferring nonessential expenses, and finding more efficient ways to operate." He paused a moment before adding, "It may also mean decreasing your staff." That was an outcome Shane hoped to avoid.

John Parker, the head of food and beverage, leaned forward, his face etched with concern.

"Layoffs...this will affect our service quality. Not to mention our guests will notice, and that could drive them away."

"I agree," Cia interjected. "We're entering our busiest season. We have ten weddings and four wedding receptions booked. We have two family reunions."

John nodded. "If anything, we need more staff as we enter into our summer season."

Shane met his gaze, understanding his frustration. "I understand the stakes, John, but this is a temporary measure. For the weddings and re-unions, we can cross-train staff from other departments to assist during peak times." He glanced at Cia. "Let's also explore part-time or temporary hires to manage the workload without long-term commitments. We'll monitor the impact closely and adjust as needed, but we need to ensure the hotel's financial stability first. We must ensure that any cost-saving measures don't drastically impact the guest experience. It's going to be a challenge, but I believe we can manage it if we work together and get creative."

There was a heavy silence, and Shane could see the weight of his words settling on everyone's shoulders. He felt a pang of guilt, knowing how hard these changes would hit. But he also knew this was necessary for the survival of the hotel.

"Cutting expenses now will allow us to start modernizing the hotel—implementing online bookings, enhancing our digital marketing, and streamlining operations. These updates will not only improve efficiency but also attract more guests, ensuring long-term growth."

More silence.

"Look, I know this isn't easy," Shane said, his tone softer now. "But I believe in this team. My father believed in you." His gaze fell on Ace, whose face was stony. She hadn't said anything during the meeting, and he wondered what she was thinking. "He told me how you've overcome challenges before, and we can do it again. Let's focus on finding solutions and supporting each other through this. If anyone has ideas or needs assistance, my door is always open."

The department heads exchanged glances, their faces a mix of worry and determination.

Shane could see the gears turning as they started to process the news and think about their next steps. He hoped that, at the very least, this put to rest any rumors about a sale. He wanted his team to see that he was determined to keep the hotel afloat before it came to that.

"Thank you all for your time," Shane concluded. "Let's regroup in a week to discuss our progress and any ideas you might have. We'll get through this, one step at a time."

As the meeting adjourned and the department heads slowly filed out, Shane noticed that only Ace remained seated.

He hoped she understood that he had taken the first step in steering the hotel toward stability and that the real work was just beginning. The road ahead would be tough, but he was determined to lead by example and guide his team through the storm.

ACE SAT AT the other end of the table, her body rigid, eyes narrowing as the other managers left the conference room. She was fiercely loyal to the hotel's traditions and to Shane's father. Today, her loyalty felt like a looming wall between her and Shane.

When they were alone in the room, she spoke up, her voice steady but with an edge to it. "These budget cuts you want to make…laying off the staff…"

Shane turned to face her, his jaw set with determination. "I'm only doing what is absolutely necessary for our survival, Ace."

She crossed her arms, her gaze unyielding. "Your father had a vision for this hotel, Shane. He wanted it to retain its Southern charm, its traditions, and he wanted his employees to feel secure in their jobs."

"I understand this, but we are in dire straits," Shane retorted, frustration simmering beneath his calm exterior. "We can't survive on charm alone. We need to evolve."

Ace blinked in anger. "Evolve? By stripping

away everything that makes this place unique. Your father—"

"Isn't here anymore," Shane interrupted, his voice hardening. "Angus Jr. left me in charge. This was his dying wish, Ace. For me to take over and bring this place into the future."

"Your father would never consider laying off an employee." Angus Jr. had gone above and beyond to *help* his staff. He wouldn't leave them jobless.

"You're right. He wouldn't," he agreed. "My father would also allow people stay here without paying—"

"People who fell on hard times and were evicted from their homes," she responded. "He believed in community. He loved this island, and he cared about the people here."

"As do I," Shane countered. "Ace, if we keep down this same path...there won't be a Polk Island Hotel and then no one will have a job."

Ace took a deep breath, her fingers curling into fists at her sides. "You might be in charge now, but if you think you can just bulldoze over everything he built, then you're sorely mistaken. I won't let you destroy what he loved."

She saw the moment his patience snapped, and his face shuddered. "I'm not here to argue with you, Ace. Either get on board with the changes or get out of my way."

She stared at him, a mix of betrayal and defiance swelling in her. Without another word, she stood up, turned on her heel, and walked out of the conference room.

SHANE WATCHED ACE'S retreating form, the door closing behind her with a soft click that felt far louder in the charged silence of the room.

He exhaled sharply. This was supposed to be a fresh start, but if this day was any indication, it wouldn't be easy.

He turned back to the window, the view of the lush gardens doing little to calm his nerves.

His father's presence was everywhere in this hotel, from the meticulous landscaping to the carefully curated interiors. It was a place steeped in history and sentiment, a living monument to Angus Jr.'s dreams.

Shane shook his head, pushing aside the doubt. He had to move forward.

He needed to make this work, to find a balance between honoring the past and embracing the future. His thoughts were interrupted by a knock on the door.

"Come in," he called.

It was Janie Merck, the human resources director.

Shane had consulted with her prior to the meeting today about the potential staff cuts. She'd been thorough, offering insight on how to handle the layoffs with as much care as possible should it come to that.

"I heard the meeting didn't go so well," Janie

said, folding her arms as she leaned against the doorway.

Shane sighed. "That's an understatement. I had to announce the budget cuts. Everyone's tense, and the possibility of layoffs didn't go over well. I'm going to need your help navigating this. I hate having to do this to the employees, but I really don't have any other choice."

Janie nodded, her expression serious. "I'll make calls to my contacts—there are a few recruiters in Charleston and Hilton Head, and I know some hiring managers here on the island. In the event layoffs are required, we can at least try to find them new opportunities."

"Thanks," Shane said. "We're going to need all the help we can get to ease this transition."

Janie gave him a reassuring smile before heading back to her office.

Shane watched her leave, feeling a small spark of relief. At least he had some allies willing to help guide the staff through the rough waters ahead. But one thing still nagged at him—he needed to talk to Ace again. He wouldn't approach her right away… She probably needed time to digest the latest news.

She wasn't just his father's head of security, she was a keystone in the hotel's community. Winning her support was going to be crucial if he wanted to pull the hotel through this storm.

# CHAPTER SEVEN

ACE DRAGGED HER tired feet through the hotel lobby, feeling the effects of a long day's work. She was relieved that Shane hadn't announced his intention to sell the property so far, but at the same time, she couldn't accept the idea of laying off dedicated employees who had been with the hotel for years.

Angus Jr. was a man of integrity who always put his employees first. He would never even dream of resorting to layoffs, knowing the hardship it would create for his beloved staff. Instead, he would tirelessly search for alternative solutions, determined to keep everyone employed and cared for.

The moment Ace spotted Misty and her youngest daughter, Fawn, waiting for her in the lobby, a wave of warmth washed over her. Her exhaustion melted away as a genuine smile spread across her face. As they approached, she scooped up the little girl in a tender hug, her spirits instantly lifted.

"Ace. *Ace.*" Fawn's excited voice echoed in the lobby as she wrapped her small arms around her neck.

Misty's eyes shone with gratitude as she took Ace's hand, guiding her to a nearby chair. "Fawn has something she wants to tell you," she said.

Fawn beamed up at Ace, her dark curls bouncing with excitement. "I helped Mommy make you cookies," she exclaimed, her eyes twinkling with pride.

Ace felt tears prick at her eyes as she looked at the plate of peanut-butter cookies in Misty's hands. "These are for me?" she asked, her voice catching in her throat.

Fawn nodded enthusiastically. "Yes. I mixed the dough and *everything*. All by myself!"

Ace hugged Fawn tightly, the simple gesture overwhelming her with emotion. She whispered, "Thank you," into Fawn's ear, her voice thick with gratitude. "You did such a great job. I can't wait to eat them."

As they chatted, Ace couldn't help but feel a pang of longing in her chest. Seeing Fawn's innocent joy and Misty's nurturing stirred a deep yearning within her. She had always wanted a child of her own, but her diagnosis of polycystic ovary syndrome made her feel as if her chances of becoming a mother were slipping away.

Misty seemed to notice the faraway look in Ace's eyes. "You okay?" she asked gently.

Ace forced a smile. "Yeah, just a bit tired. But seeing you two made my day."

"You know," Misty said, squeezing Ace's hand,

"Fawn looks up to you so much. You're like a su-perhero to her."

She chuckled softly. "A superhero, huh?" She grinned at Fawn. "Well, I think she's pretty super herself."

Yet, despite the lighthearted exchange, Ace knew what she truly wanted—a traditional family, with both a mother and father raising their child to-gether. It was a dream she had cherished for as long as she could remember, but as the years passed, it felt increasingly out of reach.

As Misty and Fawn said their goodbyes and left, Ace sat alone with her thoughts.

The lobby, usually bustling with activity, now seemed overwhelmingly quiet. She wondered if she would ever get the chance to be a mother like Misty. The uncertainty gnawed at her, a persistent ache that refused to be ignored.

With a deep sigh, Ace stood up and headed to-ward the employee exit. Each step felt heavy with her unfulfilled desires. The staff meeting earlier also left her feeling uncertain about the future.

Tomorrow was another day, and she clung to the fragile hope that it might bring her a step closer to the life she so deeply desired. For now, all she could do was keep moving forward, one day at a time.

She pushed through the exit doors and into the evening air.

Her SUV was parked at the far end of the lot,

and she walked briskly, her thoughts shifting to her next task.

Ace headed to Charleston. Her self-defense class had become a cornerstone of her week, offering her a sense of purpose and a way to channel her energy.

She arrived at the YMCA and hurried inside.

Her students were already gathering, chatting and stretching in the brightly lit room.

After changing into her workout clothes, Ace took a deep breath and steeled herself, mentally donning her instructor persona. She meticulously folded away her personal conflicts, locking them in a mental drawer so she could focus solely on the task ahead. The gym was a sanctuary, both for her and the women who came to train under her guidance.

"All right, ladies," Ace called out, clapping her hands to capture their attention. Her voice echoed through the spacious room, bouncing off the mirrored walls.

"Let's start with some warm-ups. Remember, you're stronger than you think," she added, her tone imbued with conviction. She'd set aside her worries about the hotel and focus on this class. It was one of the ways she found strength in uncertain times.

As they began their routines—stretches flowing seamlessly into high-intensity drills—Ace moved among them, as usual correcting forms and offering words of encouragement.

Each punch thrown and kick executed seemed to chip away at the heavy fog clouding her mind. The rhythm of physical exertion provided a meditative escape from her internal strife.

The class progressed smoothly and by the end of the session, sweat glistened on every brow, but there was also a shared sense of accomplishment that radiated through the space. For Ace, this collective energy lightened her load; it felt as though the burdens she carried had been momentarily lifted by the camaraderie and focus within the room.

"Great job tonight, everyone," Ace said warmly, smiling with encouragement. "See you next week."

With those final words, she watched as her students dispersed, chatting animatedly among themselves. She lingered for a moment longer in the now-quiet gym, savoring the fleeting peace it offered before she'd inevitably return to confront her personal battles once more.

After freshening up and changing, she climbed back into her SUV for the drive home, the night sky a dark canvas dotted with stars.

Ace's thoughts drifted back to the hotel, to Fawn, and to her own unfulfilled dreams. She knew the road ahead was uncertain, but tonight, as she drove through the quiet streets, she allowed herself a small measure of hope.

Maybe, just maybe, tomorrow would bring her a step closer to the life she yearned for.

SHANE STEPPED INTO the Polk Island Café, the familiar scent of freshly brewed coffee and baked goods greeting him as he crossed the threshold.

He was there for a quick breakfast and a moment of peace before meeting London for her doctor's appointment. The café was a comforting haven amid the chaos, a place where he could gather his thoughts.

As he approached the counter, his eyes landed on a woman sitting alone at a corner table. His heart sank as recognition set in.

It was Barbara Clanton—his mother's friend… and the woman he had caught his father with years ago. Seeing her brought back a rush of emotions he had buried deep within him: anger, betrayal, and a lingering sadness.

He had hoped to never see her again, especially now.

She looked up and their eyes met. There was a moment of hesitation before she stood up and approached him. Her face was a mixture of sorrow and determination.

"Shane," Barbara said softly, her voice trembling slightly.

He stiffened; his initial instinct was to turn and leave. But something in her expression stopped him.

"I wanted to offer my condolences," she began,

her voice low. "I heard about your father's passing, and I'm truly sorry for your loss."

He remained silent. Shane didn't trust himself to speak yet.

She took a deep breath, seeming to gather her courage. "I know I'm probably the last person you want to see right now, but there's something I need to say. Something I should have said a long time ago."

He folded his arms, leaning back slightly. "Go on."

She looked down at her hands, fidgeting nervously. "What happened between your father and me...it was a mistake. A moment of weakness. I pursued him, and he regretted it deeply afterward. Angus Jr. told me repeatedly that he loved Madelyn and that what we did was wrong. He never wanted to hurt her."

"Why are you telling me this?" Shane asked. Years had passed since he'd caught them together and he wanted to forget all of it.

Tears welled up in her eyes. "Because I need you to understand that your father wasn't a bad man. Angus Jr. made a mistake, and he regretted it every single day. He loved your mother deeply, and he loved you and your siblings. Looking at you, I can see how much pain I caused, and I'm truly sorry."

Shane clenched his jaw, struggling to contain the flood of emotions threatening to overwhelm him. His heart was a tangle of anger, confusion, and disbelief. The memories of that day—walking into the hotel to find them together in his father's office—hit him like a freight train. It wasn't just the betrayal that stung. It was the crushing weight of feeling like his world had been shattered, like everything he'd believed about family had been a lie.

He could still see them, her hands on his father's chest, his arms around her. The last thing he'd wanted to witness, but it had burned into his memory, leaving no room for doubt. His own father, the man he'd admired, had broken the trust that was supposed to hold them all together. That moment, that discovery, had been a turning point in his life. "What do you want from me?"

She reached out her hand as if to touch his, but she pulled back at the last moment. "I'm not asking for anything other than your forgiveness. I know it's a lot to ask, but I can't carry this guilt any longer without at least trying to make amends."

Shane took a deep breath, his mind racing. He thought of his mother, her strength and dignity, and the legacy his father had left behind. He thought of the pain and betrayal he'd felt, and how much he wanted to protect his family from any more hurt.

"I don't know if I can forgive you," he said slowly, each word carefully measured. "But I appreciate your honesty."

She nodded, tears slipping down her cheeks. "I'm so sorry."

Barbara left the café, leaving Shane alone with his thoughts.

He sat there for a while, staring out the window

as the island's morning bustle continued around him. The conversation had reopened old wounds, but it had also given him a sliver of closure he hadn't known he'd needed.

Taking a deep breath, Shane rose from his seat. He had a lot to process, but he knew he needed to focus on the tasks at hand. London and her baby needed him, and he wouldn't let her face her appointment alone. He ordered a quick breakfast and coffee to go, thanking the server who handed him the bagged meal ten minutes later.

As he left the café, he felt a renewed sense of determination. He would honor his father's memory by being the man Angus Jr. had hoped he would become, flaws and all. And perhaps, in time, he would find it in his heart to forgive—not just Barbara, but his father and himself as well.

SHANE SAT IN the waiting room of Dr. Meyer's office, tapping his foot nervously against the tiled floor. London was seated beside him, her hands resting protectively over her small baby bump. The sterile smell of the clinic mingled with the faint scent of honey lingering on London's clothes—a reminder of her flourishing business.

He glanced at her, noticing the tension in her posture.

"You okay?" he asked, his voice soft with concern.

London nodded but didn't meet his eyes. "Just a bit anxious, that's all."

"You know that Mom would be here with you if she hadn't had to go to her own doctor appointment," Shane said.

"I know. She offered to reschedule her checkup, but I told her not to do it. Her blood pressure has been on the high side since Dad died." London glanced over at him. "I'm glad you're here, though. We have quite a bit to catch up on."

"She told me her pressure reading was normal this morning before she left for her appointment. I don't think it's anything serious."

"I'm sure you're right."

Shane hesitated before broaching the topic that had been weighing on his mind. "London, I wanted to ask you about...the father of the baby."

London's gaze hardened slightly. "Shane, I really don't want to talk about that right now. I need to focus on bringing this baby into the world healthy and strong. And building LW's Honey business. That's all that matters to me."

Shane nodded, respecting her boundaries, though the curiosity and concern gnawed at him. "I understand."

She studied him. "Let's talk about you...why did you leave the island?" London asked. "And I know it's not just because of the job opportunity with Alexander-DePaul. I know that something happened between you and Daddy. What was it that tore you two apart?"

Shane sat there, grappling with London's piercing question. Her words echoed in his mind, each syllable laden with unspoken truths and buried pain. He knew he couldn't evade her forever.

"Dad and I..." Shane began cautiously, his voice tinged with reluctance. "We had our differences."

He hesitated, choosing his words carefully, unwilling to expose the searing wound within him— the knowledge of his father's infidelity. Running into Barbara had brought that pain to the forefront, despite that he was determined to find it in him to forgive her.

London's unwavering gaze demanded honesty. She studied Shane intently, as if sensing there was more that he wasn't saying.

The air in the waiting room grew heavy with unspoken words, creating a suffocating silence that stretched between them. It was as though the very walls held their breath, waiting for Shane to break his silence.

London reached out and placed a gentle hand on Shane's arm. "Whatever it is, you can trust me. Please, don't bear this burden alone," she pleaded softly, her voice filled with sisterly concern.

Finally, unable to withstand her concern and his own guilt any longer, Shane took a deep breath. He met London's eyes, seeing in them a reflection of his own turmoil, and began to speak. "Dad... he wasn't faithful to Mom," Shane admitted, his voice barely above a whisper. "He had an affair."

London's expression shifted from curiosity

to shock, her face paling as disbelief and anger flashed across her features. Had he just shattered her image of their father as the unwavering pillar of their family?

"He loved Mama," London protested softly, her voice trembling as if she hoped Shane would take it back. She withdrew her hand from his arm, her gaze drifting away as she tried to process the bombshell that had just been dropped on her.

"I can't believe it," she said, shaking her head as if willing the words to disappear. "You're saying Daddy had an affair? That's not the man I knew. He was always there for us. He would never—" Her voice cracked.

He shook his head sadly. "I know it's hard to accept, but it's true—"

"Hard to accept? It's impossible!" she interrupted, her frustration bubbling to the surface. "Dad was the one who taught me about loyalty and love. How could he betray everything he stood for? He loved us, Shane. He loved Mom. He would never hurt her like that. You're just—" She paused, her breath hitching. "It must be some kind of misunderstanding."

Shane felt her disbelief, wishing he could ease her pain. "I wish it were that simple. I caught Dad with the other woman. There was no mistaking what was going on." He paused a moment, then added, "Like you said…he wasn't perfect."

"Daddy made a mistake then," she interjected,

her tone defensive. "A big one…" Her voice trembled, but she clung to her denial like a lifeline.

After what felt like an eternity, London turned back to him, her eyes glistening with unshed tears. "I can't believe he would do that." She paused a moment, then asked, "Does Mama know about this?"

"No, and I don't want her to ever find out," he responded.

She nodded. "She can't hear about this. It would break her heart."

London's words struck a chord within Shane. He appreciated her strength in that moment.

"I'm sorry I didn't tell you sooner," he repeated softly, feeling heavy with remorse.

"Do you know who she is? Was it some random guest at the hotel or someone we know?" London asked quietly.

Shane hesitated briefly then, his voice steady, he replied, "It doesn't matter now."

A nurse appeared, putting an end to their conversation. Though Shane had to admit that despite the mixed feelings about his father's past, he felt lighter having told someone.

THE MORNING SUN was just beginning to filter through the blinds of Ace's office, casting a soft glow over the organized chaos of her desk. Reports, security footage, and a mug of half-finished herbal tea cluttered the surface, but her mind was razor-sharp.

She was reading over the latest incident report. A male guest had caused trouble while intoxicated and attempted to enter a room that wasn't his. Thankfully, one of Ace's team members had handled the situation, but the woman staying in the room was understandably disturbed by the ordeal.

Shane walked into the room, his presence immediately creating tension in the small space. Ace looked up, her eyes narrowing slightly as she took in his neutral expression.

"Good morning," Shane began, his tone clipped. "We need to talk."

She set down the report and leaned back in her chair, crossing her arms. "What is it, Mr. Worthington?"

He closed the door behind him and stepped closer, his hands clenched at his sides. "I've been reviewing your updated budget and the security department's expenses are too high."

Ace's heart sank, but she kept her expression neutral. "*Too high?* We were already operating on a tight budget. Any more cuts and we won't be able to guarantee the safety of our guests or staff. Did you hear about what happened last night?"

Shane sighed, taking a seat opposite her. "I did. I actually spoke with the guest that was staying in the room a few minutes ago. She's still shaken by what happened."

"I need every member of my team."

"I understand that, but we're hemorrhaging money. We need to find a balance."

"Balance?" Ace scoffed, unable to keep the frustration from her voice. "You want me to *balance* security with cutting costs? How am I supposed to do that? By taking away the very tools and personnel we need to keep this place safe?"

Shane's jaw tightened. "There are some areas we can streamline." He leaned closer and she tried not to notice the cologne he wore or the deep timbre of his voice. "Maybe we don't need round-the-clock surveillance in every part of the hotel. Or perhaps we could reduce the number of guards on the night shift."

Ace stood up, her chair scraping against the floor. "That's reckless. We've had incidents in the past, and with the recent high-profile guests, security needs to be tighter than ever. You can't just make these decisions without understanding the implications."

His eyes flashed with irritation. "I've worked in this industry my entire life and I do understand the implications, Ace. We can't keep running things the way we did when my father was alive. Changes must be made in every department."

Ace took a deep breath, trying to rein in her temper. She wanted to work with him and she would as best she could. "I get that. But compromising on security isn't the answer. If something happens because we cut corners, it won't just be your family's legacy that's affected—it'll be people's lives."

Shane stared at her, his expression unreadable. "You're overreacting."

Ace felt a surge of anger. "Overreacting? Do you have any idea what it's like to be responsible for the safety of hundreds of people every day? To know that one mistake, one oversight, could lead to disaster? I'm not overreacting, Mr. Worthington. *I'm doing my job.*"

The silence that followed was heavy, the air thick with unspoken words.

Finally, Shane sighed, rubbing the back of his neck. "I didn't come here to argue. I came to try and find a solution." The hardness in his expression melted away to reveal the vulnerability she'd seen in him the night they met. The wish to comfort him and the urge to hold her ground warred within her.

Ace watched as he got up, turned, and walked toward the door, his shoulders tense. The door clicked softly behind him, leaving a thick quietness in the room.

She had always prided herself on her professionalism and her ability to handle any situation, but this was different.

This was personal.

She could resign… Why stay and work for Shane when everything she loved about this place was changing?

But as the thought crossed her mind, a memory surfaced. It was a promise she had made to Angus Jr. in the dim light of his hospital room. His frail hand had gripped hers, his eyes filled with a mixture of pain and determination.

"Promise me, Ace," he had whispered, his voice weak but resolute. "Promise me you'll look after Shane. He'll need your support."

Ace closed her eyes, the words of her mentor sinking in. Angus Jr. had believed in her, trusted her to be the rock that Shane would need. She couldn't walk away now, not when things were getting tough. But she also couldn't stand by and watch Shane make decisions that could jeopardize everything they had worked so hard to protect.

As the day wore on, the hours seemed to stretch, and Ace felt the time pressing on her. She decided it was time for a walk to clear her head—her mind needed a break.

Plus, it was nearly time for the n check-in with her evening staff before she could head home. Instead of using the two-way radio, she'd personally visit her team members.

The weight of her promise to Angus Jr. pressed heavily on her shoulders. She needed to find a way to balance supporting Shane and ensuring the hotel's security remained uncompromised.

Ace stepped off the elevator on the third floor and spotted Calvin, one of her evening security staff, making his rounds near the hallway.

"How's everything looking up here?" she asked.

Calvin adjusted his earpiece and gave her a quick smile. "All clear so far. No disturbances, and I just finished checking the stairwells. Quiet evening."

"Good," she replied, glancing down the empty corridor. "Any issues with the cameras or radios before I wrap up for the night?"

"Everything's running smooth," Calvin confirmed. "Just the usual late check-ins. Had one noise complaint earlier, but it was an easy fix."

Ace nodded, relieved. "Sounds like things are under control. I'll do a quick final sweep, then I'm clocking out. You know the drill—if anything comes up after I leave, just give me a call."

"Will do, Ace. Have a good night," Calvin said, giving her a thumbs-up.

"Thanks, Calvin. Keep things steady," she said with a smile.

Lost in her thoughts, she almost didn't notice Oliver standing at the end of the hallway, leaning casually against the door of her office when she exited the elevator.

His presence immediately put her on edge. He'd been a guest of the hotel for a while now, and with his sharp suits and even sharper words, Oliver struck her as someone who was constantly scheming.

"Ace," he called out, pushing off the wall and

walking toward her with casual, confident strides. "Can we talk for a moment?"

She considered brushing past him, but something in his tone made her stop. "What can I do for you, Mr. Worthington?"

He smiled, a predatory glint in his eyes. "I couldn't help but overhear your little discussion with Shane earlier. It sounded like things were getting pretty tense between you two."

Ace crossed her arms, her gaze unwavering. "Do you make a habit of eavesdropping on other people's conversations? Maybe we should restrict your access to the gallery and keep you out of the administration area."

Oliver chuckled, shaking his head. "You and I both know Shane is making some poor decisions. Decisions that could put everyone at risk."

Her eyes narrowed. "What's your point?"

"My point," he said, stepping closer, "is that maybe it's time you reconsidered your loyalty. Shane is out of his depth. You, on the other hand, have the experience and the insight to make the right calls. Why should you let him drag this hotel down with his misguided attempts at leadership?"

Ace felt a flicker of doubt, but quickly extinguished it. "Shane has extensive experience in managing hotels—five-star hotels, Mr. Worthington."

Oliver's smile widened, but it didn't reach his eyes. "Loyalty is admirable, Ace, but it shouldn't be blind. Shane is making decisions that could endanger us all. If I were in charge, you could ensure the hotel's safety and security without compromise."

Ace took a step back, her posture rigid. "If you're so concerned about the hotel, maybe you should focus on supporting your cousin instead of trying to undermine him." Despite being frustrated with Shane, Oliver was being unfair. She might not agree with Shane's tactics, but he was an accomplished hotelier and cared about his family. She admired that about him. He was knowledgeable, poised...dangerously good-looking... Which was not how she should be thinking about her boss.

Oliver sighed, a hint of frustration in his voice. "If you're set on this course, so be it. Just remember, when things fall apart, you had the chance to make a difference."

With that, he turned and walked away, leaving Ace standing alone in the hallway.

She took a deep breath, steadying herself. Oliver's words had planted a seed of doubt, but she knew she couldn't let them take root. Her loyalty to Shane and her promise to Angus Jr. were more important than ever.

As she continued down the hallway, Ace resolved to find a way to bridge the gap between her and Shane. For the sake of the hotel, and for the memory of the man who had trusted her with so much, she would not give up.

# CHAPTER EIGHT

THE FOLLOWING DAY, Shane made his way through the bustling hotel lobby. He caught sight of Ace through the partially open door of the security office, her focus fixed on the computer screen in front of her.

She may have challenged him, but he respected her boldness and determination to protect jobs. Her refusal to back down only strengthened his realization that he needed her by his side.

Taking a deep breath, Shane hesitated before finally turning back toward her office. Perhaps it was time to see where they stood now.

He tentatively stepped into the office, unsure of how to break the tense silence that hung in the air between them.

"Hey," he began, his voice hesitant yet determined. "I wanted to apologize for yesterday. I didn't mean to sound dismissive about your role here."

Ace turned to face him, her gaze steady and unwavering. There was a softness in her eyes that belied the toughness of her exterior. "No need to apologize," she replied. "I understand your wanting to save the hotel. However, I stand by what I said about my department. I also don't think that laying off employees who've been here for years is the right way to go."

"This isn't something I arrived at lightly," he responded. "All I'm trying to do is save the hotel, even if this means layoffs in some areas. I'm looking into possible alternatives, Ace."

"I realize this but let that be the last option. After every other option has been exhausted."

"I'm open to that. However, we really don't have a lot of possibilities. Can we at least try to find some common ground?"

She looked at him, the hard lines of her face softening just a fraction. "I don't want to see this place lose what makes it special."

"I understand. And the hotel needs you, Ace."

She nodded. "I'll try and keep an open mind."

It was a small victory, but Shane would take it.

As they stood there, the gentle trickle of the fountain in the background, he felt the first tentative steps toward a new beginning.

"I thought about quitting," she said bluntly. "But I made a promise to your father that I would support you, and I'm not going to break that promise. But you have to know I won't support decisions that compromise the safety of this hotel."

"You promised my dad that you'd support me?"

Ace crossed her arms, her expression softening. "I did. Angus believed in you, and he meant a lot to me. He gave me a chance when I had nowhere else to turn."

Not for the first time, he found he wanted to know her better. He was so drawn to her. She hesitated for a moment, her gaze distant. "Before I came to Polk Island, my life was full of uncertainty and instability. Angus offered me not just a job, but a sense of belonging. I can't turn my back on that."

Shane's heart ached at her words. He understood more than she realized about uncertainty. "I guess we'll have to find a way to make this work without breaking the bank."

"And we will," Ace replied, her tone firm but conciliatory. "Cutting corners on security is not the answer. We need to find other areas where we can save money without putting anyone at risk."

Shane nodded slowly, the tension in his shoulders easing slightly.

If he could gain the support of all the department heads, they would protect the legacy of the Polk Island Hotel and ensure its future.

OLIVER SPOTTED KENYON just inside the kitchen, sipping from a glass of lemonade and chatting with another member of his team.

He leaned casually against the counter. "Hey, cousin," Oliver began, keeping his tone light and nonchalant.

Kenyon's smile faltered slightly, a flicker of defensiveness crossing his features. "Guests aren't allowed back here."

"I'm not just a guest and you know it."

"Regardless, you can't just walk into my kitchen."

As the clatter of plates and pans filled the air, Oliver said, "You know, it's funny how history repeats itself."

Kenyon glanced over at him, raising an eyebrow. "What do you mean?"

"I mean," he continued, lowering his voice conspiratorially, "how Angus Jr. overlooked you for Shane just like our grandfather overlooked my dad."

Kenyon paused, his expression hardening slightly. "That was a different time, Oliver. Things have changed. And there were reasons why our grandfather did what he did."

Oliver pressed on. "Have they really? You're the eldest, just like my father. Yet here we are again. Are you gonna tell me that it's never bothered you that Shane was being groomed for the GM role while you slaved away in the kitchen?"

Kenyon sighed, shaking his head. "I've never been interested in running the hotel, Oliver. I love being a chef. Even as children, I found myself in the kitchen. Chef Damon taught me how to cook. He was my mentor."

"But don't you see?" Oliver persisted, lowering

his voice further. "This is exactly how it started between my father and uncle. One gets the title, the other gets left out. It's what tore them apart."

Kenyon's gaze hardened, his jaw tightening. "I'm not Uncle Jacob, and Shane is not my dad. I won't let it come between us."

Oliver leaned in, now speaking with the urgency he felt. "All the way back to Asa, the tradition has always been the eldest son or daughter inherits and oversees the hotel until death."

Kenyon turned away briefly, busying himself with checking an order, then met his gaze again with a determined look. "I appreciate your concern, Oliver. But I'm not interested in the GM position. Shane is my brother, and I won't betray him."

He felt a surge of frustration and disappointment, realizing he had failed to sway Kenyon to his side. Oliver had hoped to ignite a spark of doubt, to make Kenyon see Shane's ascent as a threat rather than an inevitability. But Kenyon's loyalty ran deep, anchored in familial bonds that Oliver couldn't undermine.

With a resigned nod, he straightened up, a bitter taste of defeat settling in his mouth. "I get it. Family loyalty and all that."

Kenyon placed a reassuring hand on his shoulder, his tone softening slightly. "You're my cousin, Oliver. But you've done a lot to try and hurt this family. Just stop…"

His attempt to sway Kenyon had failed, leaving him more determined than ever to find another way to assert himself in the face of Shane's seemingly unstoppable rise. He had another few tricks up his sleeve—now he needed to put them into action.

SHANE, STANDING TALL behind the polished mahogany desk in Guest Services, was engulfed in a tempest of emotions amid the serene elegance of the opulent lobby.

His peaceful morning had been shattered by the unexpected chaos that unfolded with the Thompson reservation issue, a seemingly innocuous event that was about to erupt into a full-blown crisis.

Mr. and Mrs. Thompson, a pair of elderly lovebirds celebrating their fiftieth wedding anniversary, had arrived at the Polk Island Hotel only to be met with the shocking news that there was no reservation in their name.

When Mr. Thompson presented his confirmation number, nothing came up in the computer. The reservation seemed to have vanished into thin air. The Thompsons had meticulously planned this annual getaway, and their excitement had soured as they stood in the lobby, bewildered and frustrated.

"I don't understand." Mrs. Thompson's voice wavered, disbelief resonating in each syllable. "We always make our reservation before we leave for the next year. My husband even spoke with someone last week to confirm. They assured us that bungalow ten would be ready and waiting for us."

Micah, the epitome of poise and professionalism, replied smoothly, "I'm very sorry, Mrs. Thompson. I'm not sure how this happened. Let me check our system again."

As he feverishly tapped away in the hotel's reservation software, Shane came up beside him, seeing the gaping hole in the system where the Thompsons' reservation should have been. The problem was, all the bungalows, including ten, were now booked.

"Could it have been a system glitch?" Shane asked.

"Maybe," Micah replied, but clearly, he wasn't convinced. The Polk Island Hotel was known for its impeccable service and seamless operations. A glitch like this was unheard of.

"I'm really sorry about this," Shane apologized to the Thompsons. "We're going to do everything we can to make this right."

Mr. Thompson, a tall man with a kind but weary face, sighed deeply. "We've been looking forward to this trip for months. This hotel has always been special to us. This is where we spent our honeymoon fifty years ago. Every year we've stayed in the same bungalow. Number ten. We came all the way from New Jersey."

Shane couldn't help but feel a pang of guilt. He knew the significance of the Polk Island Hotel to many of their guests, especially for special occasions like this one. "Mr. and Mrs. Thompson. Please, give us a moment. We'll find a solution."

"While you're waiting, we'd like you to have lunch on us. You can choose South Winds or North Winds…it's your choice," Micah said.

"I'd like South Winds," Mrs. Thompson responded.

Micah handed them vouchers. "Enjoy your lunch. And don't worry." He smiled reassuringly. "We will make this right."

When they left the lobby, he called Kenyon. "Hey, a Mr. and Mrs. Thompson are on the way there. Please send a bottle of champagne to their table. Their reservation got screwed up somehow." He hung up.

Shane was grateful for Micah's quick thinking.

"Shane, that reservation was in the system," Micah said. "I get a list of all the guests on their honeymoons, celebrating anniversaries, birthdays…"

"It's not there now," Shane responded. "How do we fix this?"

"The only thing we have available is one of the suites. We could put them in the Magnolia Suite."

The Magnolia Suite was the most expensive and lavish room in the entire hotel. It was a huge upgrade, and they wouldn't make their usual revenue on the room.

Shane nodded. "Book it. These guests have been loyal to us for fifty years. We can't let their anniversary go unnoticed or be ruined because of our mistake." Micah gave him a grateful smile and quickly made the arrangements. "I've also ordered a bouquet of roses to be sent to the suite."

Shane felt a sense of satisfaction mixed with guilt. They may have appeased the guests, but this mistake would leave a dent in the hotel's profits, and perhaps their reputation if the Thompsons remembered the mix-up and told others.

Shane walked to South Winds to personally inform the Thompsons and give them the keys.

Mr. Thompson wore a look of disbelief when he was told they'd been upgraded.

"I knew your grandfather, and the service at this hotel is unchanged since his time," Mr. Thompson said. "The first time we came here, we booked a regular room because it was all we could afford. Angus Sr. heard us mention that we were on our honeymoon and upgraded us to bungalow ten."

Shane smiled. He was pleased that his guests were happy. Yet he couldn't shake the feeling of unease. The incident had exposed a vulnerability in their system, and he knew they had to do better.

He and Micah would have to sit down to figure out what had gone wrong. He hadn't gotten to the bottom of his email being hacked yet, despite bringing it to the attention of the manager at Springhill Event Services. Something told him this reservation mix-up wasn't a system glitch but a deliberate act. He couldn't change what had happened, but he could make sure it never happened again.

# CHAPTER NINE

SHANE SPENT THE latter part of the morning fielding calls and messages about the latest piece of gossip threatening the hotel. The stakes had never felt higher—if the rumor wasn't squashed quickly, the hotel's reputation would take a serious hit. He called an emergency meeting with Cia and Micah.

Closing the door to the conference room, he announced, "There's a story circulating in the media about the Polk Island Hotel being sold to the Alexander-DePaul chain."

Cia's eyes widened in shock. "How did something like that get out? Especially since it's not true."

Shane gritted his teeth, sensing the storm that was about to hit. "I don't know. But if people believe it, it's going to create chaos and confusion for us."

Cia rubbed her temples in frustration. He understood her stress—he'd spent the better part of yesterday helping her resolve a wedding-cake order, which, according to their usual vendor, the hotel had canceled ahead of a huge wedding they were hosting this weekend.

"We need to find out who leaked this and set the record straight immediately," Cia insisted.

"I completely agree," Shane replied, his voice now steely with determination. "But right now, our top priority is ensuring that the wedding taking place this weekend goes off without a hitch. I'll handle the media and damage control."

After the meeting, he retreated to his office, only to be met by an incessant ringing from his phone.

Shane answered with trepidation, already anticipating what was coming next.

"Is this Shane Worthington?" a shrill voice demanded.

"Yes," he responded warily. His heart pounded in his chest. "Who is this?"

"Clara Sams with the *Polk Island News*," the reporter said. "Your hotel is making headlines about its sale to another company. I'd like you to hear from you whether the rumors are true that you're selling to Malcom Alexander."

Shane took a deep breath, forcing himself to remain calm even as her statement sank in. "I'm sorry, but that information is incorrect. The hotel is not being sold."

But inside, his mind was racing. He had considered selling the hotel—had almost convinced himself that it was the right move. After all, the financial strain and pressure to live up to his father's expectations had been crushing. Part of him still wondered if it would be easier to let it go, to walk away from the overwhelming responsibility. Wasn't that the logical choice?

Yet now, standing here, being in this office as he had the past few weeks, it wasn't just about business anymore—it was about the family legacy, about everything his father had built. If the sale rumors gained momentum, they could cause a media storm and shake the staff's confidence. Worse, it would betray Ace, who had stood by him out of loyalty to his father.

He realized with a jolt that the idea of selling no longer felt like an option he could stomach. The thought of seeing this hotel in someone else's hands made him feel as if he'd be failing both his family and the people who had trusted him to lead. People like Ace. He felt a twinge in his chest as he thought of her. She seemed to believe in him—or she trusted his father's instincts about him, anyway. Why did her opinion mean so much to him? Because he admired her... She was beautiful and so intriguing...

He couldn't let things spiral out of control. This hotel was staying in the family. He just had to make sure no one—especially not the media—found out how close he'd come to selling. As the morning wore on and he fielded more calls about the news story, he realized that the extent of the storm brewing—he needed to quell it before it was too late.

ACE LEANED AGAINST the railing of the Polk Island Hotel's rooftop terrace, sipping her herbal tea as the afternoon sunlight bathed the ocean in a golden hue. She glanced at her watch, knowing Shane would be joining her any minute now. He had requested that she meet him here.

The door to the terrace swung open, and Shane stepped out, his expression a mix of frustration and determination.

Ace recognized that look—Shane was on a mission to solve a problem.

"Hey," he greeted, his voice tinged with tension. "Thanks for meeting me up here."

She nodded, then set down her cup. "What's going on?"

Shane sighed, running a hand through his hair. "It's been a rough couple of days. First, the Thompson reservation disappears without a trace, and then a wedding-cake order was canceled. Cia placed that order eight months ago, and we've never had an issue with that vendor before. On top of that, this morning I've had to deal with calls from guests and reporters wanting to know if I'm selling the hotel to Malcolm Alexander. I spoke with him briefly—reporters are calling his office as well. Just so you know, I turned him down after talking to my family. Malcolm is very supportive and has offered his help if we need it."

Ace raised an eyebrow. "That's great news. However, this is quite a series of unfortunate events. Any idea what happened?"

Shane leaned against the railing, looking out at

the water, his shoulders slumped. "I've been going through everything with Cia and Micah, and we can't find any logical explanation for either incident," he said, his voice laced with frustration. "At first, we thought the IP address we traced might give us a lead, but it ended up pointing to one of our vendors. When we followed up, it was a dead end—nothing suspicious on their end."

He let out a sigh, shaking his head. "I'm starting to believe that someone is deliberately trying to sabotage us. There's no other way to explain how all of this is happening at once."

Ace considered his statement, her mind racing. "Why do you think someone would do this on purpose?"

Shane clenched his jaw. "I'm not sure, but I have a strong suspicion that it might be Oliver. He's probably the one contacted the newspapers."

That surprised her. "Your cousin? Why do you think it's him?"

Shane's voice dropped as he said, "He's been resentful ever since my grandfather passed the hotel to Angus Jr. instead of his father. Uncle Jacob's been gone over twenty years… Oliver's made it clear he believes that he should be the one running things."

Ace nodded. "He definitely wants to be in charge, but this is pretty extreme."

Shane shook his head. "I don't have any proof—it's just a gut feeling." He leaned heavily on the railing, his large form so close, his dark eyes unfocused. She wanted to reach out to him, comfort him, but she squashed the thought. He'd come to her because she was his head of security, and he needed solutions.

She took a deep breath, choosing her words carefully. "Oliver left the island three days ago. He told Guest Services that he wasn't checking out—just going to spend a few days with his mother in Charleston."

Shane rubbed his temples. "This can't just be a coincidence."

Ace considered the possibilities, trying to see the situation from all angles. "Look, I know it feels personal, but sometimes these things do happen. Systems glitch, vendors make mistakes. It could be just a string of bad luck. Things haven't always run smoothly here…minor issues. As for the newspaper… I don't know."

Shane shook his head, frustration evident. "I don't buy it. Up until now operations, logistics, and our systems have always run smoothly. Two major screw-ups like this back-to-back? It doesn't add up. Something's off."

It was definitely suspicious; she'd give him that. "Let's not jump to conclusions just yet," she responded. "We need to investigate this thoroughly. If someone is sabotaging us, we'll find out who. But we also need to consider that it might just be random mishaps."

Shane nodded slowly, though Ace could see he was still troubled.

"The important thing is to stay calm and methodical. We can't let these incidents shake us," Ace said, trying to keep the edge out of her voice. Despite the chaos surrounding the hotel, they needed to stay focused, even if standing this close to Shane made it hard to ignore her attraction to him.

"Thanks, Ace. I appreciate your level-headedness. I just hate seeing the hotel's reputation take a hit like this." Shane managed a small smile.

She nodded, feeling the weight of his words. "We all do," she agreed. "Your father faced challenges before, and we've always come out stronger. We'll get to the bottom of this, one way or another."

Now he smiled fully, and their gazes held for a moment.

Ace felt a flicker of something—an ease between them that hadn't been there before. It felt good to be on the same side, working toward the same goal. But she quickly reminded herself to stay professional. Ace couldn't afford to let down her guard, not after what happened with her ex. There was too much at stake here, and getting too close to Shane could complicate everything.

There was no room in business for personal entanglements—not now, and especially not with him. Shane took a deep breath, nodded resolutely and straightened. "Thank you again."

"Anytime," Ace replied, watching as Shane made his way back inside.

She picked up her cup, staring out at the ocean once more. As much as she wanted to believe it was all just a coincidence, a nagging feeling in the back of her mind told her Shane was right about someone sabotaging the Polk Island Hotel, and if that was the case, she needed to find out who—and fast.

AFTER HIS MEETING with Ace earlier, Shane had filled Nelson in on everything that had happened. When Nelson investigated, it had come to their attention that several other supply orders had been canceled. Nelson then called for Shane and Ace to meet him in his office immediately.

Shane stepped out of his office when he heard a knock on his door. Ace. "Ready?" he asked by way of greeting when he saw her.

She nodded, and together, they walked down the hall to the IT department.

Seated in Nelson's office a few moments later, they discussed a plan of action.

Nelson said, "We need to secure all the employee email accounts."

"Agreed," Shane replied. "But how do we do that?"

Nelson began typing on his computer keyboard. "We change all the passwords and make sure they're strong and unique. No more using the same password for multiple accounts. I'll also enable two-factor authentication for an extra layer of security."

Shane nodded. "That's a good start. What about our suppliers? How do we make sure they know what's happening and don't fall for any more fake cancellations?"

Ace thought for a moment. "We should contact all our suppliers personally and inform them about the situation. Tell them that from now on, any changes or cancellations must be confirmed with a phone call from one of us directly. *No exceptions*."

"That makes sense," Shane said. "But what about finding out who's behind this? We can't just sit around and wait for them to strike again."

"I'll start by reviewing our account logs and seeing if I can trace where these unauthorized messages and cancellations are coming from," Nelson responded. "My team can help track any suspicious activity."

Shane looked relieved. "That sounds like a solid plan." He rose to his feet. "Let's get to work."

Shane and Ace left Nelson's office.

By the time Shane returned to his desk, Nelson called to say that an unfamiliar IP address had accessed several email accounts multiple times over the past few weeks. It would take Nelson some time to pinpoint the exact location, but it was a start.

An hour later, Shane's phone buzzed with a notification. It was another news alert about the supposed sale of the Polk Island Hotel.

His heart sank as he read the headline: Historic Polk Island Hotel to be Sold to Corporate Giant Alexander-DePaul.

His phone rang.

"Mom—"

She interrupted him, and asked, "Did you see the news?"

"I saw it," he muttered. "We intend to release a statement denying these stories immediately. I've asked my admin to draft something up. We need to reassure our guests and staff that the hotel is not being sold."

"Cia told me about the near fiasco with the wedding cake. You need to find out who's behind this and stop them before they cause any more damage," Madelyn stated. "If they're willing to go this far, who knows what else they're capable of?"

Shane vowed to uncover the truth. After the call ended, his mind drifted to Ace. She was sharp and grounded in a way that both calmed and challenged him. He knew he should keep his distance to keep things professional, yet he couldn't deny that her presence was anything but ordinary.

Later, as he passed by her office, he couldn't resist knocking on the door, half hoping she'd read his mind and half dreading that she might.

Ace looked up from her desk, raising an eyebrow. "I thought you were gone for the day."

"I'll be here for a while this evening," he said, stepping inside and closing the door behind him.

Their eyes locked for a moment, the air between them charged with an unspoken tension that neither wanted to acknowledge yet couldn't ignore. "I'm trying to get to the bottom of this mess," he stated. "And I could use your help."

Her gaze lingered on him, warm and steady. "If you're up for working late to get to the bottom of this, so am I."

# CHAPTER TEN

OLIVER STOOD ON the porch of his mother's house, gazing out at the sprawling garden that she had tended for years. The air was warm and fragrant with the scent of blooming roses and jasmine.

He could hear the distant sound of laughter from children playing in the yard across the street, a reminder of the close-knit family he felt increasingly disconnected from.

Oliver sighed with disappointment after reading his text from Emma.

Shane had managed to save the day for the guests whose reservation had disappeared and to find a bakery to supply a wedding cake. However, the hotel's reputation had taken a hit. It wouldn't be an easy fix to stop the rumors that he was selling to Malcolm Alexander, especially now that local news outlets had reported on it.

Oliver's phone buzzed, and he glanced down at the screen. Another text from Emma. She'd followed up to let him know she had contacted two former hotel employees and arranged to meet with them.

A slow smile spread across his face.

*Perfect.*

This was exactly the kind of progress he had been hoping for. He knew disgruntled ex-employees were often the easiest to manipulate, especially when their departure had been less than amicable. People who had been fired rarely needed much convincing to air their grievances, and even less to lend a hand in a little sabotage.

He could hear their complaints already—the familiar litany of blame and frustration.

It wouldn't take much to stoke that fire, push them to take actions they might not have considered on their own. And Emma, well, she had a way of getting people to open up to her, to feel comfortable enough to spill their secrets. It was one of the reasons he'd involved her in this plan from the start.

Oliver tucked his phone back into his pocket, satisfied. Things were moving in the right direction. If they played their cards right, Shane wouldn't know what hit him.

Oliver was the natural leader for the hotel. He had ideas to make it prosper. He'd silently observed the financial woes plaguing the family business from afar. He knew about the decline in occupancy rates, the dwindling profits, and had seen the desperation in his cousins' eyes whenever they discussed the hotel's future. And yet, he hadn't shared his thoughts with them—like implementing green practices, such as solar panels, water conservation and water reduction. Not because he lacked solutions, but because of the bitter resentment that simmered within him.

His mother stepped out onto the porch, carrying a tray with two glasses of iced tea. She set the tray down on the small table between their chairs and handed him a glass.

"Thank you," Oliver muttered, taking a sip and avoiding her gaze.

She settled into the chair beside him, her eyes filled with a mixture of concern and determination. "Son, we need to talk," she said softly.

Oliver sighed, knowing where this conversation was heading. "Ma, we've been over this. I don't want to discuss it."

"We have to," Alice insisted. "I can't stand seeing you so unhappy and estranged from the family. You need to make peace with your cousins."

Oliver shook his head, his frustration simmering just below the surface. "They treat me like an outsider, like I don't belong." He couldn't help but dwell on the stark contrast between his life and that of his cousins.

"That's not true," Alice said gently. "They've always welcomed you with open arms. It's you who keeps pushing them away."

Oliver's jaw tightened. "They only tolerate me because they have to. I'm as much of a Worthington as they are, but they act like I'm some distant relative who doesn't matter."

He recalled the day his father had been ousted from the family business, a decision that had shattered their lives and driven a permanent wedge between them. Oliver's father had never recovered from the humiliation and failure, and neither had Oliver. The bitterness had taken root early, fueling his ambition and determination to prove himself worthy of the family name, even if they had cast him aside.

Yet, despite his resentment and the jealousy that sometimes gnawed at him, Oliver knew deep down that maybe his mother was right. Maybe his cousins weren't to blame. They were simply born into a life of privilege and expectation, just as he was born into one of struggle and defiance. It was the hand fate had dealt them all.

Alice reached out and placed a hand on his arm, her touch warm and comforting. "You are a Worthington, Oliver. No one is questioning that. But your attitude and the way you approach them—it's driving a wedge between you and your cousins. They haven't done anything to hurt you."

He pulled his arm away, his irritation rising. "They've taken everything, Ma. The hotel should have gone to Dad. Grandfather promised it to him, but instead, it went to Angus Jr. And now Shane's running everything. It's not fair."

Alice sighed, her expression pained. "I know you're hurt, Oliver. But holding on to this anger isn't going to change anything. It will only make you more miserable. You need to let go of the past and try to build a future with your family."

Oliver stood up abruptly and began pacing the porch as he tried to rein in his emotions. "I can't just let it go. It's not that easy. Every time I see them, I'm reminded of everything we've lost. I should oversee the hotel, not Shane. It's my rightful place."

She stood and approached him, her eyes filled with tears. "Son, I want you to be happy. Truly happy. Not consumed by bitterness and resentment. You have so much potential, so much to offer. But you're letting this anger define you."

Oliver stopped pacing and looked at his mother, his heart aching at the sight of her distress. "I will be happy, Ma," he said quietly. "But only when I'm in my rightful place. I can't just accept things as they are."

Alice reached up and cupped his face in her hands, her touch gentle but firm. "Your rightful place is with your family, Oliver. Not as an adversary, but as a cousin, a nephew, a son. You need to find a way to work through this, to forgive and move forward."

Oliver closed his eyes, feeling the weight of his mother's words but unable to let go of his anger. "I don't know if I can do that," he admitted.

Could he put aside his bitterness and resentment for the greater good? Could he set aside his pride and offer his ideas, knowing they might save the hotel and restore his family's fortune? It was a question Oliver wrestled with.

For now, he would continue to work silently from the sidelines, refining his business ideas and preparing for the moment when his cousins might finally acknowledge his contributions.

"You can," Alice whispered. "You have a good heart, son. I've seen it. You just need to let it guide you."

Oliver pulled away and turned to look out at the garden again, his mind a whirlwind of conflicting emotions. He wanted to make his mother happy, to be the son she believed in. But the bitterness and sense of betrayal ran deep.

"I'll try," he said finally, though his voice lacked conviction.

Alice smiled sadly, understanding the struggle within him. "That's all I ask. Just try. For your own sake."

Oliver nodded, but his thoughts were already drifting back to the hotel, to the legacy he felt had been stolen from him. He couldn't shake the feeling that his place was there, leading the family business as he believed his father should have. Making peace with his cousins seemed like an impossible task, one that would require him to give up his dreams and accept a reality he couldn't reconcile with.

SHANE DESCENDED the staircase of the Polk Island Hotel, his thoughts preoccupied with the latest batch of guest complaints and upcoming events. The morning sun streamed through the large windows, casting a warm glow over the opulent foyer.

As he reached the bottom of the stairs, he turned toward the gallery, which was the hotel's pride and joy, housing family heirlooms and precious artifacts that had been passed down through generations of Worthingtons. Shane's great-grandfather had overseen the initial collection, and each generation added to it. The centerpiece of the collection was the priceless sculpture by the artist Lorne. Although he had dropped the Worthington surname, Lorne and Asa remained close cousins.

When Shane entered the gallery, his heart sank. The protective glass case that housed the heirloom had been shattered, shards littering the floor like broken dreams.

The sculpture itself was gone.

Shane's stomach clenched as he stared at the empty display case. "No," he whispered, his voice barely audible over the pounding of his heart. He rushed to the empty pedestal, his mind racing. *How could this have happened?*

The Worthington Gallery was supposed to be one of the most secure parts of the hotel. He felt a wave of panic and dread crash over him.

His mind spiraled with questions. Could this be the work of the same saboteur, or had he been so consumed by the chaos at the hotel that someone else had taken advantage? He wasn't sure anymore.

The sense of certainty that had driven him was now riddled with doubt.

He stared at the empty pedestal, his heart pounding harder. Could Oliver have orchestrated this entire thing, or was there someone else lurking in the shadows? In the confusion of the last week, with so many distractions pulling at him, it was possible that someone else had swooped in and stolen the statue while his guard was down. He was supposed to be leading this hotel into its future, yet all that awaited him was uncertainty.

He called Ace and she entered the gallery a few minutes later.

"What's going on?" she asked.

He turned to her. "It's gone. Someone stole it."

Ace's eyes widened as she took in the scene. "How? This place is secure."

"It must have happened right after night security came through."

Shane shook his head. "I don't know. I don't know how I'm going to tell the family. This statue has been here since Great-Grandfather's time. It's irreplaceable."

She placed a reassuring hand on his shoulder. "We'll figure this out, Shane. We'll find out who did this. But right now, we need to think about how to handle the immediate situation."

Shane took a deep breath, trying to steady himself. "We can't let anyone know it's missing. Not yet. It would cause a panic, and the guests might lose trust in us if they found out the hotel had been robbed."

Ace nodded. "Agreed. We need to keep this quiet while we investigate."

Shane hesitated, then nodded. "I'll tell the family that we've moved the statue to a more secure location off-site. I'll also announce that we're revamping the hotel's security system to ensure this doesn't happen again."

Ace gave him an encouraging smile. "That sounds like a good plan. I'll start looking into the security footage and questioning the staff. We'll find out who did this."

Shane felt a flicker of hope, the weight on his chest lightening just a bit. Ace had a way of calming his storm, grounding him when everything felt out of control. It wasn't just her competence; it was her unwavering presence, the way she stepped in when he needed it most, sometimes without him having to ask.

"Thanks, Ace," he said softly, meeting her eyes. "I don't know what I'd do without you."

She squeezed his shoulder, her touch firm but reassuring. "We'll get through this together. Now, let's get to work."

As Ace left to begin her investigation, Shane stood alone in the gallery, staring at the empty pedestal. He felt a crushing weight of responsibility settle on his shoulders. The hotel had always been a symbol of his family's strength and unity, and now it felt as if that symbol had been shattered along with the glass case.

He made his way to his office, his mind racing with a thousand thoughts. How had someone managed to get past their security?

Shane picked up the phone and called a family meeting.

An hour later, his mother and siblings gathered in the small conference room adjacent to his office, their expressions ranging from curiosity to concern.

"Thank you all for coming on such short notice," Shane began, trying to keep his voice steady. "I have some important news regarding the gallery."

Madelyn looked at him with a mix of anxiety and expectation. "What is it, Shane?"

He took a deep breath. "We need to upgrade the security there, but in the meantime, I've decided to move all the items to a more secure location off-site. Given the recent security concerns with mysterious cancellations, Ace and I believe this is the best course of action to protect our family heirlooms."

There were murmurs of surprise and concern around the table.

Micah nodded in agreement. "It's a good idea. Better to be safe than sorry."

Madelyn looked worried, but nodded, too. "I trust your judgment."

Shane felt a pang of guilt but forced a smile. "Mom, it's only temporary."

As the family dispersed, Shane returned to his office, feeling both relief and dread. The immediate crisis had been managed, but the underlying problems remained. He had to find the statue and the person responsible for its theft, and he had to do it quickly. The reputation of the Polk Island Hotel—and the legacy of the Worthington family—depended on it.

Shane spent the next few hours poring over security reports and making calls to tighten their defenses. He knew Ace was out there, working tirelessly to uncover the truth. Despite the chaos, he felt somewhat relieved. Like Ace had said, the hotel had faced challenges before, and they would overcome this one, too.

They had to.

As the sun set over the island, casting long shadows across the hotel grounds, Shane looked out the window of his office, feeling a renewed sense of determination. The fight was far from over, but he was ready for whatever came next.

SHANE'S HEART THUMPED in his chest as he paced back and forth in the office. His mind raced with thoughts of the stolen heirloom had been taken right under their noses. Every fiber of his being continued to point to his cousin being the culprit. Oliver had proven himself deceitful before, and this felt like another one of his schemes. Without hesitation, Shane ordered a thorough search of Oliver's suite, determined to find evidence to support his suspicions.

His mind raced as he rummaged through Oliver's belongings, desperate for any clue to the missing statue. Each mundane item only added to his frustration and disappointment. The only thing found was a notebook filled with notes, research, and strategies to increase hotel revenue.

"You've been a very busy boy," Shane whispered as he put the notebook back where he'd found it. "Too bad you'll never get the chance to implement any of it."

Ace watched him closely, her presence a reminder of the weight on his shoulders. "It's not here," she said flatly, but with a hint of understanding in her voice.

Shane's heart sank even lower at her words. Could he have been wrong about his own cousin? His cousin hadn't been staying in his suite for almost a week.

He reasoned that it was because Oliver wanted a solid alibi. When he returned, Shane intended to keep a close watch over him. For now, they had to figure out who else could have taken it and how they were able to steal it under his watch.

The statue held more than just monetary value—it was a symbol of his family's legacy, passed down for generations. And now, it was gone, all because of his inability to protect it—his father had mistakenly placed too much faith in him.

Oliver burst unannounced into his office at the end of the day, shortly before Shane was about to leave.

"How was your visit with Aunt Alice?" Shane asked tersely as he shut down his computer. "Mom told me you were in Atlanta."

"She's fine. Still got a lot of fight in her," he responded. "I stopped by the cemetery earlier to visit Dad and Uncle Angus. I met someone interesting there."

Shane could sense there was much more weight behind those words than his cousin was letting on, but he remained silent.

"Barbara Clanton was there. I believe you know her. She was sitting there at the foot of Uncle Angus's grave, crying. Suddenly, she just starts pouring her heart out to me. You may not know this, but she was in love with Uncle. She wanted to say a final goodbye before she left the island."

Shane's heart sank at the realization that this could only mean trouble. He couldn't let this information reach his mother.

"I was shocked to learn that it was Aunt Maddie who encouraged Uncle to hire Barbara as his executive assistant. She was even a bridesmaid in their wedding." Oliver smirked. "What happened next is quite surprising to me. All this time, I thought my uncle was a saint—"

"Oliver, stay out of this," Shane commanded, his tone brooking no argument. He knew his cousin well enough to suspect that he would try to use this information as some sort of leverage. And the person who'd be hurt was his mother.

"Just thought you'd want to know. Get ahead of any rumors…"

"Get out of my office," Shane demanded. This confirmed it—his cousin was only here to stir up trouble.

He glanced outside at the darkening sky, feeling the weight of his responsibility heavy on his shoulders. The ominous clouds mirrored the growing sense of dread inside him, as if his fragile peace was hanging by a thread, ready to snap at any moment. Shane knew that the storm brewing wasn't just outside—it was already here in the hotel.

And at the center of it all was Oliver.

As SHANE SAT beside Ace in the dimly lit security room, he could feel the tension growing—not just from the investigation but from her closeness.

Ace leaned forward, her finger tapping the screen. "Look. Right there. See how the screen jumps? That's not normal."

Shane squinted, leaning in closer to the monitor. "Yeah, I see it," he muttered, his jaw clenching. The footage had been tampered with; frames edited to hide something—someone. His frustration was mounting, but Ace's presence seemed to steady him. Her quiet focus was unwavering, and he found himself stealing glances at her, more aware than ever of the calm she brought him.

Ace played the footage back several more times, and Shane felt exhaustion creeping in.

Suddenly, Ace froze. "Wait. There…" She pointed again.

In the corner of one frame, a faint reflection—a hooded figure moving toward the sculpture.

Shane's breath caught. "Is that…?"

"It's something," Ace said, standing up, her voice filled with cautious excitement. "I'm heading back to the gallery. I need to take another look in person."

Shane nodded, pushing himself out of his chair. Should he accompany her? No. He needed some space from her and the way she drew him in. "Call me if you find anything."

Ace gave him a small, encouraging smile. "Will do."

As she turned to leave, Shane hesitated. He wanted to say more, to thank her, but the words caught in his throat.

Instead, he simply nodded.

She seemed to catch his uncertainty because her eyes softened as she said, "We'll find it, Shane."

He silently considered the chaos that had overtaken the hotel. She moved closer, reached up a hand as if to touch him, then pulled back. "This was out of your control. Don't blame yourself." He and Ace stood together in the quiet of the office. He wanted to lean even closer, cup her face in his palm.

"I'd better get back to work," Ace said, suddenly stepping back.

"Let me know if you find anything," Shane responded.

She nodded and left. He needed to clear his mind, maybe take a walk on the beach. As he exited his office, Oliver caught up with him, and asked, "Why is the gallery closed? What happened?"

"We're revamping security," Shane answered. "I've had the entire collection moved to a secure location."

Oliver looked surprised. "When will it reopen?"

"Once we've updated our security system. It's nothing to worry about." Shane knew he couldn't keep this secret forever, but for now, he couldn't risk causing his family any more pain. He just hoped they would understand when the truth finally came out. Ace would find whoever had done this.

Shane let out a long breath as he left the hotel and headed for the beach. He ran a hand through his hair, trying to shake the growing distraction Ace was becoming. He needed to stay focused—on the theft, on protecting his family's legacy. But as the thought of her lingered, so did the realization that keeping his distance from her wasn't going to be as easy as he'd hoped.

# CHAPTER ELEVEN

ACE SAT IN the surveillance room, surrounded by the glow of multiple monitors displaying footage from the gallery's cameras. The hours had stretched into the evening as she meticulously reviewed every frame for any clue that could lead them to the person who had stolen the priceless sculpture.

Her eyes were tired, but determination fueled her as she continued to analyze more of the footage around the time of the theft. Ace had always been thorough, but tonight she was relentless. She enhanced each frame, zooming in on details, hoping to catch a glimpse of anything out of the ordinary.

As she scrolled through the footage from another camera, her breath caught in her throat. There, in a split second of clarity, she saw it—a reflection of the person dressed in dark clothing, gloves, and a cap pulled low over their face. They moved with purpose to where the sculpture had been prominently displayed.

Ace's heart raced with excitement and urgency.

She rewound the footage, zooming in on the mysterious figure.

She dialed Shane's cell. "I think I've found something," she said when he picked up. "Can you join me in the surveillance room?"

He arrived within minutes.

Shane leaned in closer, his arm nearly brushing against hers, Ace's heart skipped a beat. She could feel the heat radiating from him, and his focused intensity only made her pulse quicken. She tried to steady her breathing, focusing on the screen instead of the proximity of the man beside her. "Who is that?" Shane's voice was low, and the way his brow furrowed in concentration sent a shiver through her. "Can you enhance it?"

Ace nodded quickly, hoping her face didn't betray the flush she felt creeping up her neck. She began typing, her fingers moving swiftly over the keyboard, grateful for the distraction.

As she applied the filters, her mind raced, not just about the image, but about Shane. He had always been composed, professional, even though he was under immense pressure to keep the hotel afloat—but here, in these stolen moments of closeness, Ace couldn't ignore how drawn she was to him.

The image on the screen sharpened, but it was hard for Ace to focus on anything other than how Shane's nearness made her feel—like the world outside this room could fall apart, but in here, she was safe.

"It's coming into focus," she said, her voice slightly breathless as she zoomed in further, trying to push aside her thoughts.

Shane's eyes stayed glued to the screen, but Ace couldn't help but wonder if he felt it, too, or if he was so wrapped up in the crisis that he hadn't noticed the attraction simmering between them.

As the image revealed more details of the figure's attire, Ace stole another quick glance at Shane, her chest tightening. He had no idea what he did to her, and she had to keep reminding herself—he was her boss, and now wasn't the time for distractions.

But she couldn't deny that being this close to him made focusing on anything else nearly impossible.

"They're wearing gloves, probably to avoid leaving fingerprints," she observed. "And look at the way they move—confident, like they know exactly where they're going."

"We need to identify this person," Shane said firmly. "Pull up any other footage from that night. They must have entered or left the gallery at some point."

Ace nodded, her focus unwavering as she searched through the archives for any additional footage.

Minutes passed in tense silence broken only by

the clicking of keys and the hum of the monitors. Finally, she found what she was looking for—a glimpse of the figure slipping out a side entrance of the gallery.

"I've got them leaving," Ace announced. "If we're lucky, we might be able to track their movements from the hotel to a vehicle... Whoever this is, they seem to know where all the cameras are located."

"This is either an inside job or the thief is working with someone who knows this hotel very well," Shane stated. "They know all too well how to avoid every single camera. Maybe this is a result of the pending layoffs. It's possible that somehow the employees found out that we're considering it, or they could believe that I'm selling the hotel." He was very familiar with the employee grapevine and how quickly rumors spread.

"I don't know, but I'm not giving up," Ace uttered.

He smiled at her. "I never imagined you would."

WALKING TO HIS OFFICE, Shane couldn't shake the image of Ace from his mind. Her eyes, intense yet soft, seemed to pierce right through him. He tried to focus on the task at hand, but his thoughts kept drifting back to her. The hotel commanded his full attention now.

The financials were a mess, occupancy numbers were declining, and the competition from newer, flashier resorts was fierce. He couldn't afford any distractions, especially not now. Yet, Ace was a distraction he couldn't seem to avoid.

His father's voice echoed in his mind, urging him to be practical, to make the tough choices that would ensure the family's stability. But every time Shane thought about cutting jobs or selling the hotel, he imagined Ace's disappointed eyes, the way her face had softened just a fraction when they had found a small piece of common ground.

Shane sat down at his desk, trying to drown his thoughts in spreadsheets and reports. Numbers danced before his eyes, but the only image that stayed clear was Ace's face. He remembered the way her lips pressed into a thin line earlier, when she was deep in thought, scanning the security footage. He found himself smiling despite the turmoil around him.

The sound of footsteps broke his reverie. Shane glanced up to see Janie and Lilly passing by, offering polite nods.

He straightened in his chair, forcing his attention back to the documents in front of him. He couldn't let his feelings for Ace cloud his judgment. But the more he tried to focus, the more his thoughts strayed to her.

Shane recalled a conversation, how she had looked him directly in the eye and told him she had thought about quitting but stayed because of a promise to his father. Her loyalty was unwavering, and it matched his own commitment to the hotel.

He stood up and walked to the window, looking out over the courtyard. The thought of being close to Ace, of feeling the electricity that sparked every time they were near each other, made his heart race.

With a sigh, Shane turned back to his desk. The pile of work was daunting, but it was nothing compared to the emotional battle raging within him.

Ace made him feel alive in a way he hadn't in a long time. Every smile, every touch—even unintentional—lit something inside him that he wasn't ready to face. He couldn't deny that her presence made him feel like he could take on the world. But falling for her could tear down everything he'd worked to protect. His focus had to remain razor-sharp, especially with his leadership being questioned.

The stolen statue gnawed at him, adding to his already mounting stress. The thought of someone within the hotel's circle betraying them stung deeply.

He knew he would have to confront his attraction to Ace eventually. He was saved from thinking further on that by a knock at the door.

Cia popped her head in. "Are you free?"

He waved her in, then sat back in his chair, absentmindedly rubbing his temples as if to dispel the lingering doubts that gnawed at him.

Cia settled into the adjacent armchair.

"I keep thinking about what happened with that wedding cake and trying to figure out who would go as far as to cancel it. It had to be someone who worked at the hotel for a while. The order was placed eight months ago."

"I agree," Shane responded. "Do you think it could be one of your staff members?"

"I considered it," Cia answered. "But after speaking with them one-on-one… I don't think it was."

"Has anyone quit within the past year?"

Cia hesitated for a moment, seemingly weighing her words before she spoke. "Not in my department. But there was a guy that worked in IT. He was fired about eleven months ago. He was caught stealing a case of rib eye from the kitchen. And then there was this employee… Selena. She worked in accounting and had been funneling money into a personal account. She was fired as well. Daddy made her pay back the money she stole."

*Two employees had stolen from the hotel.* His father hadn't said… He'd need to ask Ace about this, too, since it would've involved her department. As the implications of the revelation settled in, Shane's unease grew. "Do you think they could be behind this?"

Cia shrugged. "It's possible. Mark was furious about losing his job and vowed to get even. He had extensive knowledge of the hotel's inner workings, particularly its computer systems. The bakery said that it was a woman who canceled the order."

"I still think Oliver is behind everything," Shane said. "He has the motive."

"Doesn't make sense to me," replied Cia. "Why would he try to sabotage the hotel?"

"I don't know, but my gut keeps telling me that Oliver's up to something. I've learned to trust my instincts where he's concerned."

THE NEXT MORNING, Shane went to the house to help his mother sort through the remnants of his father's life. Each item held a cherished memory, and as they divided them among the siblings, it felt like they were letting go of a little piece of their shared history. The task took them until noon to complete, and by then, their hearts were weary.

Now, sitting across from Madelyn at the Polk Island Café, Shane's mind was in turmoil. He toyed with his salad, barely paying attention to the crisp greens as he struggled to push away the conflicting thoughts threatening to consume him.

The missing statue only added to Shane's anxiety and sense of betrayal. And speaking of anxiety, he needed to rein in his thoughts about Ace—it wouldn't do to be mooning over one of his department heads.

"I really appreciate your help with this, my dear," Madelyn said with a sad smile, breaking through his inner musings. "I don't think I could do it alone."

Shane nodded, understanding the task. "Anything for you, Mom."

She chewed a bite of her food. "You know, you're more than welcome to stay with me at the house until you find your own place," she offered tentatively.

Shane forced a smile and shook his head. "Thanks, Mom, but I need my own space. The suite is fine for me."

Madelyn's concerned eyes bore into him, and he could feel her worry radiating off her. "Are you sure?"

Shane shrugged nonchalantly, masking the real reason why he couldn't bear to stay in the family home—because it reminded him too much of his late father.

His mother reached out and squeezed his hand in support. Shane felt grateful for her understanding but also guilty for wanting to distance himself from the family home during this difficult time.

"Do you have any plans for later?" Madelyn queried.

"I'm going to Leon's birthday party," Shane announced.

"I hope you have a great time. It's about time you got out and had some fun."

He grinned. "Are you trying to say that I'm boring?"

"I'm saying you work too hard, son. You need to find a balance between work and a social life."

"I'm good." Shane planted a kiss on her cheek. "See you later, Mom."

SHANE STOOD ON the front porch of Leon and Misty's house, the warm glow of light spilling out from the windows and the faint hum of music drifting through the air.

He adjusted his collar, feeling a mix of anticipation and anxiety. While Shane was looking forward to celebrating with his friend, he couldn't shake the nervous energy that had settled in his chest since he knew Ace would be here.

He stepped inside, the room bursting with life and laughter. Leon was surrounded by friends and family, his face alight with joy. Shane mingled with the guests, exchanging pleasantries and catching up with familiar faces. Yet, his eyes kept drifting to the doorway, as he waited for Ace to arrive.

When she finally walked in, Shane felt his breath catch in his throat. She was wearing a simple yet elegant dress that hugged her curves in all the right places. He was used to seeing her in the dark suits and polos she wore to work. The soft, flowing fabric of her dress moved gracefully with her every step, and Shane couldn't take his eyes off her. She looked stunning, and the sight of her made his heart race.

Ace spotted him and made her way over, a warm smile on her lips.

"Hey," she said, her voice a soothing balm to his frayed nerves. It had been a stressful week.

"You look amazing," he said before he could think better of it.

She broke into a grin. "Thank you for the compliment."

Their gazes held as the music shifted to a slow, romantic tune.

Couples began to pair off and dance.

Shane glanced at Ace, his heart pounding. "Would you like to dance?" he asked, extending his hand.

Ace hesitated for a moment, then placed her hand in his. "I'd love to."

They moved to the center of the room, the world around them fading as they swayed to the music.

Shane's hand rested on Ace's waist. The feeling of her in his arms sent a shiver down his spine.

They moved in perfect sync.

"You know," Ace said softly, looking up at him, "it's nice to see you outside of the hotel for a change."

"Yeah," Shane agreed, his voice barely above a whisper. "It's nice to just enjoy the moment."

As they danced, Shane's thoughts raced. He couldn't deny how he was attracted to her, the way she made him feel alive and grounded at the same time. But he also knew that this wasn't the right time for romance. There were too many things that demanded his focus—it was more than one person should have to handle at once. And his attraction to an employee would only make his chaotic life even more complicated.

Yet, with Ace in his arms, he wanted to hold on to this feeling, to the way she fit perfectly against him. It was intoxicating, and he found himself getting lost in her eyes.

When the song ended, they reluctantly pulled apart. The spell was broken, and reality came crashing back. He never should've held her like this. Now, he wouldn't be able to forget what being so close to her was like.

Shane forced a smile. "Thank you for the dance."

Ace smiled back, her eyes holding a hint of sadness, as if she could sense him pulling away. "Anytime."

With that, she turned and walked away.

# CHAPTER TWELVE

THE FAMILIAR SCENT of freshly brewed coffee and buttery croissants greeted Ace as she pushed open the door to Polk Island Café on Saturday morning. She'd had a wonderful time at the party last night with Shane.

The memory of their dance lingered, a warm embrace and electric connection that awakened buried emotions. When the music ended, she'd been left cold and conflicted. The attraction to Shane and her fears battled inside her, making it difficult to navigate being around him.

She couldn't resist breaking into a wide grin when she saw a salt-and-pepper-haired figure sitting at a corner table, stirring her black coffee with slow, deliberate movements.

"Miss Eleanor, it's so good to see you," Ace said, making her way over to the table where Leon's grandmother sat.

"Alison…" Eleanor replied, squinting up at her. "I can't remember the last time I saw you."

"It's been a few weeks now," Ace said, pulling

out a chair and joining her. The Alzheimer's was slowly robbing Eleanor of all her memories. She didn't recall that Ace worked at the hotel or that she'd seen her recently at the memorial service.

"Do you work on the island?" the older woman asked.

"I'm head of security at the Polk Island Hotel," Ace answered. But she knew that Eleanor wouldn't remember their conversation even five minutes from now. Her granddaughter-in-law owned the café and was likely keeping an eye on Eleanor this morning.

Eleanor leaned in closer, studying Ace's face intently. "You know my nephews, don't you?"

"I do. I saw Trey and Leon last night," Ace stated. "We celebrated Leon's birthday."

"That's right…he had a birthday. I need to pick up a card for him."

Smiling, she nodded, feeling a pang of sadness for Eleanor.

"You know, Alison," Eleanor began, her voice gentle yet filled with conviction. "Life has a way of surprising us. Sometimes it brings us exactly what we need when we least expect it."

Ace furrowed her brow slightly, intrigued by Eleanor's cryptic words. She had known her to speak in riddles from time to time, but there was something about her tone that resonated deeply within Ace.

SHANE STEPPED THROUGH the wooden door of the Polk Island Café, where the atmosphere enveloped him in a cloud of nostalgia. The familiar smells of fresh-brewed coffee and sizzling bacon immediately brought him back to his childhood. He scanned the room and spotted Ace, who was deep in conversation with Eleanor Rothchild.

His heart skipped a beat as he saw Ace's face light up, and he made his way over to their booth, taking in the sight of her long, loose braids cascading down her back, like they had last night. It was a stark contrast from her usual tightly bound bun.

"Good morning, ladies," Shane greeted. "Do you mind if I join you?" He knew he shouldn't. His feelings for Ace confused him, but after last night, he wanted to see her again.

"Shane…what a wonderful surprise," Eleanor exclaimed. "I'm so glad to see you. How long are you in town?"

Ace slid over, making room for Shane. "Have a seat."

"I'm back home for good, Miss Eleanor."

Shane's own words caught him off guard as they slipped from his lips. He hadn't returned to the island with the intention of staying for good. But the longer he was home, the more he liked it.

As he settled into the chair, his father's voice echoed in his head, reminding him of his permission to sell if needed: "Shane, you have my blessing to do what you must to save the hotel."

The weight of those words hung over him as he'd debated his options. Selling to Malcolm Alexander was a tempting offer that would allow him to escape from the responsibilities of the hotel and return to his fast-paced life in California. But in doing so, he would lose everything he held dear— his family's legacy, the rich stories embedded in the walls of the hotel, and the vibrant community surrounding it.

"I hope you brought your appetite," Eleanor said, her eyes twinkling with mischief.

"I did," Shane responded, eager to dive into the menu and indulge in the delicious offerings of the café.

"I remember the time you came in here and tried to order a dozen pancakes." Eleanor settled back, chuckling. "That look your mama gave you…"

Shane laughed at the memory, the familiarity of the moment bringing a comforting rush of memories to the forefront of his mind. "She wasn't happy. Especially since we'd already had breakfast at home. Miss Eleanor, I loved your pancakes."

"I don't cook anymore. I've become a little forgetful over the years."

The conversation flowed easily between the three of them, with each person sharing stories and reminiscing about the past.

Shane glanced up just as Oliver entered the restaurant, his tall figure casting a long shadow across the sunlit floor.

His gaze bore into his cousin. "I thought you would've left the island by now."

Oliver laughed, a hint of bitterness in his tone. "It's my home. I never realized just how much I miss being here." It struck him that they had something in common—hadn't Shane just been thinking the same thing?

"Is that Jacob's son?" Eleanor asked.

"It's me," Oliver said. "How are you, Miss Eleanor?"

She looked at him with a motherly concern, her eyes softening. "I'm fine," she responded. "How is your mama?"

"She's good," he answered.

The older woman nodded. "Oliver, you staying out of trouble?"

Oliver grinned. "Yes, ma'am, Miss Eleanor."

*Yeah, right.* Shane glanced over at Ace, who gave him a look to remind him to keep his composure. He clenched his jaw.

After a few parting words to Eleanor, Oliver walked up to the counter to place an order.

"That young man didn't know how to stay out of trouble," Eleanor said, keeping her voice low. "I surely hope he's grown out of that by now."

Picking up a menu, Shane didn't respond. Instead, he carefully studied the options, his mind racing with memories of shared meals at the café with his family in the past. The taste of those delicious pancakes brought a smile to his lips, a small comfort amid an emotional reunion.

With all their talking, the two of them hadn't

ordered food yet. Eleanor took Shane's order and carried it to the kitchen.

"Is she still working?" he asked Ace.

"No, she just likes to come and help. Misty thinks it calms Miss Eleanor to come here every now and then."

Speaking of former jobs... "Tell me what you know about any of the employees terminated in the past year," Shane said.

She leaned forward, her expression serious. "Well, there was one in accounting and one in IT. Recently, we had to let go of a housekeeper who was stealing from hotel guests' rooms. We caught her trying to hide jewelry in between the sheets on her cart."

Shane nodded. "And these three incidents are all unrelated in your opinion?"

Ace hesitated for a moment, then shook her head. "As far as I can tell. Nora—that's the house-keeper—started months after Selena and Mark were terminated."

A server walked over with their food and placed it on the table.

Shane picked up his fork, a plan forming in his mind. "I'd like to see if there's any connection to Oliver. Especially the one who worked in IT... Mark." He thought of the leaked emails—could his cousin have gotten a former IT employee to hack his account and make it look like the messages were sent from one of the hotel's vendors?

Ace nodded in agreement. "I'll start with reviewing his personnel files and checking for any unusual activity or contacts."

"Thank you, Ace," Shane said sincerely, meeting her eyes once more. "I'm glad you're here with me on this. The layoff notices are going out on Monday."

Her brow creased. "No-o-o..." she murmured.

"We're giving employees a two weeks' severance and a letter of recommendation. Janie's also going to connect each of them with recruiters." Shane paused a moment, then said, "I hate this as much as you do, Ace. But there is no other option right now."

"We're heading into our summer season."

"I know," he replied. "Reservations are down compared to the last two years. Meetings and conferences are down as well."

Ace gave a slight nod. "I don't like the idea of people losing their jobs, but I understand."

"Reservations for this week have been steady. I'm sure it's because of the upcoming Spoleto Festival." The gospel music festival was a huge event on the island and brought in tourists every year.

"That's good news," she replied before taking a sip of her water.

"Any plans for the rest of the weekend?" Shane asked.

"Nope. Just rest and relaxation. What about you?"

"Outside of attending church with my mom, I don't have anything else planned."

They left the café and went their separate ways.

Shane felt both determined and apprehensive. The challenges ahead were daunting—the nagging worry about the stolen heirloom and the layoffs lingered at the back of his mind, casting a shadow over his resolve.

ON MONDAY MORNING, Ace met with Janie in her office.

Janie sat behind her desk, her posture rigid and her eyes sharp, watching Ace with a mix of curiosity and suspicion. "I'm confused. Why do you want to see my personnel files?" Janie asked, her tone clipped and defensive.

Ace steeled herself. She had anticipated this reaction. Although she hadn't known Janie long, she knew that she was protective of her domain, and any request for information was seen as an intrusion.

"You mean the *hotel's* personnel files," Ace clarified, maintaining a calm and steady demeanor. "I'm asking for the files of the three most recent employees who were terminated."

Janie's eyes narrowed slightly, her suspicion deepening. "Why do you need to see them?"

Janie's scrutiny bore down on her, but Ace kept her expression neutral. "I'm not willing to get into this right now," she responded. "Just know that this is at Shane's request."

The mention of Shane's name did little to appease the HR lead. If anything, it seemed to heighten her wariness. She leaned back in her chair, crossing her arms over her chest. "I think I'll have a conversation with him. I can respond to any concerns he may have regarding personnel."

Ace shrugged in nonchalance, though inwardly she was calculating the potential fallout from this conversation. "That's completely fine."

As she watched Janie's reaction, a swirl of thoughts and emotions churned within her. Ace respected Janie's dedication but any perceived encroachment on her responsibilities was met with immediate resistance.

She recognized that Janie's defensiveness was rooted in her commitment to her job. But at the same time, she was frustrated by the lack of cooperation. She was here to help, to uncover the truth behind the recent disturbances that had been plaguing the hotel. She also knew that Janie's loyalty to Shane was matched only by her protectiveness toward the staff. Which meant today's layoff announcements would be difficult for her.

"Janie, this isn't about questioning your judgment or undermining your authority. Shane asked me to review those files. He wants to understand the circumstances around the terminations. If there's a pattern or a common thread, it could point us toward a solution. This isn't about finding fault but about finding answers."

Janie's expression softened slightly, but she still looked skeptical. "And you think reviewing the personnel files will help with that?"

Ace nodded. "It's a starting point."

Janie sighed, her shoulders relaxing a fraction. "All right, Ace. I'll get you the information. But I want to be kept in the loop. If there are any issues, I need to know about them as soon as possible."

Ace smiled, feeling a small sense of victory. "Of course, we're on the same team."

SHANE HAD JUST handed out the last layoff letter.

The burden of the past few hours settled heavily on his shoulders as he slumped in his office chair. Twenty employees, each with their own story, had looked at him with shock, disappointment, and resignation as he'd delivered the news. He wanted the news to come directly from him, rather than their supervisors, since he felt responsible. The budget cuts had demanded these sacrifices, but that didn't make the task any easier.

Shane had sat down with each one, ensuring they left with two weeks' severance, a letter of recommendation, and a list of resources to help them find employment. It was a small consolation, and he knew it.

His family had built this hotel with a sense of community and loyalty, always prioritizing their employees' well-being. Never in his wildest dreams had Shane imagined he would be in this position, dismantling the team his father had so carefully nurtured.

As the door to his office closed behind the last employee, Shane felt a wave of guilt and sorrow wash over him. He had done what needed to be done, but it didn't erase the pain he saw in their eyes. It didn't erase the feeling that he had let his father down.

Shane made a silent vow. He would do everything in his power to turn the hotel around and to ensure that one day, those who had been let go could return. For now, though, he had to live with his decisions and the hope that he was making the right ones for the future.

Later in the afternoon, Shane met with Ace to discuss the three terminated employees who may have had reason to steal the Lorne statue.

"I've looked at all three employee files," Ace said, "but nothing stands out. I thought that if we could establish a pattern or identify any connections between them, we might uncover who's behind all this."

Despite how intently Shane listened to her, he felt a weight pressing on his chest. The morning's layoffs had drained him more than he wanted to admit.

Ace, ever perceptive, noticed and leaned closer, her expression shifting from casual to concerned.

"How did it go this morning?" she asked, her voice gentle but probing.

"I hate that it came to this."

Ace nodded sympathetically, her gaze steady. "You did what you had to do. Sometimes, those choices are the hardest, but necessary for the greater good of the hotel."

He couldn't help but be impressed by her clarity of thought—she'd wanted him to seek other solutions but knew in the end this was the only one. But amid the professional admiration, another feeling tugged at him—the growing attraction he'd been trying to keep at bay. Shane found himself wishing he could reach out, to close the space between them.

Pushing away any thoughts of that, Shane refocused on the task at hand. He was intentional about setting clear boundaries with his staff, ensuring that professionalism always came first. Yet, despite his best efforts, there were moments when he couldn't ignore the chemistry between them—the way Ace's eyes lit up with excitement when they discussed strategies, or the warmth of her smile when they shared a moment of success. She was getting under his skin and Shane felt powerless to resist.

# CHAPTER THIRTEEN

ACE SAT AT her desk in the hotel's security office.

She leaned back in her chair, tapping a pen against her notepad as she reviewed the day's agenda. Her thoughts, however, drifted to a more personal matter—one she had been grappling with ever since Shane had entered her life.

Shane was not just any man; he was her boss, the heir to the hotel empire who she had come to respect and admire. From the moment she had joined the team, she had sensed his dedication to the hotel and to his family. It was both admirable and intimidating.

Ace couldn't shake the responsibility bearing down on her. As head of security, she felt personally accountable for the recent breaches. She'd worked tirelessly to honor Angus Jr.'s trust in her, but these lapses made her feel she'd failed him— and Shane. And it didn't help that her feelings for Shane were complicating everything. Despite her resolve to keep things professional, she couldn't deny the magnetic pull between them. Shane's quiet strength and steady support had softened her defenses, and she found herself drawn to him in ways she hadn't anticipated. It scared her.

She had been down this road before. Her previous marriage had been toxic, suffocating—a cycle of heartbreak and disappointment. The wounds from that experience were still fresh, a reminder of the pain she had endured. She had promised herself she wouldn't make the same mistake again.

And now, here she was, feeling drawn to Shane in ways she hadn't expected.

He was different, she told herself. He was caring, respectful, and genuinely invested in the well-being of the hotel and its staff. But she couldn't deny the risks.

Ace sighed softly, closing her eyes for a moment to gather her thoughts. She wanted to be a mother someday, to create a stable and loving environment for her children. The idea of risking her heart again, of falling in love with the wrong person, filled her with unease.

Opening her eyes, Ace refocused on her work. She reminded herself of the boundaries she had set, the importance of maintaining a professional distance from Shane.

But as she glanced at a framed photo on her desk—a picture of herself as a child with her parents, filled with love and laughter—a pang of longing tugged at her heart. She wanted that for herself, a family of her own someday.

Pushing aside her thoughts of Shane, Ace delved into her tasks for the day with renewed determination. She would stay focused, keep her emotions in check. The hotel needed her, and she wouldn't let anything jeopardize her commitment to its success.

The day wore on and meetings came and went. By the time evening fell and the hotel quieted down, Ace packed up her things and prepared to leave for the day.

As she walked through the lobby toward the exit, Shane approached her with a warm smile. They exchanged a few words before parting ways.

Ace drove home, her thoughts returned to the delicate balance she was trying to maintain. She wanted love and companionship, but not at the cost of her own happiness and stability.

Arriving at her quiet cottage, Ace settled in for the evening, a mix of emotions swirling inside her. She knew she needed to tread carefully, to protect her heart and her dreams of a future filled with love and possibility. Getting involved with her boss would only complicate that.

Later, as she drifted off to sleep, Ace made a silent promise to herself—to stay vigilant, to prioritize her own well-being, and to never settle for anything less than she deserved.

ON THE first day of the Spoleto Festival, there were a few hiccups when guests were checking in, but Micah had been able to manage them.

Shane stood at the large windows of his office, looking out over the sweeping grounds of the Polk Island Hotel. The sunlight cast long shadows across the manicured lawns. It was a perfect day for musical performances. He'd purchased tickets for himself and Madelyn to attend the gospel concert on Saturday.

His parents had attended that event for much of his life.

Oliver stormed into his office unannounced, his face twisted with anger and frustration.

"You're driving this hotel into the ground, Shane," he growled, his voice low and intense. "You have no clue what you're doing. Maybe it's time you admit that and go back to Alexander-DePaul, where you belong."

Shane clenched his fists, trying to keep his temper in check. He knew Oliver's criticisms weren't entirely baseless. The hotel was struggling, and despite his best efforts, turning things around had proven more challenging than he had anticipated.

"I'm doing everything I can," Shane retorted, his voice steady but tinged with frustration. "We're facing unprecedented challenges, and I'm trying to navigate us through them."

Oliver scoffed, taking a step closer until they were almost nose-to-nose. "Trying isn't good enough, Shane. Our family's legacy is at stake here. Uncle believed in you, but I'm starting to think his faith was wasted."

The words hit Shane like a physical blow. He had always felt the weight of his father's expectations, but hearing Oliver voice his doubts cut deep. Could it be true? Was he really failing the hotel and their family's legacy?

Before Shane could respond, the office door swung open with a bang. Ace stood there, her presence commanding attention. "That's enough," she said firmly, stepping between the two cousins. "This isn't helping anyone."

Oliver glared at Ace, his jaw clenched in frustration. Shane took a deep breath, grateful for her intervention. He knew Ace had a knack for defusing tense situations, but this time, the damage had already been done.

Oliver turned on his heel and stormed out of the office without another word.

Shane watched him go, feeling anger and self-doubt swirling inside him.

After Oliver left, Shane sank into his chair, rubbing his temples wearily.

Ace hovered nearby, concern etched on her face. "Are you okay?" she asked softly.

Shane looked up at her, his expression weary. "I don't know," he admitted quietly. "Maybe Oliver is right. Maybe I'm not cut out for this. Maybe I should have stayed at Alexander-DePaul."

Ace shook her head. "Don't say that, Shane. You've been working tirelessly to save this hotel. You're doing everything you can."

"But is it enough?" Shane muttered, more to himself than to Ace.

"You can't give up now," Ace insisted, her voice unwavering. "We'll figure this out together, just like we always do."

Shane managed a faint smile, grateful for Ace's steadfast support. "Thanks," he said sincerely. "I needed to hear that." Somehow, those words coming from her—a person he admired and whose opinion mattered—provided the comfort he needed.

She smiled and exited the office, closing the door quietly behind her.

Still, Shane couldn't shake the doubt that gnawed at him as the day unfolded. He had always strived to live up to his father's expectations, but now he wondered if he was falling short.

His father's belief in him had been unwavering, but now, faced with mounting challenges, Shane wondered if he could live up to that faith.

He knew he couldn't give up—not yet. But a sense of uncertainty lingered in his heart, and he wondered if Oliver was right after all.

THE GRAVEL CRUNCHED beneath Shane's tires as he pulled into the familiar driveway of his mother's house. Evening settled in gently, casting a soft glow over the front porch, where his cousin stood, hands in his pockets, his expression unusually serious.

Approaching Oliver, Shane could already sense the weight of what was to come. "I'm not really surprised to see you here," he uttered, trying to keep his voice steady despite their blowup earlier. "What do you want? Money? Is this an attempt to blackmail the family by threatening to expose my dad's affair?"

Oliver hesitated, glancing toward the front door, but then met his gaze. "Shane, I—I think Aunt Maddie needs to know the truth."

Dread settled in his stomach like a heavy stone. "Oliver, we can't—" he began but was cut off as the door swung open and Madelyn appeared.

"The truth about what?" she asked, looking from one to the other. "I guess you two better get inside."

Oliver exchanged a brief, conflicted look with Shane before walking into the foyer.

Shane trailed behind his cousin, his mind racing with apprehension about the conversation that lay ahead.

In the cozy living room, Madelyn insisted on pouring them each a glass of iced tea before settling down into her favorite armchair, her eyes flickering between the men. "Let's get on with it."

Tension hung thick in the air.

Finally, Oliver cleared his throat, his voice uneasy but determined. "I—I met Barbara Clanton at the cemetery a little while ago. She mentioned something about Uncle Angus."

Madelyn's gaze landed on Shane and softened with understanding, though her brow furrowed slightly. "Ah, Barbara," she murmured thoughtfully. "So that's what this is about. Angus told me about that a long time ago."

Shane exchanged a surprised glance with Oliver. He hadn't expected his mother to already know, let alone to have known for so long.

"Uncle...he confessed?" Oliver asked tentatively, his voice barely above a whisper.

Madelyn nodded, her gaze steady. "Yes, he did. That's the kind of man he was—Angus Jr. didn't like secrets of that magnitude between us. It was a difficult time for a while, but we managed to work through it."

Shane felt a mix of relief and disbelief wash over him. His mother had carried this burden silently, shielding her children from the pain that could have torn their family apart.

"He also told me that was why you left the island, Shane." Madelyn sighed. "Your father knew you were deeply disappointed in him. He wanted to give you the time and space you needed to process everything...but each time he tried to talk to you, you'd shut down."

"I blamed him for not being a good husband to you."

Madelyn reached out, placing a comforting hand on Shane's arm. "I know, sweetheart. Angus and I had our struggles, but we chose to forgive each other. Barbara and I, however…our friendship didn't survive."

Shane listened intently, her words resonating deeply within him. Forgiveness and the resilience of familial bonds were lessons that had shaped their lives more profoundly than he had realized.

Oliver mumbled something about getting back to the hotel. As he got up, Shane was surprised that he didn't catch satisfaction in his cousin's eyes, only sadness.

After Oliver left, Madelyn turned to Shane, her eyes reflecting a lifetime of wisdom and love. "Son, laying the past to rest doesn't mean forgetting. It means finding peace within yourself and with those you love."

Her words overwhelmed him, and he nodded in silence, touched by the depth of her understanding. Despite the storms they had endured, his mother's spirit remained unbreakable, her heart always open to forgiveness and healing.

Madelyn reached out to place a comforting hand on his arm. "Shane, it's important to forgive those we love. I forgave Angus for his mistakes, and in doing so, I found peace. It's not easy, but holding on to grudges only weighs us down." She paused, searching his eyes for understanding. "You need to forgive Oliver, too. Life is too short for bitterness, my son. Letting go can set you free."

A lump formed in Shane's throat as he took in her wisdom. It was a lesson he had learned the hard way but hearing it from his mother now made it hit closer to home. He knew she was right, yet the thought of forgiving Oliver stirred up so many emotions—pain, betrayal…but also a glimmer of hope that maybe there was a way forward.

His mother's unwavering belief in the power of forgiveness provided a beacon of light in the darkness that surrounded him. As he gazed into her loving and resilient eyes, he felt some of the stress of the past began to lift, even if just a little bit.

Shane left his mother's house with a new purpose. There was one more person who needed to hear the truth.

He drove the short distance to London's place.

His sister was sitting on the porch reading a book. She looked up as he walked toward her, concern clouding her features.

"Hey, Shane," she greeted, a hint of worry in her voice. "Everything okay?"

He took a deep breath, preparing himself for another difficult conversation. "We need to talk. It's about Mom."

Her eyes widened slightly, and she gestured for him to sit beside her on the porch swing.

"What's happened?"

Shane sat down, the swing creaking under their combined weight. "I just came from her house. Oliver was there."

London frowned. "Did he do something?"

"He found out about Dad's affair and that I

knew about it. He went there to tell her," Shane explained, watching her reaction closely.

"What?" London's face paled, and she leaned forward, her voice hushed with urgency. "I don't know why I'm surprised. But how did he find out?"

Shane sighed. "He met Barbara at the cemetery recently. She was at Dad's grave. He thought Mom needed to know the truth…"

London's shock was palpable. "Barbara Clanton? That's who it was?"

"Yeah," Shane confirmed, his voice thick. "Mom already knew, though. Dad confessed to her a long time ago. They worked through it, but Mom and Barbara's friendship didn't survive."

London shook her head in disbelief, trying to process the information. "I can't believe it. Barbara…she betrayed Mom's trust like that?"

Shane placed a reassuring hand on her shoulder. "I know it's a lot to take in. Our mom…she's incredibly strong. She forgave Dad and she didn't want us to bear that burden. That's why she never let on what was really going on between them."

Tears welled up in London's eyes as she absorbed the news. "All this time, I thought Mama and Daddy had this perfect marriage. I never realized how much she had to forgive."

Shane squeezed her shoulder gently. "None of us did. But it shows how strong she is, how much she values family and forgiveness."

London wiped away a tear, her expression softening. "I hope that I'll be at least half the mother that she is."

"You're going to be a great mother."

They sat in silence for a moment.

As the stars began to twinkle in the night sky, Shane felt a sense of peace settle over him.

AS THE VIBRANT melodies of the gospel chorus filled the venue at the Spoleto Festival, Ace found herself swept away by the soul-stirring music. The rich harmonies and powerful voices resonated through the air, lifting her spirits and filling her with a sense of joy. It was a welcome escape from the daily routines and challenges she faced at the hotel.

Lost in the music, Ace almost didn't notice Madelyn's familiar figure a few rows ahead. Shane's mother was a pillar of grace and elegance, and it was no surprise to see her there. She knew that Madelyn and Angus Jr. attended the event every year.

Ace felt a surge of excitement and curiosity, wondering if Shane was also nearby. She scanned the audience discreetly, her heart skipping a beat when she spotted him walking toward Madelyn.

Shane looked dashing in a crisp white shirt and black denim jeans. He stood next to his mother, his attention fixed on the stage. Shane's presence added a layer of depth to the music, as if his passion for the arts resonated in harmony with the singers on stage.

When the chorus concluded their set with a rousing finale, Ace watched as Shane and Madelyn applauded, alight with admiration.

The audience began to disperse, and Ace hesitated for a moment, unsure if she should approach them. But before she could decide, Shane turned, and their eyes met.

"Ace!" Madelyn called out warmly, her smile radiant. "What a pleasant surprise to see you here."

She quickly made her way over, and said, "I really enjoyed the concert."

"Oh, so did I," Madelyn responded.

"I did, too," Shane said, his voice softer than usual, betraying a hint of warmth that made her heart flutter.

Ace turned to Madelyn. "I wasn't sure if you'd be attending this year."

"I wasn't, either," she stated. "Shane had to practically drag me out of the house, but I'm so glad I came. This was very uplifting." Her heart warmed—it was evident how much Shane cared about his mother and her healing.

"I'm planning to attend as many events at Spoleto as I can," Shane said. "To make up for the times I've missed."

"Son, I know we'd planned to grab a quick bite, but I'm tired. I'm going to head home. If Ace isn't busy, maybe she can join you for dinner?" Madelyn suggested. Ace couldn't help but note a twinkle in the older woman's eye that suggested she was up to something.

Shane exchanged a glance with his mother before facing Ace. "I'd appreciate the company. I'm in the mood for some of Misty's chicken wings and red velvet waffles."

"Sure, I'll have dinner with you. I was planning to pick up something, anyway," Ace said.

"I'll drop my mom at the house, then meet you at the café."

While walking toward the exit, Ace tried to keep her emotions in check. Seeing Shane outside of work settings stirred something within her—a longing she was hesitant to fully acknowledge. She reminded herself to tread carefully, not wanting to misinterpret their connection.

Ace arrived at the restaurant and secured a cozy corner booth for them. A few moments later, he arrived and took the seat across from her.

"That gospel chorus performance was truly something else," she said when they were seated and looking over the menu.

Shane nodded, his eyes reflecting genuine interest, making her feel seen in a way she hadn't experienced in a long time. "I agree. The harmonies were incredible, weren't they?" His voice held a depth that drew Ace in.

They placed their orders.

"So you grew up in Charleston," Shane said.

Ace nodded. "I did. But I've always loved Polk Island. We used to come here almost every single weekend when I was a little girl. The summer after I graduated high school, Miss Eleanor gave me a job. I worked here until I left for college."

Shane appeared to be listening intently, as if captivated by her every word.

"I don't think I fully appreciated the island until I moved to Los Angeles," he confessed. "I love the simplicity and sense of community."

Their food arrived.

As the evening wore on, they shared stories of their childhoods. Their laughter bridged the gap between their seemingly different worlds. Ace's heart felt lighter, hearing about Shane as a boy and telling him about her own girlhood.

"You know," she said, lowering her voice, "I always pictured myself married with kids by now. I love children—there's something about their energy and curiosity that brings joy to life. But after my divorce, it all felt so far away."

She paused, wondering if she'd said too much. But Shane leaned closer as if wanting to hear more. "I grew up with an abusive father. Although my ex never laid a hand on me, my marriage was…difficult. He was mentally and emotionally abusive, and by the time I left, I felt like I'd lost a part of myself. It took a while for me to feel whole again."

He nodded. "That's understandable. I've spent

so many years in Beverly Hills consumed by work that I almost forgot what truly matters—family and community. I think being back here is helping me remember who I am."

Ace met his gaze as understanding bloomed between them. "It's amazing how places can ground us, isn't it?" she said, her eyes brightening with a hint of hope. "This island, your family… It all holds such potential for a future."

She'd realized over the past few weeks that beneath Shane's polished exterior lay a man of depth and complexity, one who cherished family traditions as much as she did. His admission stirred something inside her, a feeling that maybe their lives were more aligned than she initially thought.

After dinner, when they finally stepped outside the café, the warm glow of the evening wrapped around them like an embrace as they walked through town in comfortable silence. They were getting close to her house.

"Enjoy the rest of your weekend," Ace said, her heart racing with hope and trepidation.

"You, too," he responded, his voice steady but his eyes revealing the same unspoken connection she felt.

The night air carried with it a sense of possibility that lingered between them, igniting an undeniable spark. She couldn't escape the feeling that there was more to him she had initially thought, and she wanted to know him deeply. As they stood there, words unspoken but understood, Ace realized that the common ground they'd found tonight left her with something other than doubt… It left her with hope.

# CHAPTER FOURTEEN

ACE COULDN'T SEEM to shake Shane from her mind. It wasn't just his rugged charm or the way his eyes seemed to see right through her defenses; it was the way he made her feel—safe and understood, yet terrified.

As she walked through the hotel on Monday morning, her eyes landed on a young family in the lobby. The mother cradled a newborn, while the father doted over them both with pure adoration.

Ace felt a pang of longing deep in her chest, the kind of yearning that made her heart ache. The image stirred up memories she had buried deep inside—dreams of a family, of love and laughter, that had once seemed so attainable.

But those dreams had turned into nightmares during her marriage. The promises of forever had shattered, leaving her with scars that had never fully healed. Her ex-husband had been charming, too, at first. But that charm had quickly turned to control then cruelty. Ace had escaped, but the wounds were still raw, the fear of repeating that cycle ever-present.

Falling for Shane felt like the worst idea imaginable. He was her boss, for one, and mixing business with personal matters could lead to disaster. But more than that, opening her heart again meant risking it all—risking the chance of reliving the pain and betrayal that had nearly broken her.

Ace shook her head, trying to dispel the turmoil within. She was good at her job, and right now, she needed to focus on finding the stolen sculpture. Yet, even as she poured over the notes and leads, her mind kept drifting back to Shane. His kindness, his strength, his unspoken understanding—all of it drew her in, making her question her resolve.

Her fingers traced the edge of the desk as she stared at the scattered documents. The sculpture was important, not just for the hotel, but for her sanity. Solving this case would prove that she was in control, that she could handle anything thrown her way. It was a distraction she desperately needed.

*But the heart wants what it wants.* And Ace's heart was a battlefield of conflicting desires. She longed for the warmth of a family, for the chance to love and be loved again. Yet, the fear of opening herself up to potential heartbreak was paralyzing. Every happy family she saw was a reminder of what she had lost, and what she might never have.

Taking a deep breath, Ace forced herself to focus. The sculpture had to be found, and the culprits brought to justice.

Determined, she dived back into her work, hoping that the task at hand would drown out the emotional storm brewing inside her. Deep down, she knew that ignoring her feelings for Shane was like trying to ignore a rising tide. Sooner or later, it would come crashing down, and she would face the truth she was so desperately trying to avoid.

SHANE SAT AT his desk, numbers of the latest financials blurring together as his mind wandered, fixating on Ace. Her sharp wit and the way her eyes lit up when she talked about her summers on the island had captivated him. But the thought of falling for her sent a wave of anxiety crashing over him.

Falling for her was becoming less a matter of choice and more a compulsion he couldn't ignore. With each shared story, the stakes grew higher; they had started to trust each other, and the thought of jeopardizing that closeness also terrified him. Shane felt both excited and apprehensive about the path unfolding before him, knowing that the deeper he fell, the harder it would be to protect his heart.

He looked around his office at the framed photos of his father, grandfather, and great-grandfather, the men who had built the Polk Island Hotel into what it was today. The legacy they had left behind was more than just bricks and mortar; it was a testament to their hard work and dedication, a beacon of the Worthington family's identity. Keeping the hotel in the family meant finding a way to keep the business afloat. Reservations and event bookings were still down, even with the boost from the Spoleto Festival, and he needed to turn things around fast. Not to mention, they had to find the missing Lorne piece.

Shane's duties gnawed at him, preventing him from making any clear decisions. His inner turbulence around the hotel extended to his feelings for Ace. He couldn't afford to let his emotions cloud his judgment, not when so much was at stake.

Getting involved with her felt like a dangerous distraction, one that could compromise his ability to make the tough decisions needed to save the hotel. He'd feared letting her down with the recent layoffs, after all. His thoughts were a tangled mess, his heart and mind at odds.

His phone buzzed on the desk, pulling him out of his reverie.

It was Cia, reminding him of their lunch meeting.

Shane sighed, pushing aside his conflicted feelings. As he made his way to North Winds, he tried to steel himself and keep his churning thoughts at bay.

Cia was already there.

They ordered their meals, and for a while, their conversation was light and easy.

"You wouldn't believe the theme for this upcoming wedding," Cia said, her voice bubbling with excitement. "The bride wants doves in gold birdcages hanging all over the room. It's going to be magical but quite the logistical challenge."

Shane chuckled, trying to imagine the Grand Ballroom filled with birdcages. "Sounds like you've got your hands full," he said, admiring her passion.

"I do, but I love it," she replied, leaning back in her chair. "And the annual cancer fundraiser is shaping up to be spectacular. We're pulling out all the stops to make sure it's a night to remember. Hopefully it will mean a booking for their fundraiser next year and more interest in the hotel."

He smiled. "Amen to that."

"I'm thrilled to have you back home. The hotel needs you, Shane. We need you," Cia said, her tone becoming more serious.

Shane nodded, his sister's words sinking in. "I laid off twenty people last week."

"You did what was needed," she responded.

"It still doesn't make it any easier," Shane admitted, his gaze dropping to the pristine white tablecloth.

The clinks and murmurs of the restaurant surrounded them, a stark contrast to the heavy conversation weighing down their lunch.

Cia reached across the table, her hand finding his in silent support. "You're shouldering a lot,

Shane," she said softly. "I wish there was something more I can do."

He squeezed her hand gratefully before releasing it. "Everything will work out," he replied with forced confidence. But deep down, he was filled with doubt and fear.

Their food arrived, and they shifted the conversation to lighter topics, a temporary escape.

Cia took a sip of her iced tea. "I meant to ask… how are we funding the security overhaul for the gallery?"

"We won't be able to start that project until later," he answered, trying to keep his tone steady, but his stomach was in knots.

Appearing confused, Cia asked, "But why did you shut it down?"

"I just…think it's necessary to keep our collections more secure," he responded vaguely, avoiding her gaze.

Cia frowned, clearly sensing that something wasn't right. "Has something happened? Is everything okay?"

Shane shook his head, unable to meet her concerned eyes. He hated lying to her, to all of them. The secrets felt heavier than ever, especially the promise he'd made to Angus Jr. about selling the hotel if it came to that. Keeping his family in the dark about the missing statue had been a bad move—one that gnawed at him daily. He didn't want to lie to them again, didn't want to keep them tethered to the shadows of his mistakes.

"Hey, meet me at Mom's after work," Shane suddenly said. "I need to talk to everyone together."

The furrow in Cia's brow deepened. "Is everything all right?"

"Yeah," Shane lied again, forcing a smile. "I just want to give everyone an update."

But inside, he was churning with anxiety. What he really wanted was to confess the truth about the stolen statue that he had hidden for far too long. Today was the day he would come clean, but the thought made him sick with guilt. He could almost hear his mother's voice urging him to be honest, to let go of the burdens he had been carrying alone.

The truth loomed over him like a storm cloud, ready to break open, and Shane knew he couldn't delay it any longer. It was time to step out of the shadows and confront the reality he had been trying to escape.

STANDING TALL ON the porch of his mother's house, Shane's heart pounded in his chest.

As he entered the house, he was greeted by the familiar warmth and scents of home. Madelyn bustled in the kitchen, preparing snacks and drinks for the family gathering. She looked up and smiled, but Shane could see the worry in her eyes. She had always been able to sense when something was amiss.

"Shane, honey, you look tired. Everything okay?" she asked, her voice tinged with concern.

He forced a smile, trying to mask his turmoil. "Yeah, Mom. Just a lot on my mind."

Madelyn's brow furrowed, but she didn't press further. Instead, she continued setting the table, and Shane took a seat in the living room, waiting for the rest of the family to arrive.

Soon, the sound of the front door opening and closing signaled the arrival of his siblings.

First to arrive was Aiden, who was back in town to attend some Spoleto Festival events. He walked in with a broad grin, carrying a box of pastries. "Look who brought the good stuff."

Shane managed a genuine smile at his brother's enthusiasm. "Hey, Aiden. Good to see you."

Aiden plopped down on the couch beside Shane. Next came their sister London. She gave Aiden and Shane both quick hugs.

Her sharp eyes studied him. "Shane, you look stressed. Everything okay at the hotel?"

Before he could respond, Kenyon walked in, followed by Cia and Micah.

With everyone gathered, Shane knew it was time. He cleared his throat, drawing everyone's attention. "I asked you all to meet me here because there's something I need to tell you. Something important."

Silence fell over the room, punctuated only by Shane's trembling hands as he took a deep breath.

He knew this was going to be difficult, but facing his family with the truth was proving to be harder than he had imagined.

"The Lorne sculpture was stolen."

The reactions were immediate—gasps of shock, expressions of disbelief, and questioning glances exchanged between family members. London's hand flew to her mouth in horror, while Cia looked at Shane with hurt and confusion in her eyes. Kenyon's face showed a mix of anger and concern, and Aiden and Micah seemed bewildered.

"When did this happen?" Kenyon demanded.

"Two weeks ago," Shane replied, his voice strained. "That's why I shut down the gallery."

"Why didn't you tell us?" London's voice rose in accusation. "How could you keep something like this from us?"

Shane felt a pang of guilt. "I—I thought I could handle it on my own. I didn't want to worry you all."

Cia's soft voice cut through the tension. "That's not how we work, Shane. We face things together."

His guilt intensified at her words. "I know... I was wrong. I thought I could fix it, but... I failed. And now I feel like I've let you all down."

London crossed the room and placed a comforting hand on his shoulder. "You haven't let us down, Shane. You don't have to carry this burden alone."

Aiden's tone was serious as he leaned forward.

"Yeah, man, we're a team. We should've been in this together from the start."

Kenyon's steady voice joined in, "We understand why you did what you did, but you should have come to us."

Cia reached over and squeezed Shane's hand. "We're upset because we care. You're not a failure, you're our brother and we love you."

Tears welled up in Shane's eyes as he felt the overwhelming support of his family breaking through his walls of regret and shame. "Thank you," he choked out. "I was so scared... So scared that I'd let you all down. That I'd let Dad down."

His mother's voice echoed through the room, "Your father shouldn't have placed so much on your shoulders. We will all share this burden going forward."

"We'll find a way to get the statue back," Kenyon stated with determination. "I have a friend who may be able to help."

Despite the support of his family, Shane couldn't shake off the feeling of failure lingering within him. He knew they were there for him, but he couldn't help but wonder if he had really let them down by not coming to them sooner.

"My friend works for the FBI," Kenyon continued. "Charles Beck, in the art-theft program."

For a moment, Shane was speechless, a flicker of hope igniting within him. "The FBI? You think they would help us find the statue?"

Kenyon nodded. "I think it's worth a shot. They have resources and connections that we don't. Then again, my friend just might see what he can find out. Not really sure how all that works."

Shane felt a wave of gratitude and relief wash over him. "Thank you. I really appreciate it. I was starting to feel like we had no options left."

"Do you have any clues as to who might have taken it?" Micah asked. "The hotel has cameras everywhere."

"Whoever stole the statue knew how to avoid them. I have Ace looking through files of employees who were terminated last year. Maybe one of them decided to steal the statue in retaliation."

Micah leaned back, frowning. "That's probably a good start, but what if it's someone who is still on the inside?"

"I'm thinking Oliver has something to do with it," Shane announced. "He's familiar with the security system. He's got motive."

Kenyon considered this for a moment, eyes narrowing thoughtfully. "If it's Oliver, he'd know exactly where to hit. But if he's really behind it, we need more than a hunch—we need proof."

Shane nodded in agreement. "I know. I'm working on it. Ace is combing through every detail, and if I'm right… Oliver is going to jail. I'm not letting him off easy just because he's family."

An uneasy silence fell across the room.

# CHAPTER FIFTEEN

ACE PULLED HER car into a spot across the street from the Polk Island Café. The sun was shining brightly on this beautiful mid-June afternoon, and she couldn't help but smile as she stepped out of her car to enjoy the weather.

She furrowed her brow in confusion as she stood near the entrance, her curiosity piqued by an unexpected sight. Emma, who worked in Guest Services, had claimed to have no connections on Polk Island before accepting the job at the hotel a few months ago, yet here she was, seated with Mark and Selena. Both had been terminated well before Emma's arrival, and Ace distinctly recalled that Mark had been especially bitter about it.

Her instincts flared. Why would Emma, someone who seemed so unassuming and had distanced herself from any prior association, be fraternizing with two disgruntled ex-employees? Ace's mind raced with questions as she took a cautious step back. What was their relationship, and what could they possibly be discussing? Had Emma been less forthcoming about her past than she let on?

Trying to remain unseen, Ace quickly retrieved her phone. She positioned herself discreetly, ensuring she was out of their line of sight while capturing a few photos. Her hands were steady, but her mind raced with questions and suspicions.

Once Ace had a few good shots, she waited patiently until the group exited the café. She recalled Emma telling her that she was from Atlanta. She said she'd visited the island once and fell in love with the place, so she began looking for employment.

Several of the employees shared that same story—it made sense to Ace. Polk Island had also seduced her with its beauty, warmth, and sense of community. After Angus Jr. hired her, the locals welcomed her enthusiastically and soon became her family.

After the trio left, she got out of her car and walked back to the café to pick up her order. Ace strolled up to the counter and was greeted by Misty. "Hi there. Your order will be up shortly," she said with a smile.

"Thanks, and can you add one of your delicious chocolate raspberry brownies," she replied, her voice steady but her thoughts still racing.

As she waited for her food, Ace replayed the scene she had just witnessed. Emma and the two ex-employees seemed extremely comfortable with one another, very familiar. It could be nothing, but her gut told her otherwise. It was too coincidental.

The café was bustling with life, people chatting and laughing, yet Ace felt a growing sense of isolation.

Her take-out order arrived.

On the way back to the SUV, Ace bit into her brownie, taking a moment to savor the rich, decadent treat.

Jumping to conclusions without all the facts could lead to unnecessary conflict. She had to piece together the puzzle, find out Emma's connection to Mark and Selena. It was possible they knew each other some other way that had nothing to do with the hotel.

Ace sat in her vehicle, finishing her sandwich with one hand while scrolling through the photos she'd snapped of the trio. She studied every detail—their expressions, shifts in body language, any hint that might reveal the thief among them. Determined, she vowed to track down the person responsible, no matter how deep she'd have to dig or how many sleepless nights it might take.

OLIVER SAT IN his car, his hands gripping the steering wheel tightly. The engine hummed quietly as he kept a watchful eye on the entrance of the Polk Island Café. He was supposed to meet with Emma, Mark, and Selena, but he'd hesitated when he spotted Ace heading to the restaurant.

With their extensive knowledge of the hotel's inner workings, Mark, Emma, and Selena were able to exploit back doors and vulnerabilities left unchecked. Together, they'd caused chaos by bypassing security, accessing sensitive data, and manipulating reservations and payment systems. Their actions revealed the glaring weaknesses of the hotel's outdated cybersecurity measures. Once he was in charge, he intended to fix that.

Oliver slid down lower in his seat, ensuring the brim of his baseball cap cast a shadow over his face. He couldn't risk being seen by Ace because he knew that she would run straight to Shane.

After Emma and the two ex-employees left, Oliver watched as Ace went inside.

He couldn't shake the feeling that she was piecing things together. He drummed his fingers anxiously on the steering wheel as he watched her head back to her car.

Oliver's gut tightened. He reached for his phone and dialed quickly, never taking his eyes off Ace.

The call connected, and a feminine voice answered on the other end. "Where were you? We waited over an hour. I was late getting back to the hotel."

Oliver uttered, "I think Ace is starting to put two and two together."

There was a pause on the other end before the voice replied, "What makes you say that?"

"I just saw her at the Polk Island Café," Oliver

explained, trying to keep any hint of panic out of his voice. "Emma, she saw you with Selena and Mark."

There was a pause on the line. "That doesn't prove anything. I'm not worried."

"I am," Oliver insisted, clenching his jaw. "If she figures this out, everything we've worked for goes down the drain."

"I've got to go," Emma said. "Micah's watching me."

Oliver ended the call, slipping the phone back into his pocket. He took a deep breath, trying to steady his nerves. The stakes were higher now, and the margin for error had just gotten smaller.

He started the car, blending into the traffic as he followed Ace at a safe distance, his mind racing with the need to stay one step ahead of her. He needed to make sure his plan remained intact.

SHANE STOOD ON the porch of Ace's house, the scent of blooming jasmine mingling with the ocean breeze. He knocked gently on the door, feeling a mixture of anticipation and nervousness. It had been a long day, and he looked forward to the solace of her company. After discovering a shared love of shrimp tacos at work earlier, she'd invited him for dinner. He'd had too long a week to do anything but accept.

She opened the door, her face lighting up with a warm smile. "Hey. C'mon in."

"Hey," Shane replied, stepping inside. The comforting aroma of shrimp and spices filled the air. "Smells amazing."

She laughed lightly. "Hope you're hungry."

"Starving," Shane said, his stomach growling in agreement.

They made their way to the kitchen, where Ace had laid out a spread of tortillas, seasoned shrimp, fresh salsa, guacamole, and various toppings. They chatted about their day as they assembled their tacos, the atmosphere easy and relaxed.

As they sat down to eat, Ace reached for a folder on the counter. "I wanted to show you something," she said, opening it to reveal several photos. "I took these earlier at the Polk Island Café. Take a look."

Shane examined the photos closely. "I recognize her. She works in Guest Services."

Nodding, Ace responded, "Yeah. Her name is Emma. The other two people used to work at the hotel. Selena and Mark."

"They look like a couple. Maybe they're all friends." Shane eyed her. "What are you thinking?"

"Emma told me that she didn't know a single person on the island when she relocated here. She moved from Atlanta after accepting a job offer from the hotel. Mark and Selena were fired months before she came—so I'm curious how they know each other. Of all the people on this island, why connect with those two? It's more than a coincidence."

Shane sighed, setting the photos down. "We just need to figure out how they fit into all of this. If at all."

They continued to eat, while discussing the various possibilities. Not for the first time, he admired Ace's sharp mind and dedication. She had a way of making complex things seem simpler.

After they finished dinner, Ace cleared the table, then gestured toward the living room. "How about we watch a movie? Something to unwind a bit?"

Shane smiled, feeling a warmth spread through him at the invitation. "Sounds good."

They settled onto the couch, a comfortable silence falling between them as the film started.

He felt the tension of the day melting away, replaced by a growing awareness of Ace beside him. Her presence was calming but also stirred something deeper within him. Shane found himself stealing glances at her, admiring the way the light from the screen played across her features.

As the movie progressed, he felt an urge to move closer. Shane fought the impulse, reminding himself that they had a professional relationship to maintain. Yet, the more time he spent with Ace, the more attracted he became.

When the movie ended, Shane knew he needed to leave before he did something he'd regret. He turned to Ace, a soft smile on his lips. "Thanks for dinner and the movie. I needed this."

She smiled back, her eyes warm. "Anytime. I'm glad you came."

Shane stood up, hesitating for a moment before making his way to the door. "I'll see you on Monday," he said, his voice steady despite the tumult of emotions inside him.

"Good night," Ace replied, her gaze lingering on him.

Shane walked out into the cool night air, his mind racing. As much as he wanted to stay, to explore whatever it was that was growing between them, he knew he had to be careful. There was too much at stake, and he couldn't afford to let his feelings cloud his judgment.

He drove back to the hotel, his thoughts a whirlwind of possibilities and regrets.

Shane couldn't shake the image of Ace from his mind. He knew he had to find a way to navigate his feelings while still focusing on working together. But one thing was certain—his feelings for Ace were becoming impossible to ignore.

ACE STOOD AT the kitchen sink, the remnants of their dinner still lingering in the air, the warmth of the evening still fresh in her memory. She washed the dishes slowly, her mind replaying the moments she'd shared with Shane. It had been a long time since she'd felt so at ease, so comfortable in someone's company. She shouldn't have invited him to stay after dinner, but being with him felt too good.

As she scrubbed the last of the dishes, she allowed herself to reflect on the evening, letting the feelings wash over her like a gentle tide.

Shane had arrived with his usual quiet confidence, his presence immediately filling her small house with a sense of calm and assurance. She had been nervous at first, worried that the casual dinner might feel awkward or forced, but those fears had quickly melted away.

The conversation had flowed easily, punctuated by shared laughter and thoughtful silences. They had talked about the investigation, of course, but there had been moments when the conversation veered into more personal territory, and those moments had felt like a revelation. She couldn't remember the last time she had felt such genuine interest from someone.

She had convinced herself that she didn't need anyone, that she was strong enough on her own. But Shane had a way of breaking through those defenses, of making her feel alive in a way she hadn't felt in a long time. When she'd invited him to stay, Ace had chosen a lighthearted comedy, something to help them unwind after the intense discussions about the case. As they sat together on the couch, she'd felt a sense of contentment settle over her. It was a simple pleasure, watching a movie with someone she cared about. Her stomach knotted at that thought… She did care about him.

She had stolen glances at Shane throughout the

film, his profile illuminated by the flickering light of the screen. There was something about him that drew her in, made her want to let him into her world.

Now, standing in her quiet kitchen, Ace dried the last dish and put it away.

She leaned against the counter, staring out the window into the dark night. The loneliness she had felt for so long seemed a bit more distant, replaced by a flicker of possibility. Shane made her feel things she had thought were lost to her—hope, excitement, and a sense of connection.

As she stood there, the cool glass of the windowpane met her warm fingertips, causing a slight tingling sensation that sent shivers down her spine. Ace knew she had to be careful. Their professional relationship needed to remain intact. But as she thought about the way Shane had looked at her, the way he had made her laugh and feel understood, Ace wondered what might happen if she allowed herself to take a chance on him.

She sighed, pushed herself away from the counter, and turned off the kitchen light. The room plunged into darkness, only the dim glow of the moonlight filtering through the curtains.

Ace made her way to her bedroom, feeling a warmth in her chest that had been absent for far too long. The sensation was both unfamiliar and comforting, like a long-lost friend she had finally rediscovered.

For the first time in a long time, she felt a spark of optimism about the future.

# CHAPTER SIXTEEN

THE NEXT MORNING, Shane sat in his office, still digesting the implications of what Ace had shown him earlier. His thoughts were interrupted by a soft knock at the door.

It was Micah.

Shane motioned for him to come in and close the door.

"Hey, I need to talk to you about something," he began, leaning forward in his chair.

"Sure, what's up?" Micah replied, taking a seat across from him.

Shane took a deep breath. "Ace saw Emma at the Polk Island Café yesterday... She was with Selena and Mark—two employees that were terminated for theft."

Micah's eyes widened in surprise. "Emma? Really? I was under the impression she really didn't know anyone on the island outside of work."

"Do you know anything about her? Any issues we should be aware of?" Shane asked, his tone serious.

Micah shook his head slowly. "Emma started working here a few days before we lost Dad. She's quiet, keeps to herself mostly. I haven't had any issues with her. She seems to know computers. We had an issue, and she knew exactly what was going on. Emma told me that she studied IT but didn't finish her program."

Shane frowned, tapping his fingers on the desk. "That's interesting, especially given the email situation. We need to keep a closer eye on her."

Before Micah could respond, the door burst open, and Kenyon rushed in, his face flushed.

"Shane, you need to hear this," Kenyon said, barely catching his breath. "I just got word from my friend that whoever stole the heirloom is trying to sell it. There's a rumor of an underground auction scheduled to take place in two weeks. It's by invitation only. Charles is talking to his supervisor about how to proceed. This thing sounds like it's much bigger than we know."

Shane felt his stomach drop. "An auction? Are you sure?"

The room fell silent for a moment as the gravity of the situation sank in. Shane felt a wave of fear and frustration. "It might be too late," he muttered.

Ace, who had been standing by the door, stepped forward. "It's not too late, Shane. I spoke to a police officer here on the island and gave him Charles's information. There's still a chance to find the culprit and stop the auction. We just need to let law enforcement take over."

Shane looked at her, drawing strength from her confidence. "I'm not just going to sit idly by and do nothing."

Ace crossed her arms, thinking quickly. "I know how you feel, but there isn't anything we can do. Let's let the FBI handle this."

Shane nodded, feeling a renewed sense of determination. "Okay. They have fourteen days to stop this sale and get the heirloom back. Micah, you keep an eye on Emma. Kenyon, ask Charles to find out everything he can about this auction."

They all agreed.

As they left his office, Shane couldn't shake the feeling of unease, but he refused to let fear consume him, for his family's heirloom and their legacy were too precious to lose.

SUNDAY MORNING, OLIVER SAT on a weathered bench in a quiet corner of the park in Charleston, the breeze from the nearby harbor rustling the leaves of the ancient oak trees that shaded the area. The sun cast a warm, golden hue over everything, but Oliver's mood was anything but serene.

He tapped his foot impatiently, scanning the park for any sign of Emma.

After a few moments, he saw her approaching, her steps hurried and her expression tense.

She slid onto the bench next to him, casting a

furtive glance around to ensure they weren't being watched.

"You're late," Oliver said, feeling irritated and anxious.

"Sorry, I got held up. What's so urgent?" Emma replied, brushing a strand of hair out of her face.

Oliver leaned closer, his eyes narrowing. "Did you forget that Ace saw you with Selena and Mark? Two people you're not supposed to know..."

Emma's eyes widened momentarily before she composed herself. "So? This isn't a very big island. I could've met them anywhere."

Oliver clenched his fists, struggling to keep his voice low. "You're getting careless, Emma. This whole thing could blow up in our faces if we're not careful."

Her demeanor remained calm, almost too calm for Oliver's liking. "Relax, Oliver. Ace can't prove anything. We were just having lunch. There's no crime in that."

Oliver shook his head, frustration evident in his expression. "This isn't a game. Shane already suspects something and if they find out what we're planning—what I'm planning—it's over. Everything I've worked for, everything I deserve, will be gone."

Emma placed a hand on his arm. "Look, we've been careful up until now, and we'll continue to be careful. No one's going to find out."

Oliver pulled away, stood up and paced in front

of the bench. "You don't get it. I've been waiting for this chance my whole life. The hotel, the legacy, it should be mine. Not Shane's, not anyone else's. I won't let anyone take that from me."

Emma watched him, her expression unreadable. "We'll get what we deserve, Oliver. But you need to stay focused. We're so close. Don't let paranoia ruin everything."

Oliver stopped pacing and sat down again, taking a deep breath. "You're right. We need to be smart. We can't afford any more slipups. We have to prove that the hotel is floundering under Shane's leadership."

Emma nodded. "Consider it done, *dear husband*. They owe you more than that eight-point-eight-nine percent. A share of the hotel your family built." She placed a hand to her stomach. "This is our baby's legacy, too." She leaned over and kissed his cheek. "I love you, Oliver."

His heart softened. She'd stuck by him all this time and she'd keep helping him. "I love you, too."

With that, Emma stood up, giving him one last look before walking away. "You're coming to the apartment later tonight, right? I really miss waking up beside you."

He nodded.

Oliver watched her go, his mind racing. Emma had always understood the stakes, and together, they would take back what was rightfully his.

Shane, the golden boy who had always had everything handed to him, didn't deserve it.

Oliver clenched his fists, determination coursing through him. He had come too far to let anyone stop him now. Failure was not an option. The price of victory was high, but Oliver was willing to pay it.

# CHAPTER SEVENTEEN

A FEW DAYS LATER, Ace spotted Mark near the hotel pool while on her rounds. He no longer worked there, so why was he on the property? Could he be a guest? She intended to find out.

Ace slipped on her sunglasses to ward off the sunlight; her mind was set on one thing—confronting the former employee.

However, when she looked around, he was nowhere to be found. Ace scanned the pool area before walking back inside.

She spotted Shane engrossed in conversation with a guest in the lobby and approached him with a friendly smile.

"Can I have a word with you in private?" she asked, her tone indicating the seriousness of the matter.

Shane nodded, excusing himself from the guest before turning his attention to Ace. "What's on your mind?" he asked, his expression curious yet cautious.

"Mark is somewhere here on the property. He was near the pool. I walked out there but he'd disappeared."

Shane hitched one shoulder. "He's allowed to be here until he does something wrong."

"I'm going to alert my team. Have them keep an eye on him," Ace responded.

"Do you think he would be this blatant if he had stolen the statue?"

She hesitated for a moment, weighing her words carefully. "I'm not sure. But we can't rule anything out."

Shane nodded; his jaw clenched. "Keep me updated. We can't afford any more surprises."

Mark's presence here, after everything that had happened, felt deliberate.

Just as she reached her office door, her cell phone buzzed with a message from Calvin, one of her team members. The text read:

Mark spotted heading to one of the storage rooms.

Ace's heart pounded in her chest as she quickly changed direction, her steps brisk and purposeful. Mark no longer had access to the hotel storage. That area was for staff only. Whatever Mark was up to, she intended to find out—and she hoped it wasn't too late to prevent further damage.

SHANE SAT ALONE in his office, the only source of light coming from the soft glow of his computer screen. He was startled when Janie appeared at his door.

He gestured for her to come in. "What can I do for you?" he asked.

Janie glided into the room, radiating compassion and understanding. "I just wanted to check on you," she said softly. "I know you're still grieving amid everything happening. Loss can be a difficult burden."

A hint of gratitude mixed with hesitation filled him. He appreciated Janie's concern.

"I hope I'm not intruding..." she continued cautiously.

"No, not at all," he responded earnestly. "Please, tell me... How are things going with you?"

Her smile was warm as she said, "Exceptionally well. Working here at the hotel has been a joy, and Polk Island is absolutely stunning."

Shane couldn't help but feel curious. "Where are you from originally?"

"Philadelphia," Janie revealed softly. "My roots are deep there."

Shane's interest sparked. "What led you to this new chapter of your life? If you don't mind sharing."

Janie let out a gentle sigh. "After being a caregiver to my parents until they passed away, I needed a fresh start. Their absence left a void that I am still learning how to fill."

Their eyes met, silently conveying unspoken understanding between them. Could Janie know the turmoil raging inside Shane after losing his dad?

The inner conflict tearing at his soul? He'd spent years upset with his father, and yet losing him had made Shane miss him terribly.

"Just know that I'm here if you ever need someone to confide in," Janie offered tenderly. "Sometimes, knowing someone else is on a similar path can bring light to the darkest moments."

Shane managed a strained smile and nodded gratefully. "Thank you," he whispered.

"I'll let you get back to your work."

"Janie..."

"Yes?"

"When did you start to feel some sense of normalcy again?"

A melancholic smile played on her lips as she replied, "To be completely honest... I'm still waiting for that moment."

Shane's gaze lingered on her retreating figure, her words resonating deeply within him. His thoughts drifted to Ace—fierce, independent Ace, whose presence both comforted and unsettled him. Spending time with her lately had helped him start to feel normal again.

The sound of footsteps approaching interrupted his reverie, and Shane looked up to see Micah standing at the doorway. His youngest brother wore a concerned expression, a stark contrast to his usual carefree demeanor.

"Shane, you okay?" His voice held a note of genuine worry as he stepped farther into the office.

He managed a small, tired smile, attempting to mask the exhaustion he'd felt the past few weeks. "I'm fine, just a lot on my mind," Shane replied.

Micah narrowed his eyes, clearly unconvinced. "Is it about Dad?"

Shane nodded slowly, knowing he could never hide anything from Micah. "Yeah, it's about him… I really miss him."

His brother moved to sit across from him, his expression softening with understanding. "I picked up my phone twice to call and check in. Then I remember that he's gone."

"And he's never coming back," Shane murmured.

ACE DECIDED TO call it a night. All she wanted was to get home and unwind, though frustration gnawed at her for letting Mark slip through her grasp. A few moments after getting the text about him, she got another that he'd slipped out an employee exit and was seen heading off the hotel grounds. She knew she'd allowed her growing attraction to Shane to cloud her focus, a distraction she couldn't afford.

Her car was parked in a dimly lit area, but she had walked this route countless times before, always feeling safe within the familiar surroundings of the hotel grounds.

As Ace approached her car, a sudden noise behind her made her freeze.

She turned quickly, scanning the lot, but saw nothing.

Just her imagination, she told herself, shaking off the eerie feeling. But her instincts, honed by years of law-enforcement experience and self-defense training, screamed at her to stay alert.

She quickened her pace, keys clutched tightly in her hand, ready to use as a weapon if needed.

She reached her car and fumbled to unlock the door when she heard footsteps rapidly approaching. Her heart pounded in her chest, adrenaline surging through her veins.

Before she could react, a figure emerged from the shadows. Even under the hood pulled low over his face, Ace could tell he was a man—the broad shoulders, the confident stride, the way he filled the space with an imposing presence. Her training kicked in instantly, and she pivoted to face him, dropping into a defensive stance, ready for whatever might come next.

"What do you want?" she demanded, her voice steady despite the fear gnawing at her.

The man didn't answer. Instead, he lunged at her, his movements swift.

Ace blocked his initial strike with precision, countering with a quick jab to his side. She pivoted on her foot and aimed a kick at his knee, hoping to incapacitate him. But he moved with surprising speed, dodging her attack and grabbing her arm in a vise-like grip.

She tried to break free, but he was strong—too strong. He forced her against the car, the cold metal pressing into her back. She used every technique she had to break his hold, but he outmatched her.

Panic began to creep in.

The man's grip tightened mercilessly; then, he suddenly slammed her head against the car window.

Stars erupted in her vision as searing pain radiated through her skull.

She fought desperately to stay conscious but felt herself slipping away into darkness as she crumpled to the ground.

She lay there helpless with shadows surrounding her fading vision. She heard the man retreating across the parking lot. She tried to call for help, but the words sounded jumbled even to her. A spark of determination ignited within her even as the blackness closed in around her.

# CHAPTER EIGHTEEN

WHEN ACE AWOKE, she was disoriented, her head throbbing with pain.

She was lying on the cold ground, the night sky spinning above her. She tried to sit up, but a wave of dizziness forced her back down. Taking slow, deep breaths, she fought to gather her scattered thoughts.

Where was he? Was he still here?

Ace forced herself to her feet, her body protesting with every movement. She glanced around, but the attacker was gone, leaving no trace of his presence.

She stumbled to her car, gripping the door for support, and managed to open it with shaking hands. She sank into the driver's seat, locking the doors behind her, and fumbled for her phone.

With trembling fingers, Ace dialed Shane's number.

It rang twice before he picked up, his voice filled with concern.

"Ace? Where are you?"

"Shane," she whispered. "I… I was a-attacked…"

"Where are you?" he repeated urgently.

"In my car."

"Stay right there. I'm coming," Shane replied, his voice firm and reassuring. "Don't hang up."

Ace nodded, though he couldn't see her.

She leaned back in the seat, clutching the phone to her chest. The pain was overwhelming, but she focused on the sound of Shane's voice, grounding herself in the knowledge that help was on the way.

She felt like she couldn't breathe.

Ace opened the door.

A wave of dizziness struck as she stepped out of the vehicle. Tiny black dots filled her vision and grew larger until total darkness consumed her once more.

PUSHING OPEN THE door of his mother's car, Shane's breath caught in his throat at the sight before him.

The door to the SUV was open and Ace was lying on the ground of the hotel parking lot, unconscious. Blood trickled down her forehead, marring her face.

Shock paralyzed him for a moment, but then a surge of emotions flooded through him—fear, anger, guilt.

"Ace…" Shane dropped to his knees beside her, gently shaking her shoulder. "Ace, can you hear me?"

She remained unresponsive. Shane's mind raced, the panic threatening to overwhelm him. With trembling hands, he pulled out his phone and dialed 911, his voice barely steady as he gave them the details.

"One of my employees—" his voice faltered as he said it, knowing she was more than that "—has been attacked. She's unconscious," he said urgently. "She needs help."

The operator assured him that help was on the way and instructed him to stay with Ace until they arrived. Shane sat by her side, holding her hand tightly, whispering words of comfort into the deafening silence.

Minutes stretched like eternity as he waited for the ambulance. He looked at her vulnerable form, feeling a fierce protectiveness rise within him. He realized then, with startling clarity, just how much she meant to him.

Finally, the wail of sirens pierced the night, and Shane breathed a sigh of relief.

Paramedics swiftly assessed Ace's condition and lifted her onto a stretcher. Shane followed closely as they hurried her out to the ambulance.

At the hospital, he paced the waiting room, unable to sit still.

When a doctor finally approached him, Shane's heart leaped into his throat.

"Are you here for Alison?" the doctor asked.

Shane nodded eagerly. "Yes, how is she?"

"She has a concussion and some bruises, but she

should recover," the doctor replied calmly. "We're keeping her overnight for observation."

Relief flooded through Shane, almost bringing tears to his eyes. "Thank you," he choked out.

He'd been a brief visit with Ace before they took her away for further treatment. In that time, he crossed the street to file a report at the police department.

Once Ace had been settled in a hospital room, Shane watched over her while she slept, feeling an overwhelming sense of relief that she was safe, yet a lingering fear about what had happened to her.

As she stirred awake, her eyelids fluttering open slowly, Shane's heart skipped a beat. "Ace?" His voice was thick with emotion as he gently squeezed her hand.

She blinked a few times, as if trying to focus on his face. "Shane?" Her voice was weak and raspy.

"I called for help, and now you're here in the hospital."

Ace's eyes widened in confusion, then filled with realization. "Who?"

"We don't know yet," Shane replied, his brow furrowed with concern. "But I promise you, I'll find out who did this to you."

Ace managed a weak smile before drifting off again, her breathing steady and peaceful. Shane sat vigil by her side until the nurses requested that he leave, his mind racing with questions and plans for finding the culprit the whole time.

Before leaving the hospital, Shane made a silent promise to himself to protect Ace at all costs and bring justice to whoever had caused her harm.

OLIVER WAS LIVID, his face burning with anger and frustration as he entered the studio apartment. Emma was working so he'd had to come alone.

"Where's Mark?" he demanded.

"I'm not sure," Selena responded.

"What were you thinking? Nobody was supposed to get hurt. What if she dies? I'm not going to prison for anyone. This ends now." The words escaped his lips like bullets.

Selena opened her mouth to defend herself, her voice small and timid. "I told Mark that he went too far. He was only supposed to scare Ace. Not beat her up." She threw her hands up in a gesture of helplessness, her shoulders slumping.

"You never should've involved her in the first place!" Oliver retorted, his voice still filled with fury. He paced angrily back and forth across the room, his footsteps heavy on the floor.

Shrugging, Selena growled, "Ace should have just minded her own business. It wasn't my fault." Her voice held a hint of defiance.

"If I were you… I'd consider leaving town. Like, *today*," Oliver said, his anger an open wound. He looked her dead in the eyes, his gaze unyielding. He felt a cold determination to end this once and for all. "Y'all have been nothing but careless."

"I'm not going anywhere." Selena crossed her arms. "They can't connect me to what happened with Ace. Mark was wearing a hood or something. He said it looks like a random mugging at best. Oliver, you just need to calm down." Selena's voice wavered slightly, betraying her own fear and uncertainty. "Besides you promised us money—something we have yet to receive."

"There may not be any money now." Oliver's words hung in the air. There'd be nothing for any of them if they were caught.

"You're panicking," she uttered, her voice now more assertive. "I thought you wanted to take the hotel from Shane."

"And if Ace doesn't make a full recovery?"

"You just need to calm down." Selena's voice was firm now. "You can't let this ruin everything we've worked for." She raised a brow, as if daring him to lose faith in their cause.

Shaking his head, he uttered, "I'm done with all this." Oliver clenched his jaw tightly as he glared at her. "You don't get it, do you?" His voice was low, seething with restrained anger. "This was never supposed to go this far. I didn't sign up for this level of violence."

Selena's expression hardened as she met Oliver's gaze head-on. "We can still salvage this situation. Shane is vulnerable right now. We can use that to our advantage if we play our cards right."

Oliver shook his head, the weariness of their predicament settling over him. "You don't know him like I do. Right now, we're not doing anything."

"I know," Selena replied softly. "Things got out of hand, but we can still recover this without resorting to further violence."

Oliver paced the room, his mind racing. "I don't want blood on my hands. Put a leash on your boyfriend, Selena."

"Understood."

THE HOSPITAL ROOM remained quiet except for the occasional nurse checking in on Ace. Finally, she woke up again, this time more alert. Gratitude washed over Shane as her gaze met his.

"Shane," she whispered hoarsely.

He leaned closer. "I'm here, Ace. How are you feeling?"

"I'm sore all over," she admitted, wincing as she shifted slightly on the bed. "But I'm glad to feel anything at all. I can't believe someone was able to get a jump on me." She offered it lightly, but he could tell she felt vulnerable.

"I'm glad it's not worse," Shane confessed. "I don't want anything to happen to you."

The sincerity in his voice seemed to calm Ace. "I'm going to find whoever did this," she whispered.

"I filed a report with the police. Your team is going through the surveillance tapes."

"They're good at their job," she responded. "If

there's anything to be found—they will find it." Shifting her position, Ace added, "I need to get out of here. We must be getting close."

Shane hesitated for a moment, torn between his instinct to protect her and his respect for her determination. He knew that she was capable and strong, but this situation was escalating beyond their control. So were his feelings for her. The sound of her voice on the phone after the attack... It had made him desperate with wanting to protect her. The news that she'd been hurt made him realize just how deeply he cared for her. He was falling for her and never wanted to see harm come to her.

"I understand your need to solve this, Ace," Shane began carefully. "But we can't ignore the danger you're in. We need to consider all options to ensure your safety."

Ace's eyes flashed with a mix of frustration and determination. "I can handle myself, Shane. This is my job, my responsibility."

Shane reached out and took her hand gently. "I know you can handle yourself, Ace. But you don't have to do it alone. Let me help you."

There was a brief pause as Ace considered his words, her gaze softening slightly. "Okay," she finally relented, a reluctant acceptance in her eyes. "But we do this my way, understood?"

Shane nodded, a small smile tugging at the corners of his lips. "Your way, Ace. I'm right here with you."

"It just occurred to me that I know someone who is well connected to the art world," she stated. "He might be able to get Kenyon's FBI friend an invite to that auction."

Shane was taken aback. "An underground auction?"

Ace gave a slight nod. "He used to be involved in that sort of thing."

"From your law-enforcement days?"

"Actually, he's related to my ex-husband—his brother."

Shane wasn't sure about this. He knew what her marriage had been like. "Are you sure you can trust him?"

"He owes me," she responded. "For a favor I never collected on. I'm calling it in."

Shane nodded. "Fine. Give me his information and I'll pass it on to Charles."

"All I have is a name. but I'm confident they'll know exactly who he is," Ace responded. "He has a criminal past. It's possible he still does."

# *CHAPTER NINETEEN*

RAIN DRIZZLED LIGHTLY from the overcast sky, casting a dreary atmosphere over the island as Shane paced the floor of his suite. His thoughts were a chaotic swirl of worry and determination, amplified by the nervous energy coursing through his veins.

Ace's former brother-in-law had come through and secured an invitation to the secret auction where the stolen heirloom was rumored to be sold. Shane had forwarded the info to Agent Beck. Now they were in the tense period awaiting the outcome of the auction, where every minute felt like an eternity.

Shane checked his phone for what seemed like the hundredth time, but there were no updates yet.

He drummed his fingers anxiously against the screen, his mind racing with scenarios of success and failure. The recovery of the statue and finding the person who attacked Ace. Shane suspected the two incidents might be connected, but he had no proof.

Ace, who was lying in a hospital bed recovering

from the attack that had put her there. The thought gnawed at Shane's gut like a persistent ache. Whoever had stolen the statue had not hesitated to harm Ace, and Shane was determined to make them pay dearly for it.

He closed his eyes, trying to push back the worry that threatened to overwhelm him. Ace was strong, resilient, but seeing her in that hospital bed had shaken him to the core.

A notification from his phone snapped Shane out of his reverie. He quickly unlocked it, his heart racing as he read the message from Agent Beck: Inside. Auction about to start. Will update ASAP.

Relief flooded through Shane, but it was tempered by the tension still coiled tightly in his chest. He typed back a quick reply: Stay safe. Keep me posted.

As he pocketed his phone, Shane took a deep breath, trying to steady his nerves.

The next moments would be critical. He had to trust Kenyon's friend to gather the information they needed, but uncertainty gnawed at him. He wished he could be inside, overseeing the operation firsthand, but his role now was to wait and react based on the updates they received.

He got another text.

The statue is here.

Shane felt a surge of adrenaline at the news and

responded: Do you have eyes on it? Any sign of Oliver? He left the island early this morning.

He didn't know where his cousin had gone. Only that he'd requested a car to Charleston and his suite had been vacated.

Minutes passed like hours as Shane waited for any update of the identity of the thief. His jaw clenched; they couldn't afford to let the statue slip through their fingers again.

Hours later, his phone rang.

Agent Beck's voice crackled over the device. "They've been caught. Security is escorting the thieves out now."

Relief flooded through Shane, mingled with a fierce satisfaction.

"And, Shane," Beck continued. "One of them is a hotel employee—she revealed herself during the arrest. Janie Merck."

The air left Shane's lungs. *Janie?* His HR lead… was the thief? He couldn't process the information but murmured a thanks and hung up.

They had done it; the heirloom was safe. Janie and her accomplice would be taken into custody.

But as he exhaled deeply, a profound sense of exhaustion settled over him. The weight of the past few days, the worry for Ace, and the intensity of the moment had taken its toll.

It was a solid victory in a larger battle, and it was significant. The thief would face consequences, and the heirloom would be returned to its rightful place.

He was still trying to process Janie's part in all this. Shane never once suspected that she was behind the theft. She'd always seemed so genuine. Was she also behind the cancelled reservations and supplier orders?

Half an hour later, Shane went to the hospital.

He sat in a hard plastic chair next to Ace's hospital bed, his hand tightly clasping hers. The rhythmic beeping of the machines and the strong scent of antiseptic filled the room. He watched her chest rise and fall with each breath, his heart heavy with relief and worry.

His phone buzzed with a text on the bedside table, interrupting the quiet.

Shane glanced at the screen and saw multiple missed calls and from his family. He'd been so zoned out, with his phone on silent, that he'd missed them. Panic set in as he quickly opened the message from his mother.

London is in labor. We're at the hospital. Baby's coming early. Please come.

His stomach twisted with anxiety. His sister wasn't due for another six weeks. He looked at Ace, torn between staying by her side and rushing to be with his family. He knew London needed him more, but leaving Ace alone was not an option.

Finally, he made up his mind, then leaned over and whispered in Ace's ear. "I'll be back soon. I promise." He gave her hand a gentle squeeze before hurrying out of the room.

Navigating through the maze of corridors, Shane found himself outside the maternity ward.

The atmosphere was tense as he spotted his worried family huddled together outside a delivery room.

"Mom, what's happening?" Shane asked, concern evident in his voice.

Madelyn turned to him, tears streaming down her face. "London went into labor early," she sobbed. "We're all so scared."

Shane's heart clenched as he embraced his mother tightly, trying to offer comfort.

"Before you texted me, I was on a call with Agent Beck. He was able to secure the statue before it was sold." Maybe some good news would calm her and boost her spirits. "He has the people who stole it. Janie was one of the people arrested."

Madelyn looked shocked. When she finally responded, she said, "I'm so glad to hear this. I was beginning to feel like we're losing everything. Now I just need for London and the baby to be okay."

"They will be," Shane said. "They have to be."

For the next several hours, the family waited in tense silence. In intervals, Shane paced the waiting area, hoping for news. Occasionally, he slipped back to Ace's room to check on her, then returned to the maternity ward. After what felt like an eternity, a doctor emerged from the delivery room with news.

"London has delivered a baby girl," the doctor announced solemnly. "But she's small and will need to stay in the neonatal intensive care unit for a while."

Relief and joy washed over Shane, but he still felt a twinge of fear for his tiny niece. After being invited to meet the baby, the family followed the doctor to the NICU, where Shane saw London resting in bed, looking exhausted yet relieved.

"Hey, big brother," she greeted him with a weak smile.

Shane stepped forward to take her hand, trying to hide his concern. "You did great," he said softly. "How are you feeling?"

"Tired," London admitted with a small laugh. "But I'm okay. How's the baby?"

"They're taking good care of her," Shane reassured her. "She's going to be just fine."

Tears filled London's eyes as she nodded. "I was so scared, Shane."

"I know," he said, gently stroking her hand. "But both of you are safe now. Just rest and get your strength back."

After spending a few more precious moments with London, Shane made his way to the tiny incubator where his niece was lying, surrounded by tubes and monitors. His heart swelled with love and protectiveness as he watched over her, their family by her side, knowing she was a fighter just like her mother.

As he stood there, a sense of resolve washed over him. He would do everything in his power to protect this family and ensure they all recovered fully. Shane would do anything to make it happen—no matter the cost.

ACE WAS LYING IN the hospital bed, her mind racing. She found her thoughts drifting to Shane more often than she would like. He had been there for her, a constant presence over the last few days, refusing to leave her side even when she insisted she was fine. His steady comfort and quiet strength had become her anchor in a storm she hadn't anticipated.

When she had been attacked, the first person she thought of—the one she needed to hear from—was Shane. It had surprised her at first, how natural it felt to reach for him, how safe she felt knowing he was on the other end of the phone.

Shane had been there when she came to, a mix of worry and relief on his face.

But now she realized something even deeper—she was falling for him.

"How are you feeling?" His gentle question snapped her from her thoughts. He was standing in the doorway, his presence bringing some solace.

"Better," Ace replied, offering a small smile,

even though her mind was still processing the events of the last few days. "Thanks to you."

Shane's gaze was soft, but there was something behind it—an exhaustion, a worry that went beyond concern for her. He looked like he was carrying more than just her pain.

"There's something I need to tell you…" he began, his voice lowering. "London went into labor last night. Six weeks early."

Ace's heart clenched, a mixture of emotions swirling inside her—worry for Shane's family, joy for the new life entering the world, and a sudden, aching awareness of the life she had always imagined for herself. Motherhood, something she had longed for but had pushed away after her divorce, now seemed so close and yet so far.

"She delivered a healthy little girl, and my sister's doing fine. The baby is being monitored in the NICU."

"That's amazing," she said sincerely, trying to hide the wistfulness in her tone. "Congratulations, uncle."

Shane smiled back at her.

"What happened at the auction? Have you heard anything from Agent Beck?"

"He was able to secure the statue," he responded. His expression changed. "They arrested Janie and a male accomplice."

Ace gasped. "Janie Merck, the director of human resources?"

Shane nodded. "I think she and Oliver may be in cahoots. I just need to find a way to prove it. But all that matters right now is that the statue is safe. Agent Beck has it in his possession and it will be returned to the hotel."

"That's wonderful news," Ace said. "But… I'd like to know why Janie would do something like this." And had her colleague had Ace attacked? Why?

Shane shrugged. "Greed."

"You're probably right." She reached out, taking his hand. "Thanks for everything."

Shane sat down next to the bed and squeezed her hand gently. "I care about you, Ace. Seeing you like this…it's made me realize how much."

Her heart fluttered at his words, but she quickly pushed down the feeling, not wanting to read too much into it. "I care about you, too, Shane. And I'm so grateful for everything you've done."

As they sat together, unspoken feelings hung heavy in the air. Ace's mind drifted to the tiny baby in the NICU, triggering an ache inside her for something more. But before she could dwell on it too much, Shane broke the silence with a soft declaration. "Seeing my niece for the first time… it made me think about the future. About what really matters."

Ace looked up at him, tears threatening to spill from her eyes. "Yeah, it does put things into perspective."

Shane nodded, his gaze holding hers steadily. "It does. And I know one thing for sure—life is too short to waste any more time."

Her heart soared at his words but also trembled with fear of opening up and being vulnerable. She gave him a small smile, hoping it conveyed everything she couldn't say out loud.

"One step at a time?" she suggested softly.

"One step at a time," Shane agreed, squeezing her hand reassuringly once more.

SHANE STOOD IN the hospital corridor, his thoughts swirling around Ace and his newborn niece. The day had been a whirlwind of emotions, and he was trying to catch his breath.

He looked up when he heard the elevator doors ding open, revealing his cousin stepping out with a bouquet of flowers and a cluster of balloons.

Oliver's arrival immediately set Shane on edge. He'd disappeared suddenly and now he was back.

Oliver approached with a broad smile, scanning the hallway. "Shane! Heard about London and the baby. Thought I'd drop by and bring some cheer." Everyone in the family knew his history, his relentless ambition, and his desire to control the Polk Island Hotel. Shane's instincts told him that Oliver's visit was more than just a gesture of goodwill.

Shane forced a smile, though he remained wary. "Thanks, Oliver. London's room is down the hall, second on the left."

He nodded. "Thanks. I'll head in and see her. How's the baby doing?"

"She's stable. Still in the NICU, but the doctors are optimistic," Shane replied, his tone clipped.

Oliver nodded again, then made his way down the hall. The man had always been a source of friction, his intentions often cloaked in a veneer of family loyalty. What was he up to now?

Shane stood just outside of London's room, straining to hear the low murmur of voices inside. He didn't feel comfortable leaving Oliver alone with his sister; he couldn't trust his cousin. While he had no evidence linking Oliver to Ace's attack or the missing heirloom, Shane had a gut feeling that something wasn't right. He knew that Oliver was up to something, and he couldn't shake off the sense of unease that it caused him.

When his cousin finally emerged from London's room, Shane stepped forward. "Can we talk for a minute?" he asked, keeping his voice steady.

"Sure thing," Oliver replied, following Shane to a quieter corner of the hallway.

Shane crossed his arms, narrowing his eyes. "Why are you really here, Oliver? You've never been the type to make hospital visits."

He feigned a look of hurt. "Come on, Shane. She's family. I'm here to show support."

"Support?" Shane scoffed. "Or is it because you

want to keep tabs on us and the running of the hotel?"

Oliver's smile faded, replaced by a more serious expression. "I admit, the hotel is an opportunity I'm interested in. But I wouldn't do anything to harm the family. You know that."

"Do I?" Shane countered. "You've always had your own agenda. And right now, the last thing we need is more stress. If you're here for London, then fine. But don't think for a second that I'm not watching you."

Oliver raised his hands in mock surrender. "All right, all right. No need to get defensive. I'm just here to help."

Shane stepped closer, his voice low and firm. "Then help by staying out of our business. Focus on being a cousin, not a competitor."

Oliver's eyes flashed with annoyance and amusement. "Message received. I'll be on my best behavior."

Shane watched as Oliver walked away, a knot of tension tightening in his chest. He knew his cousin well enough to recognize that Oliver wouldn't back down so easily. The battle for the Polk Island Hotel was far from over, but right now, Shane's priority was his family. He turned back toward London's room, determined to protect what mattered most.

Shane entered and placed a gentle hand on London's shoulder. "Everything okay?" he asked softly.

London nodded, a tired but content smile on her face. "Yeah, everything's okay. Thanks for being here, Shane."

"Always," Shane replied. "I saw my niece and she's beautiful, London." London beamed in response.

No matter what Oliver's plans were, he would stand firm. He would protect his family, safeguard the legacy of the hotel, and—no matter how complicated things got—he was determined to build something more with Ace. She had become a part of the foundation he was fighting to preserve, and he wouldn't let anything tear that down.

THE FOLLOWING EVENING, Shane stood outside Ace's cottage, a large paper bag filled with takeout from North Winds in his hands. The tantalizing aroma of her favorite Italian dishes—lasagna, eggplant Parmesan, and garlic bread—wafted up, mingling with the warm summer evening air.

Ace was finally home from the hospital, and he wanted tonight to be perfect. He took a deep breath, trying to steady himself before knocking gently on the door.

The door opened, and there stood Ace, her bruised face lighting up with a radiant smile. She still looked a bit pale, but the spark in her eyes was unmistakable.

"Shane, you brought dinner!" she exclaimed,

stepping aside to let him in. "I was hoping you would."

Shane smiled back, feeling a wave of relief. "Of course. I figured you could use a proper meal after all that hospital food. Raj said eggplant Parmesan was your favorite."

Ace laughed softly, a sound that eased the tension in his chest. "You're a lifesaver. It smells amazing."

They settled in the cozy living room, the coffee table now transformed into a makeshift dining area. Shane unpacked the food, spreading out the containers and utensils. They sat cross-legged on the floor, a familiar routine that brought a sense of normalcy.

As they started eating, Shane watched Ace closely, noting the way her face softened with each bite, as if the tension from the past several days was slowly fading away. He took comfort in the fact that she seemed more at ease now. But despite the peaceful moment, he knew he had something important to share, news that could change the course of everything.

"Ace," he began, setting down his fork. "The Lorne statue…it arrived earlier from the FBI. I have it locked away now with the other heirlooms and artifacts."

Ace's eyes widened as surprise and relief flooded her features. "That's—that's amazing,

Shane," she said, her voice filled with genuine awe. "You did it."

Shane smiled slightly, grateful for her reaction. "I couldn't have done it without you," he admitted. "You were relentless in helping me piece everything together, in making sure we found it."

Ace shook her head, her gaze softening as she looked at him. "No, Shane. You did this. You took control when things were falling apart. You didn't just find the statue—you resolved everything, and that's what matters. You're a great leader."

Her words settled over him. He wasn't used to this—being seen, being appreciated for something beyond the surface. He'd spent so many years focused solely on the hotel business, driven by responsibilities and old promises. But Ace, with her calm insight and steady encouragement, made him feel like he was more than just the guy trying to hold everything together.

"Thanks," Shane murmured. "That means a lot, coming from you."

Ace leaned back slightly, her expression thoughtful. "It's true. You've done a great job, Shane. You care about this place, about your family, and you're showing it in everything you do."

He met her gaze, the intensity between them undeniable now. The stakes had always been high when it came to saving the hotel, but now there was something else, something personal between them. Shane could feel it, and the more he tried to ignore it, the more it pulled him in.

"I just..." Shane said, hesitating for a moment, "I don't want to let anyone down. Not my family, not the people who depend on the hotel."

Ace smiled gently. "You won't. You've already proven that."

For a moment, Shane couldn't tear his eyes away from her. Her belief in him was like a balm to the uncertainty that had gnawed at him for months. But that belief was also complicating things, because now he was aware how much her confidence in him affected him. The connection between them was growing stronger with every word, every look, and the more they trusted each other, the harder it became to deny what was really happening.

They continued their meal in comfortable silence. The food was delicious, and the company even more so.

As the evening wore on, they moved to the couch, talking and laughing softly, the weight of recent events momentarily lifting. They'd been through a lot together.

They had recovered the statue, and Ace was on the mend. Now it was only a matter of time before they uncovered the full truth about who'd been sabotaging the hotel and brought everyone involved to justice.

For now, though, Shane was content to sit be-

side Ace and share a quiet moment of triumph and
hope. The challenges ahead seemed a little less
daunting with her by his side.

# *CHAPTER TWENTY*

THE NEXT DAY, Shane pulled up to London's house as the sun began its descent in the late afternoon sky. Kenyon and Micah were already there, unloading the flat-packed crib from Kenyon's truck.

He took a deep breath. London and her baby girl were still in the hospital, and the premature birth had put everyone on edge. But right now, they had a job to do—get the nursery ready for when his sister came home.

"Hey, Shane," Kenyon called, lifting one end of the crib box. "Glad you made it. Ready to get to work?"

"Yeah," Shane replied, pushing aside his worries for a moment. "Let's get this done."

The three brothers carried the box inside, navigating the tight hallway of London's cozy home. They made their way to the small room that London had already decorated with soft pastel colors and baby-themed wall decals. It was clear she'd put a lot of love into preparing for her baby's arrival, even if it had come sooner than expected.

Micah tore open the box and began sorting through the various pieces of the crib. "I hope this comes with instructions. I don't want to mess this up."

Kenyon laughed. "You and me both. Let's just take it step by step."

Shane grabbed the instruction manual, and began flipping through the pages. "All right, let's start with the base. We need these screws and those two longer pieces."

As they worked together, the familiar rhythm of teamwork settled in. It reminded Shane of the countless projects they had tackled together over the years. Despite their occasional disagreements, they always came together when it mattered.

"London's going to love this," Micah said, tightening a bolt. "She's been through so much already."

Shane nodded, his mind flashing back to the image of his sister in the hospital bed, exhausted but relieved. "Yeah, she deserves this. And that little girl is going to need a safe place to sleep."

Kenyon handed Shane a screwdriver, a thoughtful look on his face. "You know, this whole thing got me thinking. Life's too short to take for granted. We need to be there for each other, no matter what."

"Agreed," Shane said, his voice steady. "We've got to stick together, especially now."

As they continued assembling the crib, their conversation flowed easily, touching on memories from their childhood, hopes for the future. The crib began to take shape, each piece fitting together with a satisfying click.

Shane paused. Not long ago, he had been ready to sell the hotel and walk away, convinced that his life was still back in Beverly Hills. But now, as he fit another piece of the crib into place, he realized how much had shifted within him. Being here, working alongside his brothers, brought a sense of peace he hadn't expected, and now the thought of staying—of keeping the hotel and rebuilding his life here—didn't feel like a burden. It felt like home.

After a couple of hours, they stood back to admire their work. The crib was sturdy and secure, ready to welcome London's baby girl home.

"Looks good," Micah said, wiping sweat from his brow. "I think we did a pretty decent job."

Kenyon clapped Shane on the back. "Teamwork, right? London's going to be thrilled."

Shane smiled, feeling a sense of accomplishment and relief. "Yeah, she will be. Thanks, guys. I know she'll appreciate this."

They spent a few more minutes tidying up the room, making sure everything was in its place.

Before leaving, Shane took a moment to stand in the nursery, imagining his niece sleeping peacefully in the crib they had built. It was a small thing, but it meant everything to their family.

As they headed out, Shane glanced at the backyard through the kitchen window. He could see the circular honey-farm design London had implemented, a series of beehives arranged in concentric circles, creating a harmonious and efficient system for honey production. Each ring served a specific function, from the outermost circle of wildflowers that attracted the bees, to the innermost circle, where the hives were placed. It was a testament to London's dedication and love for her craft, and it filled Shane with pride.

"All right," Shane said, turning to his brothers. "Let's get out of here. We've got a lot more to do before London and the baby come home."

Despite the challenges ahead, he knew they would face them together.

For London, for the baby, and for their family.

ACE WALKED DOWN the softly lit corridor of the hospital, her steps slowing as she neared the nursery. She was here to visit London, but she couldn't resist a peek at the nursery. Through the large viewing window, she saw the tiny, delicate forms of newborns swaddled in pastel blankets. A nurse moved quietly among them, checking on each baby with gentle hands.

The sight tugged at Ace's heart, bringing a mist to her eyes.

She stood there for a few moments, unable to tear her gaze away. The longing to be a mother, something she had tried to bury deep within her, resurfaced with a powerful ache. She had always dreamed of holding her own baby, of feeling that bond, that indescribable connection. But after the trauma and heartbreak of her marriage, she had locked away those dreams, too afraid to let herself hope again.

Ace's thoughts drifted to her past, to the love and trust that had been shattered. The pain of that betrayal had left scars she wasn't sure would ever fully heal. She had learned to protect herself, to guard her heart fiercely. The idea of opening up to someone again, of risking that kind of pain, seemed almost impossible.

An image of Shane suddenly flashed in her mind. His steady, reassuring presence, his kindness, and the way he had been there for his family and for her. She felt a flutter in her chest, a warmth that scared her more than she wanted to admit. Quickly, she shook her head, trying to dispel the thoughts.

"No," she whispered to herself, her voice barely audible. "He's my employer. I can't... I *won't* let myself go there."

She turned away from the nursery, forcing her feet to carry her down the hall to London's room. She needed to focus on what she'd come here for—to support London and be there for her friend. London had just brought a new life into the world, and Ace wanted to offer her any comfort she could.

When she reached London's room, she paused at

the door, composing herself before stepping inside. London was resting in her bed, looking exhausted but glowing with the joy of new motherhood.

"Ace," London greeted her with a tired smile. "Thank you for coming."

She smiled back, though her heart still felt heavy. "Of course. How are you feeling?"

"Tired, but happy," London replied. "Did you see my daughter? She's perfect, isn't she?"

"I was able to get a glimpse. She's so tiny."

"She's a fighter," London said proudly.

As they talked about how London had been doing, Ace tried to focus on the conversation, but her thoughts kept drifting back to the nursery, to her own unfulfilled dreams, and to Shane. She had promised herself she wouldn't let her guard down, wouldn't let herself feel those emotions again. But being here, surrounded by new life and possibilities, made it harder to keep those promises.

For now, all she could do was be there for her friend and try to find some peace in the happiness of others. Maybe, just maybe, one day she would find the courage to open her heart again.

But today was not that day.

SHANE SAT ACROSS from Leon and Trey Rothchild at their favorite lunch spot, a quaint bistro nestled in the heart of Polk Island. The three men had ordered their meals and were waiting for the food to arrive, enjoying the relaxed ambiance and the hum of quiet conversation around them.

"Shane, you've done a great job with the hotel," Leon said, taking a sip of his iced tea. "Mr. Angus would be proud."

"Thanks, Leon," Shane replied, a modest smile on his face. "It's been a team effort, and I've had a lot of support from everyone."

Trey leaned back in his chair, studying Shane. "You know, you're at the point in your life where you should start thinking about settling down. Marriage, family, the whole package."

Shane chuckled, shaking his head. "I don't know about all that."

Leon nodded thoughtfully. "Family is important. It gives you a reason to come home, something to ground you. You've got the hotel running smoothly. Now might be the time to think about your personal life."

Shane shrugged. "I just don't have anyone special in my life right now," he admitted, glancing out the window. The words didn't feel right passing his lips… He thought of Ace and how much he'd come to care for her. "And besides, relationships can be complicated. I've seen enough to know that."

Trey exchanged a knowing look with Leon before turning back to Shane. "What about Ace? She seems like a great person… We saw you together at Leon's party."

Shane quickly dismissed it with a wave of his

hand, not wanting to let his thoughts linger on Ace. "She's my employee, Trey. I can't mix business with personal feelings. It's not professional."

"Come on, Shane," Leon said with a smile. "We've all seen you two together. There's a connection there. Maybe it's worth exploring."

Shane sighed, leaning back in his chair. "Ace is amazing, no doubt about that. She's dedicated, smart, and has been a huge asset to the hotel. But… it's just not something I want to complicate. I value our working relationship too much." He needed to be firm in this…if only to convince himself. His reaction to seeing her hurt had shaken him. He didn't realize how much she'd got under his skin in such a short time. It troubled him.

Trey leaned forward, his expression serious. "Look, I get it. Mixing business and personal life can be tricky. But sometimes, the best relationships come from those shared goals and mutual respect. Just think about it. Don't shut the door before you've even looked inside."

Shane nodded slowly, mulling over Trey's words. He couldn't deny that there was something special about Ace, but the fear of jeopardizing their professional relationship and his own hesitations about opening his heart held him back. He liked spending time with Ace, but he'd been through a lot this year with his dad passing and taking over the hotel. Plus, his family needed him. Now wasn't the right time to start dating seriously.

The waiter arrived with their meals, breaking the tension.

As they dug into their food, the conversation shifted to lighter topics—old memories, upcoming projects, and plans for the weekend. But in the back of his mind, thoughts of Ace lingered. For now, he decided to keep those thoughts buried, focusing instead on the here and now, and the responsibilities that lay ahead.

# *CHAPTER TWENTY-ONE*

SHANE ARRIVED AT the hotel early the next morning, the soft light of dawn casting long shadows across the lobby. As he made his way to his office, he spotted Ace entering through the main doors. She looked composed, though a hint of fatigue lingered in her eyes. He'd suggested she take as much time as she need of work, but he wasn't surprised when she'd wanted to come back. He recalled Trey's words from the previous day, the suggestion to consider the possibility of something more with her. It was a thought that had lingered in his mind longer than he cared to admit.

"Morning, Ace," Shane called out, walking over to her. "How are you feeling? It's your first day back after…everything."

Ace offered him a small smile, though it didn't quite reach her eyes. "Morning, Shane. I'm doing all right. A bit tired, but I'm ready to get back to work."

He nodded, admiring her resilience. "I'm glad to hear that. We've all been worried about you."

"Thanks," she said softly. "It means a lot to have your support."

They walked together toward the office area, the hum of hotel activity beginning to pick up around them. Shane could sense her determination, the same fire that had always made her such a valuable part of the team, now burning even brighter.

"So, what's on your agenda today?" Shane asked, trying to keep the conversation light yet supportive. Ace's expression tightened, her resolve clear despite the fatigue etched in her face. "Now that Mark is in custody for attacking you, the heirloom's back and Janie's behind bars, I'm focusing on the security gaps. She got into the gallery without tripping a single alarm. We were lucky to recover the piece, but if we don't fix those holes, it could happen again." She winced slightly as she shifted in her chair.

Shane admired her drive, but concern tugged at him. Even after the attack, even while still healing, Ace couldn't stop pushing herself. "You've done so much already, Ace. We all want to make sure this never happens again, but you need to give yourself time to heal, too. You're still recovering."

Ace nodded, though the resolute glint in her eyes remained. "I know," she said, her voice softer but still firm. "But knowing what we've learned about Janie—that she's an art thief who targeted us because she thought our collection was an easy score—only makes me more certain we can't afford to leave anything to chance. She exploited a weakness, and I'm going to make sure it doesn't happen again."

Shane sighed, torn between pride and worry. "Just don't forget to take care of yourself while you're at it. We need your sharp mind at its best, not worn down."

Ace offered a faint smile. "I'll be careful. But I can't just sit back, not when we were so close to losing everything."

Shane couldn't help but feel a deeper sense of respect and admiration for Ace. She was strong, capable, and fiercely committed to her work. He wished he could explore those feelings.

"Just promise me you'll take care of yourself," Shane said, his tone gentle but firm. "We can't afford to lose you, Ace. Not now, not ever."

She looked up at him, her eyes softening slightly. "I promise, Shane. And thank you, really. For everything."

He smiled, feeling a warmth spread through him. "Anytime. We're in this together."

As they parted ways to start their respective tasks, Shane couldn't help but watch her for a moment longer.

Trey's words echoed in his mind, and he wondered if maybe, just maybe, there was a future where he and Ace could be something more. For now, he would focus on supporting her professionally and ensuring the hotel ran smoothly.

Throughout the morning, Shane found himself checking in on Ace more often than usual. She was completely engrossed in her work as she sifted through reports and made calls, determined to tighten their security defenses in the gallery and find out what she could about Janie. Her dedication was both inspiring and humbling.

By lunchtime, Shane decided to take a break and clear his head. He made his way to the hotel's rooftop terrace, a peaceful spot with a view of the island and the ocean beyond. He leaned on the railing, letting the salty breeze wash over him as he thought about the growing realization of his feelings for Ace.

The sound of footsteps behind him had him turning. He saw Ace walking toward him, a pensive expression on her face.

"Hey, taking a break, too?" she asked, joining him at the railing.

"Yeah, needed some fresh air," Shane replied, smiling. "How about you? Everything okay?"

"Just needed to clear my head for a bit," she said, looking out at the horizon. "This investigation is consuming, but I know it's important."

He nodded, feeling a sense of camaraderie in their shared moment of respite. "You're doing a great job, Ace. I have no doubt you'll get to the bottom of this."

She turned to him, her eyes searching his. "Thanks. It means a lot coming from you. I just hope I can live up to everyone's expectations." He noted that these were words he'd spoken to her before.

"You already have," he said softly, putting more emotion into the words than he'd intended. "And remember, you're not alone in this. We're all here to support you."

Ace smiled with genuine warmth in her eyes. "I know. And that makes all the difference."

THAT EVENING, Ace sat in the quiet of her living room, a cup of tea in her hand. The day had been a whirlwind of emotions and challenges, but now, in the stillness of her home, she had a chance to reflect. The soft glow of the lamp cast gentle shadows around the room, creating a comforting cocoon that allowed her to gather her thoughts.

Returning to work had been harder than Ace had anticipated. She was strong—that was what everyone kept saying—but the recent attack had shaken her in ways she hadn't fully processed. The physical fatigue was manageable, but a deeper, uneasy feeling lingered, one she kept trying to push out of her mind. Seeing the familiar faces of her team again and feeling their watchful concern only seemed to intensify it. She took a slow, steadying breath, letting the steam from her tea warm her face, and tried to sort through the emotions stirring within her, determined to stay focused on the job.

Shane's words from earlier replayed in her mind.

He'd been so supportive, so genuinely concerned for her well-being. His gentle reminder to take care of herself had touched her deeply. As she sipped her tea, Ace allowed herself to acknowledge the thoughts that had been creeping in around the edges of her mind all day. She had always been cautious with her heart, especially after the painful end of her marriage.

The scars from that time were still tender, and the idea of opening herself up to someone again was both alluring and terrifying. Yet, she couldn't deny the growing bond she felt with Shane. He'd stirred feelings she had tried to bury deep within herself.

Ace set down her cup and leaned back into the cushions, closing her eyes for a moment. Images from the day flashed through her mind—the determined look in Shane's eyes as he encouraged her, the way he seemed to understand her without needing many words, and the fleeting moments of connection they had shared. She admired his leadership and dedication to the hotel. He'd steered the hotel through tightening their budget and had been compassionate in the way he handled the layoffs. He was a good man.

The day's events had shown her that she was stronger than she realized, capable of facing her fears and pushing through adversity. Perhaps there was a place for trust, companionship, and even love.

Ace made a silent promise to herself. She would

face the challenges of tomorrow with the same resilience that had carried her through today. And, as she drifted off to sleep that night, she allowed herself to imagine a future where she could find both justice for the hotel, and perhaps, a place in her heart for someone like Shane.

ACE WALKED DOWN the hallway of the inn, her steps echoing softly in the quiet. Janie's arrest and the recent attempts to sabotage the hotel had shaken everyone, and her own brush with danger had only heightened her resolve to find out who was behind it all.

Her return to work had gone smoothly so far but she was looking forward to the weekend. If only to work out how she felt about Shane. Ever since her first day back on the job, he'd been treating her differently. Checking in on her frequently all week, reminding her to take it easy, and offering to lighten her workload. It was sweet at first, like he cared, but lately it was too much. Like he didn't trust her to do her job.

As she approached Oliver's suite, she stopped abruptly, spotting Emma slipping out of the door. Emma's eyes widened in surprise and fear when she saw Ace, her face flushing a deep red.

"Emma?" Ace called out, her voice steady but her stomach tight with suspicion. "What are you doing here?"

Emma nearly dropped her purse as she tried to

come up with a plausible explanation. "I, um, I was just… I mean, Oliver needed some help with… something."

Ace narrowed her eyes as she stepped closer. "With what, exactly?"

Emma's gaze flickered to the side, avoiding eye contact. "Just some…paperwork. You know how it is."

Ace felt a surge of frustration. "Why didn't he call Micah or Shane? Or me? What kind of paperwork requires you to come to his suite so early in the morning? I'm sure you are well aware of the rules."

Emma's hesitation was answer enough.

Ace gestured to the elevator. "Let's take this downstairs to the security office, Emma. I think it's time we had a proper conversation."

Emma's eyes widened, and she seemed to consider running, but she nodded reluctantly and followed Ace.

The walk to the security office was tense, with neither of them speaking. Ace's mind was racing, piecing together the fragmented information she had. She couldn't shake the feeling that Emma knew more than she was letting on.

Inside the security office, Ace closed the door behind them and gestured for Emma to sit.

The room was stark and utilitarian, a sharp contrast to the opulence of the rest of the hotel.

Ace leaned against the desk, crossing her arms.

"Emma, I need you to be honest with me," she began, her tone firm. "What were you doing in Oliver's suite? And don't give me any more excuses about this nonexistent paperwork. The only thing in your hand is that purse."

Emma looked down at her hands and twisted them nervously. "Ace, it's—it's complicated."

"Complicated how?" Ace pressed. "I've been through a lot lately, and I need to know what's going on. The sabotage, the stolen heirloom, everything. If you know something, you need to tell me."

Emma took a deep breath, finally meeting Ace's gaze. "All right, I'll tell you."

Ace nodded, her heart pounding. "Talk."

Emma sighed, her shoulders slumping. "Oliver... he wanted to force Shane to step down as GM. He thought that if things were bad, no one would continue supporting him. Oliver figured Shane would give up and just go back to Los Angeles."

Ace's mind reeled. "Why? Why would Shane do that?"

Emma looked down again, her voice barely above a whisper. "Oliver says that Shane hates failure."

"What's in this for him?"

"Oliver's been overlooked, cheated out of what he deserves."

Ace frowned, trying to understand. "What do you mean...what he deserves?"

Emma glanced up, her eyes filled with a mix

of guilt and sorrow. "Oliver should have a bigger share in the hotel, more control."

Ace shook her head, trying to process everything. "But to go this far? To sabotage the hotel and steal from his own family? That doesn't make any sense."

Emma's expression hardened. "This is the only way to get what he deserves. We don't see it as betrayal. We view it as taking what's rightfully his."

Ace felt a rush of anger and sadness. "So all of this, the reservation glitches, the theft…it was all just to make a point?" She took a deep breath, trying to keep her emotions in check. "And you? What's your part in all this?"

Emma looked down. "I wanted to help Oliver."

"Why?"

Her expression grew sad. "Because I know how it feels to be invisible to everyone in your family. To constantly be overlooked. Nobody deserves that." She studied Ace. "You don't understand…"

She stood up, her resolve strengthening. "I understand more than you know, Emma… You're in love with Oliver."

# CHAPTER TWENTY-TWO

OLIVER STOOD OUTSIDE the hotel, the morning air cool against his skin as he scanned the quiet street for any sign of Emma. The tension in his chest tightened with each passing second. The familiar facade of the hotel loomed behind him, a silent reminder of the chaos he had orchestrated and the uncertain future he faced.

Finally, Emma appeared, hurrying toward him with a look of panic on her face. Oliver's heart sank; this wasn't going to be a pleasant conversation. She'd texted him about Ace asking questions.

"Emma," he greeted her, his voice low and strained. "What happened with Ace?"

She bit her lip, glancing nervously around as if expecting Ace to appear out of nowhere. "We need to leave. *Now.* We should get in the car and leave Polk Island before it's too late."

His eyes narrowed. "What are you talking about?"

Emma's voice wavered as she spoke. "I told Ace everything. About our attempts to sabotage Shane. Oliver, we're all going to end up in jail. Especially if Mark decides to tell the police that we hired him to help sabotage the hotel."

His heart pounded in his chest. He had expected Emma to keep their secrets, to maintain their plan. "You told her *everything*?" he repeated, disbelief mingling with anger. "Why would you do that?"

Emma's eyes filled with tears. "I couldn't lie to her. She saw me leaving your suite. She pressed me for answers and I—I couldn't keep up the facade. I'm sorry."

Oliver took a deep breath, trying to quell the storm of emotions swirling within him.

Betrayal, anger, and a deep, gnawing fear threatened to overwhelm him, but he knew he had to stay composed.

"Please don't be angry with me."

"Emma," he began, his voice softer now, "I'm not angry. I understand. This situation has spiraled out of control."

She looked up at him, surprise flickering in her eyes. "You're not upset?"

Oliver shook his head. "No. I know you were under a lot of pressure." He sighed deeply. "This is my mess, and I'll take responsibility for it."

Emma's relief was unmistakable, but her fear remained. "What are we going to do? We can't just wait around for them to arrest us."

Oliver's resolve hardened. "First off, Mark is the one who attacked Ace. Not us. I need to see my family. It's time to tell them everything. Running away won't solve anything."

Emma's eyes widened in shock. "You're going over there?"

Oliver nodded slowly. "Yes. I've caused enough damage. It's time to own up to my actions and face the consequences."

Emma looked at him, searching his face. "Are you sure?"

He met her gaze steadily. "I'm sure. If I keep running, I'll never stop looking over my shoulder. It's time to confront my demons and make things right with my family."

Emma's shoulders slumped in resignation. "All right. I'll stand by you. Whatever happens, we'll face it together."

He gave her a small, appreciative smile. "Thank you, Emma. Your support means a lot to me."

As they made their way back into the hotel, Oliver's mind raced with thoughts of the impending confrontation. He knew it wouldn't be easy, and he doubted his family would forgive him quickly, if at all. But this was the only way forward, the only way to put an end to the lies and deceit that had poisoned their lives.

He took a deep breath, steeling himself for what was to come. It was time to face his family, to reveal the truth, and to seek redemption, no matter the cost.

Oliver reached out to his aunt, asking for a family meeting.

Thirty minutes later, he and Emma stood in the living room of the Worthington home, his heart pounding as he faced the gathered family members.

"First off, I want you to know that we didn't have anything to do with what happened to Ace," Oliver began, his voice firm despite the underlying tension he felt. "I know he's been arrested, but we had nothing to do with that—he was angry with Ace because she fired him."

Madelyn raised an eyebrow but remained silent, waiting for him to continue.

"But you still conspired with Emma there to sabotage us," Cia stated.

Micah glanced over at the woman standing beside Oliver. "Emma, how much did he pay you?"

"There's something you should know," Oliver added, taking a deep breath. "Emma is my wife, and she is carrying our child."

Gasps filled the room, and all eyes turned to Emma, who placed her hand protectively on her slightly rounded belly.

She offered a small, nervous smile, clearly feeling the weight of the moment. "I only wanted to help Oliver. He just wants to be treated like a Worthington and not an outsider."

Madelyn sighed, her expression a mixture of sympathy and disappointment. "Oliver, you could have just been up-front and honest with us. There was no need for all the scheming."

Oliver felt a pang of guilt but pressed on. "I know, Aunt Maddie, but I was angry. Anytime I came around, everyone brought up my past. I have ideas that could help increase profits, but no one was willing to listen to me."

"Why didn't you sit down with Angus Jr. and discuss your ideas with him?" Madelyn asked. "I'll tell you why that never happened. Because you're just like your father. He underestimated his brother and you have done the same," she said softly. "You're both impatient, and you never try to just sit down with the family to sort out any issues. Sabotaging the hotel and stealing the heirloom…"

"Wait…*what*?" Oliver asked. "We didn't steal anything. Are you talking about the Lorne statue?"

"Are you really going to stand there and pretend you didn't take it?" Shane asked. "You do know that Janie was caught."

Puzzled, Oliver looked at his wife. "Who is Janie?"

"She's the HR director," Emma responded. "She hired me. I heard she was arrested for the theft, but I didn't know y'all thought we were a part of that."

Eyeing his cousin, Shane stated, "I believe you. I really thought you were behind the theft, but I just couldn't prove it. For my part, I'm sorry."

"Oliver, I hope you will learn that family means

more than just blood and entitlement," Madelyn stated.

His shoulders slumped slightly at her words. "I realize that now. I just wanted a future for my family. I'm sorry for everything I've done. I hope one day you all can forgive me. All I want is for my child to grow up surrounded by family and proud of the Worthington legacy."

Madelyn's expression softened further, and she reached out a hand. "It's not too late. We can work this out, but it must be done the right way. Honesty and integrity are what binds us as a family."

Oliver nodded, feeling a mix of relief and regret. "I'm ready to make things right."

Madelyn paused, and when she continued, her tone was gentle. "Before he died, your grandfather set aside a trust for you, Oliver. He left strict terms that you couldn't touch it until you had settled down—found stability in your life. That trust is yours, but you must prove to me that you're ready for it."

Oliver looked at her, stunned. "A trust? Did my father know about it?"

"No," she responded. "Jacob was financially irresponsible. He…" She hesitated briefly. "He had a gambling addiction, and it almost cost your grandfather the hotel…that's why he placed Angus Jr. in charge."

"He gambled, but it wasn't a problem," Oliver said, his voice wavering with uncertainty. He knew his dad had spent the occasional night out at the casino or bet on the odd sports game, but an addiction?

Aunt Madelyn's expression turned sad. Her eyes seemed to reflect years of hidden pain. "Why do you think your mother left him? She called me after they lost the house in Richmond. We gave her the money to move back home to Atlanta. Angus Jr. purchased a car for her, so she didn't have to take the bus back and forth to work. She was worried about leaving you alone after school."

A wave of shock washed over Oliver as he absorbed the truth. His mother's silence had shielded him, keeping him from knowing the sacrifices she made to protect him from the bitterness that had poisoned their family.

"She never told me," he said, his voice cracking. "I just figured my grandmother was the one who helped us out when we needed it. When I asked Mom why she left my father, she told me that he was sick over Granddad giving the hotel to Uncle. That's why I blamed him. I wanted to get even."

"Yes," Madelyn said. "But your actions have consequences. You can't just claim what you think you deserve without earning it. Oliver, we want to support you, but you're going to need to show us that you've changed."

Oliver nodded, feeling the truth of her words settle deep within him. The journey ahead wouldn't be easy, but for the first time, he felt a sense of clarity and purpose. He looked around the room, seeing not just obstacles, but a family that, despite everything, was willing to give him a chance.

He felt a glimmer of hope. It wasn't the smoothest path he'd taken, but with his family's support, Oliver believed he could find his place within the Worthington legacy without resorting to deceit.

"So what are your plans?" Shane asked. "Are you and Emma planning to leave the island?"

"I guess that is the plan," Oliver confessed. "But the truth is that we really don't have any place to go." He glanced at his wife. "I was thinking about going back to Atlanta, but Emma really likes it here…"

"Why don't you just stay, then?" Kenyon suggested. "Polk Island is still your home. You have family here. Perhaps we can help keep you out of trouble. That's what Dad would've done—I know he tried to get your father to change his mind about leaving the island."

Madelyn nodded in agreement. "You and Emma can stay in the Worthington II suite until you find a permanent place to live."

Oliver eyed Shane. "Are you sure about this?" He glanced back at his aunt. "You want me to stay?"

"Not only that," Shane responded. "Lilly is the assistant GM and she told me this morning that she's relocating to Long Beach, California, with her fiancé. We can discuss your replacing her.

That's if you're interested. Your ideas are solid, and I'd like to discuss them in more detail."

He looked over at Micah. "I don't want to block your moving up the ranks."

"I enjoy my job as the guest relations and reservations manager. It'll be a while before I even consider something like that. *If ever*," Micah stated. "Once I'm done with grad school… I might decide to venture into corporate America."

Oliver looked over at Emma and smiled. "I guess we're staying on the island."

Emma beamed. "I'm so glad because I really love it here. Besides, I'd like my baby to be surrounded by family."

"How long have you two been married?" Madelyn asked.

"Six months," he responded.

"You're newlyweds still," Cia said with a grin. "Did you have a wedding?"

Emma shook her head. "I really wanted one, but Oliver didn't think he'd have any family outside of his mother in attendance, so we decided to just go to a justice of the peace. No point in going through all that expense."

Cia nodded, her expression turning pensive.

"I need to get back to the hotel," Shane announced.

As he turned to leave, Oliver called after him.

"I know this isn't any of my business, but I'm gonna say it, anyway. Don't waste any more time," he said, his voice low but firm. He'd seen his cousin around Ace…there was love there, and Shane wouldn't be the first Worthington man to push away a chance to be happy. "You've got a chance with Ace—don't let it slip away like I did with everything else."

ACE WAS IN the middle of leading a self-defense class on Tuesday evening when she spotted Shane walking into the gym. His presence sent a ripple of unease through her, even as she continued demonstrating a wrist escape technique to the group of women gathered around her. She could feel his eyes on her, and it didn't sit well.

She didn't need him here. Not like this. Not watching her.

"Okay, now let's pair up and practice," Ace said, her voice steady, though her insides churned with irritation. As the women partnered up, she turned to Shane, who was already making his way toward her.

"Hey," Shane greeted, his tone too soft for her liking. "I just wanted to check in, see how you're doing."

Ace crossed her arms, keeping her expression neutral. "I'm fine, Shane. Busy, obviously." She gestured toward the class behind her, hoping the sight of her leading a group of capable women would remind him that she didn't need rescuing. He'd been treating her with kid gloves at work since she'd returned. Yet somehow, he'd pulled away, too, always keeping a distance and a professional tone, sidestepping topics that veered into the personal. Why was he here now, in her space, unannounced?

"I know," he said, glancing briefly at the group. "I just…wanted to make sure you're okay."

Her jaw tightened. The concern in his eyes made her bristle. She appreciated what he'd done after the attack—she needed help then, when she was recovering—but now? Now it felt like he was treating her like she was fragile. Like she needed to be handled with care. And she couldn't stand it.

"I'm teaching a self-defense class, Shane," she said, her voice sharper than she intended. "I think I'm doing just fine."

He blinked, clearly taken aback. "I didn't mean it like that. I just… I care about you, Ace. I don't want you to feel like you're alone in this."

She could feel the tension coiling in her chest, her frustration growing. "I'm *not* alone. I've been handling things on my own for a long time. I needed help after the attack, sure, but that doesn't mean I need someone constantly checking up on me like I'm a victim."

Shane's expression shifted, a mixture of hurt and confusion. "That's not what I'm trying to do."

Ace glanced over at her class, the women now practicing their moves, oblivious to the tension brewing between her and Shane. She dropped her arms, her stance defensive. "It feels like that's exactly what you're doing. I don't need a knight in shining armor, Shane. I don't need someone to save me. I'm not broken."

His shoulders tensed, his eyes searching hers as if trying to find the right words. "I know you're strong, Ace. That's not what this is about."

She shook her head, her irritation spilling over. "Then what is it about? Because from where I'm standing, it feels like you're seeing me as something I'm not. I've been through worse, and I'll keep pushing through. But I don't need you coming in here, checking on me like I'm some fragile thing."

The tension between them was almost suffocating now. If he cared about her, why had he pulled away? She could tell every time they interacted at work that something had shifted for him.

Shane stood there, clearly wrestling with his emotions, but Ace wasn't backing down. She couldn't. Not when she felt like he was seeing her as less than she was.

"I just wanted to be there for you," he said, his voice quieter now. "I care about you. I'm not trying to undermine your strength."

Ace exhaled slowly, her frustration still simmering beneath the surface. "I appreciate what you've done, but I can't have you thinking you need to protect me. Not like this."

He nodded, though the hurt in his eyes was unmistakable. "I hear you."

Without another word, Shane turned and walked toward the door, leaving Ace standing in the middle of her class, watching him go.

She felt a pang of regret, but she couldn't let herself get close to him. Not now. Not when she feared he'd always see her as someone who needed saving. And that was something she refused to be.

SHANE STEPPED OUT of the gym, the door closing behind him with a soft thud, but the tension from his encounter with Ace still clung to him like a heavy fog. He'd expected… He wasn't even sure what he'd expected. Maybe that Ace would appreciate him checking in, that she'd understand he was trying to be there for her. But the way she'd looked at him, the sharpness in her tone—he hadn't seen that coming at all.

He replayed the conversation in his head, trying to pinpoint where things had gone wrong. All he'd wanted to do was show her he cared. After everything she'd been through—the attack, the recovery—he thought she might need someone in her corner. Someone looking out for her. But she hadn't seen it that way. Not at all.

"She thinks I see her as a victim," Shane muttered, shaking his head.

He leaned his elbows on the car roof, staring at the pavement beneath his feet. That was the last thing he'd ever want her to feel. He didn't view Ace as fragile or weak. Just the opposite. She was one of the strongest people he knew. But somehow, his concern had come across like he was trying to fix her, or worse, like he didn't believe she could handle things on her own.

He sighed, feeling a knot form in his chest. How could he have been so off-base? Ace was fiercely independent, always had been. He admired that about her. It was one of the things that had drawn him to her in the first place—her strength, her determination. And here he was, making her feel like he thought she couldn't stand on her own two feet.

Shane rubbed his hands over his face, frustration simmering inside him. He'd wanted to be supportive while staying professional… He'd been struggling lately with his feelings for her that went way beyond colleagues or even friendship. But the men in his life—Trey, Leon, even Oliver—were making him realize he couldn't fight his feeling for her. He'd be a fool to be presented with a chance at happiness and not take it. He'd come here and tell her he cared about her. But instead, he'd made things tense, pushed her further away.

*What was I thinking?*

He walked toward his car, the echo of her words still stinging.

He realized how wrong he'd been to show up at her class unannounced. Ace was in her element, teaching those women how to defend themselves, and there he was, hovering.

He was trying to be there, to show her that he

cared. But now, it was obvious that Ace didn't need—or want—that from him. At least, not in the way he'd been offering it.

Shane opened the car door and slid inside.

He sat there for a moment, gripping the steering wheel. He knew Ace wasn't just upset about today. This was about more. She didn't trust him, didn't trust that he saw her for who she really was—strong, capable, resilient. Maybe she thought that if they got closer, he'd always try to protect her, to step in when she didn't need it. And maybe, on some level, she wasafraid of letting someone in.

Shane's chest tightened at the thought. He wanted more with Ace, but she'd made it clear she wasn't ready for that. At least, not with him. He'd have to back off, give her space to breathe. But that didn't mean he was giving up. No way. He cared too much about her to walk away now.

He took a deep breath and started the car, determination settling in. Maybe he'd gone about it the wrong way today, but he wasn't going to stop trying to show Ace that he was in this for the right reasons. She wasn't a victim, and he didn't see her that way. He just had to figure out how to prove it without pushing her further away.

*Don't waste any more time*, Oliver had said. And he wasn't going to. But this time, Shane would be careful, more thoughtful about how he approached Ace.

She deserved that.

# CHAPTER TWENTY-THREE

SHANE STARED AT the spreadsheet on his computer screen, a satisfied smile creeping across his face. After countless hours of analysis and reconfiguration, the numbers had begun to make sense. The brutal budget cuts had been necessary, but they were starting to show a glimmer of hope. Projections revealed a path forward—one that could lead the hotel out of the red and into stability if they managed things carefully.

He heard a knock on his door and said, "Come in…".

Ace stepped inside, a cup of tea in hand.

Her tentative smile was a welcome sight, but there was something in the air—an undercurrent of tension—that made him hesitate. Shane couldn't shake the memory of their last encounter at the gym, the way her demeanor had shifted when he'd shown up unannounced.

"How's it looking?" she asked, her tone hopeful as she set the cup down on his desk.

Shane gestured to the screen. "Better than I expected. The cuts are starting to make a difference. It's going to be tight for a while, but I think we can make it work."

Ace leaned over his shoulder, peering at the spreadsheets, her presence close enough that he could catch the faint scent of her perfume.

"Your father always said you had a knack for making the impossible possible. Shane, he was very proud of you."

The warmth of her words brought a smile to his face. "It's not just me. We've all been pulling together. Oliver's got some good ideas, and I'm glad he'll be coming on board next week. Turns out… Emma is finishing her IT degree and quite a few certifications, as well. She'll be working with Nelson, although she won't start until after she gives birth."

"I'm glad you and Oliver are on the same side," she said, her voice steady.

"Me, too," he replied, trying to keep the mood light.

"I just got off the phone with the FBI," Ace said, her expression turning serious. "They had some updates on Janie—well, Janine Winchester. They confirmed her real name and that she and her husband, Robert, have an outstanding arrest warrant in New York."

The revelation hit Shane like a punch to the gut. "I can't believe it. She had me fooled," he admitted, shaking his head in disbelief.

"I feel the same way," Ace chimed in, her eyes fixed on the screen as if searching for solutions within the data. "We didn't find any red flags during our background check. Maybe we should start implementing fingerprint scans."

He nodded in agreement. "It's something to seriously consider."

Shane turned back to the screen and scrolled through the detailed expense reports. "We reduced the marketing budget by reallocating more to digital campaigns, and it's paying off. The engagement rates are higher, and we're reaching a broader audience at a fraction of the cost."

"That's great," Ace replied, nodding in clear appreciation.

"I hate that we had to let people go," Shane admitted, his expression turning serious. "But those who are still here have really stepped up, and it's increasing efficiency."

"I know those decisions weren't easy. I didn't agree with them at first, but you did what had to be done. And it's working."

"Thanks, Ace. That means a lot." He felt the tension shift slightly, the air around them feeling a bit lighter.

Just then, his phone buzzed on the desk, breaking the moment. He glanced at the screen and saw a message from Micah.

Meeting in the conference room in ten. Got some ideas to discuss.

Shane's heart lifted. Micah's support had been instrumental in their efforts to revitalize the hotel's profits.

He looked back at Ace, who seemed eager to continue the conversation. "Micah's got some ideas. You want to join?"

"Absolutely. Let's hear what he has to say," she said, and they made their way to the conference room. They walked in silence, and despite the pleasant conversation earlier, Shane couldn't help but feel like things were awkward between them.

As they entered, Micah was already setting up, greeting them with a grin that radiated energy. "I've been brainstorming ways to maximize our current resources and attract new guests without breaking the bank. I've asked Oliver to join us. He should be here shortly."

"Here I am," Oliver announced, quickly taking a seat.

Shane and Ace settled in, listening intently as Micah outlined his proposals, suggesting themed weekend packages, partnering with local businesses for cross promotions, and leveraging social-media influencers to highlight the hotel's unique charm.

"These are fantastic ideas," Shane said, feeling more optimistic with each passing minute. "If we can implement these strategies effectively, we'll not only survive—we'll thrive."

Oliver nodded. "The themed weekends will give us a unique selling point and attract a diverse crowd."

Micah leaned back, appearing satisfied with their reactions. "Glad you like them. We'll need to work together to make these ideas a reality, but I have no doubt we can do it."

As the meeting wrapped up, Shane caught Ace's eye. She gave him an encouraging smile, but he couldn't shake the lingering tension.

Once back in his office, Shane took a moment to reflect. The budget cuts had been necessary, but they were only part of the solution. The real key to their success was the people—their resilience, creativity, and unwavering commitment to the hotel's future.

He turned his attention back to the budget, making a few final adjustments. The numbers were just numbers, but behind them were stories of hard work and perseverance. A deep sense of responsibility weighed on him, but he also felt a growing confidence. They were turning the tide, one step at a time.

Just then, Ace returned, knocking lightly on the open door. "Hey, can I come in?"

"Of course." Shane waved her in, the slight tension in the air returning.

"I wanted to apologize for how I reacted at the

gym," she began, her voice steady but soft. "It wasn't fair to you."

He shook his head, waving his hand dismissively. "It's not necessary. I shouldn't have just shown up like that."

"I just want you to know I'm not a victim." Her gaze connected with his. "I don't need anyone to rescue me."

"I get that, Ace. I really do," he assured her.

"It was a sweet gesture, though," she replied, a hint of a smile returning to her lips.

Shane watched as she turned to leave, the air between them still crackling with unspoken words. He wanted to bridge the gap that had opened between them, to reassure her that he was in this for the long haul. But he knew he needed to tread carefully; she was strong and capable, and he had to respect that while finding a way to show her he cared.

OLIVER STOOD IN the Grand Ballroom, his heart racing with a mixture of emotions. The room was beautifully adorned with white-and-gold streamers, and a large banner that read hung above the entrance that read, Congratulations, Oliver and Emma!

Emma, standing beside him, looked just as shocked. "This is incredibly beautiful... I can't believe they did all this for us," she murmured. "Did you know about this?"

He shook his head.

The sight of a stunning three-tier wedding cake at the center of the room left him in awe. The cake stood tall and majestic. The white icing glistened under the warm lights, delicate roses and lilies crafted from sugar adorned each tier, and the intricate details of swirls and pearls added a touch of elegance.

Soft candlelight danced off the smooth surfaces about the room, casting a warm glow. The floral arrangements around the cake were bursting with color, with shades of pink, purple, and white. It was a sight to behold, with vibrant blooms of every color cascading down from the ceiling.

Madelyn approached him with a warm smile, "We wanted to celebrate your marriage properly, Oliver. You've been through a lot, and it's time to start anew."

His eyes welled up with tears. He was unable to contain his feelings. "Aunt Maddie, this means so much. More than you'll ever know... Thank you."

Madelyn hugged him tightly. "Family always comes first."

Shane walked up to them. "We have one more surprise for the two of you."

Emma put a hand to her chest. "I'm not sure I can handle another surprise. I'm still trying to process all this."

"I think you'll really like this one," Shane replied, giving a slight nod toward the entrance.

Oliver and Emma turned in time to see her family entering the room along with his mother. It was unexpected, yet heartwarming. Their presence signified the acceptance and love that both families shared. Emma's parents and siblings greeted him with open arms.

Standing beside him, Emma leaned in and whispered, "They all came for us, Oliver. We're not alone."

He nodded, feeling a deep sense of gratitude and responsibility, knowing that this celebration marked the beginning of a new chapter in their lives.

Later, as the reception was in full swing, Oliver found Shane standing near the edge of the dance floor.

"I want to apologize again for everything I've done. I was wrong, and I'm committed to being a man worthy of the Worthington name."

Shane studied him for a moment before extending his hand. "We're family. Let's move forward together."

Oliver shook Shane's hand, a sense of relief washing over him. "Thank you, Shane. I won't let you down." He recognized that this celebration wasn't just about his marriage; it was a symbol of forgiveness, unity, and the beginning of a brighter future. He vowed to uphold the Worthington legacy with integrity and be a devoted husband to Emma.

ACE STOOD ON the edge of the ballroom, the sounds of the lively celebration echoing around her. She watched as Oliver and Emma shared a dance, their faces alight with joy. The reception was a beautiful surprise, complete with a wedding cake and decorations that spoke of a family coming together. Ace felt a warm smile tug at her lips, but her thoughts were elsewhere.

After the collapse of her own marriage, she had sworn off love, convinced it only led to heartbreak. Ace had buried herself in work, determined to keep her emotions at bay. But Shane had slowly chipped away at the walls she had built around her heart.

She glanced across the room, where Shane stood talking with some relatives. Their eyes met, and a jolt of electricity passed between them. It was as if the world around them faded, leaving just the two of them. It was overwhelming—she couldn't let herself feel this way about him. Ace took a deep breath and decided to step outside for some air, hoping to steady her racing heart.

On the terrace, the cool night air helped clear her mind. The sound of the ocean waves crashing against the shore was soothing, yet her thoughts were anything but calm. She felt both exhilaration and anxiety, caught in the emotional whirlpool that had formed between her and Shane.

Suddenly, she heard footsteps behind her and turned to see him approaching. Her heart skipped a beat as he came to stand beside her, a familiar presence that both comforted and unsettled her.

"Hey," he said softly, his voice warm and inviting, a tone that melted her defenses despite her best efforts to remain guarded.

"Hey," she replied, her voice barely a whisper, betraying her inner turmoil. They stood in silence for a moment, the tension between them palpable, like a taut string waiting to snap. Shane stepped closer, his arm brushing hers where she leaned on the balcony railing. Ace felt her pulse quicken, and a rush of warmth spread through her, reminding her just how much Shane affected her.

He pulled away slightly, his expression serious. "I wasn't out here searching for you, you know. I just needed some air."

Her heart sank slightly at his words. The memory of their encounter at the gym replayed in her mind, the way things had escalated between them when she'd reacted defensively. She appreciated his attempt to set boundaries, but part of her had hoped he wanted to see her tonight.

"Yeah, no problem," she said, forcing a nonchalant tone.

"Exactly," he replied, his eyes seemingly searching hers for understanding. "I don't want to upset you again. We're both just…navigating this."

Ace nodded, grateful he had addressed it directly, but unspoken words still hung in the air, thick and suffocating, yet intoxicating in their own right. They were trying to keep their distance, yet beneath the surface, something deeper was still stirring between them, a current of connection that felt impossible to ignore.

"Ace," he said, finally breaking the silence, his voice low and sincere. "I—"

She turned to him, her breath hitching, and felt the air around them thicken with possibility. No matter how much she wanted to deny it, the pull was there, undeniable and magnetic.

Shane spoke again, his voice low and hesitant. "There's something I've been wanting to tell you."

She looked up at him, her breath catching in her throat. "What is it?"

"This...you and me—it feels right," Shane murmured, his voice trembling.

It did feel right. Why couldn't she let herself have this? Instead of answering, she gently cupped his cheek, the feel of his skin beneath her palm sending a shiver down her spine. She moved closer, and Ace's eyes fluttered shut as he leaned in, their lips meeting in a tender kiss. It was a moment of pure emotion, all their unspoken feelings and hidden desires finally breaking free.

When they pulled apart, they were both breathless, their foreheads resting against each other. "I know," Ace whispered back. "I'm just not ready."

She felt the weight of her own words, aware that they were just as much a declaration of her vulnerability as they were a shield. In that moment, the tension between them shifted, a fragile balance of longing and caution hanging in the air. She turned away and walked back into the reception.

Throughout the evening, Ace couldn't help but compare the way she felt with Shane to her past. Her marriage had been fraught with disappointments and heartaches, leaving her skeptical of love. But Shane was different. He showed her a care and affection that began to mend her bruised heart. He gave her space all evening, though whenever their gazes met, she found understanding there. His presence in the ballroom was like a comforting anchor.

As the night wore on, Ace found herself relaxing, enjoying the festivities more than she had expected. She laughed, , danced with friends, and felt a warmth spreading through her that had nothing to do with the wine she had sipped. It was as if Shane's presence was slowly dissolving her fears, replacing them with a cautious optimism.

By the time the reception wound down, Ace felt a sense of peace she hadn't known in years. She knew the journey ahead wouldn't be easy, and there would be challenges to face, but for the first time, she believed that a second chance at love didn't have to end in pain. Shane had shown her that genuine connection and affection could heal old wounds and create new, beautiful memories. Deep down, Ace knew they had vowed not to give in to their emotions again, but she also knew that the bond between them was too strong to ignore. Whatever the future held, she was ready to face it.

# CHAPTER TWENTY-FOUR

SHANE STOOD AT the front of the house, watching as the family gathered to celebrate the homecoming of baby Arabella. The Worthington family was abuzz with excitement, and Shane couldn't help but feel a deep sense of contentment.

His eyes were drawn to Ace, who was mingling effortlessly with his family, her laughter ringing out as she spoke with London.

It was moments like these that had shown Shane the depth of his feelings for Ace. He had always thought that running the hotel would consume all his time and energy, leaving no room for a meaningful romantic relationship. But caring for Ace and watching her recover, seeing how she fit in with his family and friends, had changed his perspective entirely.

Ace turned to him, her eyes sparkling with curiosity and joy. Shane felt a surge of affection for her. It wasn't just about the attraction; it was about the bond they had formed, the way she brought light into his life. He realized then that the hotel didn't have to be a barrier to love. Instead, it could be the backdrop against which they built their life together.

He approached her. "Enjoying yourself?"

She smiled a warm, genuine smile that made his heart skip a beat. "Absolutely. I'd been meaning to come for a tour of London's place." Ace glanced around. "It's is amazing. I can't wait to come back and watch the whole process. The honey is delicious."

Shane nodded, looking around the farm. "It is. And it's nice to get away from the hotel for a bit."

Ace tilted her head. "Definitely. It's beautiful here. And it's nice to see you…away from everything."

Her words echoed in his mind. Spending time with her had become the highlight of his days. They seemed to have reached an understanding since Oliver's wedding. They'd acknowledged their connection, and while he wouldn't rush her or smother her, she'd been more open in their interactions since, as if she wanted to give them a real chance. They stuck close to each other for the rest of the party, and as the evening wore on, family members began playfully asking questions about their relationship. Shane and Ace exchanged amused glances, their connection deepening with each shared smile and knowing look.

When the celebration wound down, Shane

suggested, "How about we take a drive to North Beach? It's a beautiful evening."

Ace agreed, and they left the house, driving in comfortable silence. The sun had set, and the sky was painted with hues of orange and pink as they arrived. They walked along the shore, the sound of the waves providing a soothing backdrop to their conversation.

Shane turned to her, his voice soft. "You know, when I decided to take over the hotel, I thought it was all I had time for. That it was too demanding to allow for anything else."

Ace looked at him, her expression soft and understanding. "And now?"

"Now I realize that it doesn't have to be that way. The hotel is important, yes, but it doesn't have to be a barrier to everything else. It can be a part of my life without taking it over completely."

Ace's eyes sparkled. "I'm glad to hear you say that."

Shane nodded. "I've come to see that running the hotel and having a life outside it are not mutually exclusive. They can coexist."

She smiled, and he felt a weight lift off his shoulders. "I believe that, too. You can find a balance."

They continued their walk along the shore, the gentle sound of the ocean waves providing a calming backdrop to their conversation. Shane felt a profound sense of peace wash over him as they walked the shore and Ace spoke animatedly about her dreams, her eyes alive with passion. She painted a picture of a future filled with purpose and fulfillment, and he couldn't help but admire her even more.

"I've always wanted to create a space where people can feel safe and supported," she said, her voice brimming with determination. "A place where they can grow and thrive. I see that in the work I do, especially with the self-defense classes. It's empowering to help others find their strength."

Shane nodded, appreciating her enthusiasm. "You're incredible, Ace. You have a gift for bringing out the best in people. It's one of the many reasons I care about you so much."

She smiled at him, and he felt a warmth spread through him. But when he shifted the conversation to his own hopes, a heaviness settled over the moment, though he couldn't quite put his finger on why.

"I've been thinking a lot about the future, too. The hotel is a part of my family's legacy, and I want to honor that," he said, trying to convey his sincerity. "But I also want to make room in my life for family...just not in the traditional sense."

Ace glanced at him, curiosity flickering in her eyes. "What do you mean?"

"Honestly, I don't envision myself having kids," he admitted, feeling a twinge of discomfort in his chest. "But that doesn't mean I don't want to be a dad someday. For now, I plan to take care of my siblings, be there for Bella and any nieces and nephews I have. I want to create a nurturing environment through the hotel, a place where families can come together and feel at home."

He watched as her expression shifted, the warmth in her eyes dimming slightly. Did he say something wrong?

"That's really admirable, Shane," she replied, though her voice seemed less vibrant. "Building a family doesn't always mean having kids of your own. It's about the connections we create and the support we provide."

"Exactly," he responded, relieved that she understood. "I want to focus on investing in my siblings and the next generation, help them navigate their own paths. I want to be the kind of brother and uncle they can look up to."

For a moment, they walked in silence. Shane felt a growing sense of hope as he envisioned his future. He believed Ace was a crucial part of that vision, her strength and passion adding depth to everything he hoped to achieve. But he couldn't shake the feeling that something was off with her.

"I can see you being that uncle," she said finally, breaking the quiet. "You'd be great at it. I can imagine the kids flocking to you."

He chuckled softly, picturing the scene in his mind. "Maybe I'll become the fun uncle. The one who spoils them and takes them on adventures while making sure they know they're loved."

As he spoke, he noticed Ace's smile faltering just a bit, her gaze dropping to the ground. The warmth that had filled their earlier moments seemed to wane, and he felt a hint of sadness in the air, though he had no idea why.

"Yeah, that kind of love is what's most important—regardless of how it looks," she said quietly, but her tone was tinged with something he couldn't identify.

He felt a pang of concern. "I'm glad we're on the same page about this," he said, trying to reassure her. "It feels good to share these thoughts with you."

"Me, too," she replied, her gaze steady yet distant.

She was hiding something—something that seemed to seep into the spaces between their words. Maybe he had scared her off again with his talk of kids and family when they were supposed to be taking things slow. If only he understood the sadness in her eyes, perhaps he could find a way to ease it.

SHANE SAT IN his quiet living room, the gentle hum of the night surrounding him.

His mind wandered to the potential future he and Ace might have together. Could they truly work together at the hotel without letting their personal relationship interfere?

Ace was passionate and dedicated, qualities that

would make her a valuable partner in any venture. But the fear of what could go wrong loomed large. Shane didn't want their relationship to be a source of distraction or conflict, something that could undermine their professional roles. The hotel was still his priority, and he wouldn't do anything to jeopardize his role as the hotel's leader. They still had work to do to make the hotel the success it once was, which meant making sure the staff trusted him and his plans. Dating his head of security could jeopardize that.

Taking a deep breath, Shane tried to find clarity amid his swirling thoughts. The truth was, he couldn't imagine his life without Ace. She had become integral to his world, her support and caring giving him strength in ways he hadn't anticipated. But how could he ensure that their relationship wouldn't compromise his responsibilities?

He thought about their conversation earlier, the ease with which they'd talked about their days, shared their thoughts and dreams. There was a natural rhythm to it, a sense of partnership that felt right. Perhaps that was the key—approaching their relationship with the same dedication and commitment he brought to the hotel.

As the night deepened, Shane made a silent vow to himself. He would find a way to balance his love for Ace and his duties at work. One thing he was certain of—he didn't want to lose her.

Shane picked up his phone and sent Ace a simple message:

Thank you for being you.

With that, he finally felt a sense of calm wash over him, knowing that whatever the future held, they would face it together.

THE FOLLOWING SATURDAY, Ace sat at her favorite corner table in the Polk Island Café, chatting with Misty and eating French fries.

The afternoon light streamed through the windows, casting a soft glow over the wooden interior, and the aroma of freshly baked pastries filled the air.

"So, Ace," Misty said with a playful smile, wiping her hands on her apron. "What's been going on with you lately?"

Before Ace could respond, the bell above the door jingled, and Emma walked in, her face lighting up when she saw them.

Ace waved her over. "Emma. Come join us."

Emma smiled and made her way to their table, settling into a chair with a contented sigh. "Good afternoon, ladies. How are you?"

"We're great," Ace replied, returning her smile. "Just catching up on life."

Misty brought over a fresh cup of herbal tea for Emma and then leaned against the counter, her eyes twinkling with curiosity. "I was just about to ask Ace about her love life."

Ace hesitated, surprise and uncertainty creeping in. Her recent conversation with Shane about kids had left her feeling unsettled. "Well, Shane and I have been spending time together…which I'm sure you already know."

"I do," Misty said with a chuckle. "Leon and I saw you two on the beach last Sunday. Y'all look good together."

"He's a great guy," Ace said, her voice tinged with a mix of hope and doubt. "But I saw my doctor and my condition isn't getting any better. It's got me thinking about the future, especially about starting a family. You know how much I've always wanted to be a mom."

As Ace spoke, her voice betrayed a mixture of conflicting emotions—hope and doubt, certainty and uncertainty. Even as she praised the person in question, her mind was consumed by thoughts of her worsening condition and the implications it held for her future. The desire to start a family battled with the fear of not being able to fulfill her dream of becoming a mother.

Emma's eyes softened. "That's a beautiful dream, Ace. You'd make a wonderful mother."

Ace felt a lump form in her throat. "Thank you. But sometimes, I worry. My biological clock is ticking louder and louder. The idea of having a baby in my thirties feels daunting, with all the potential risks."

Misty chuckled, trying to lighten the mood. "Well, the first step is finding a husband, right?"

Ace laughed, though her heart felt heavy. "That's true, Misty. I'm not trying to rush anything between me and Shane. It just feels right between us. Things are progressing well."

Misty clapped her hands together, her eyes twinkling with excitement. "Well, well, well…tell us everything."

Ace's cheeks burned as she recounted the journey she and Shane had been on. Recently, they'd met a few more times for dinners and walks on the beach. They cared about each other but were taking things slow. "It's been incredible. He shows me so much care and affection, especially during times when I've needed it the most. He's been there for me in ways I never expected. I never really had that before."

Emma leaned in, her expression sincere. "I'm so happy for you. It sounds like Shane really cares about you."

"He does," Ace agreed, warmth spreading through her chest, but the weight of her doubts lingered. "And I care about him, too. I'm looking forward to what the future holds for us."

Misty's eyes sparkled with mischief. "Well, it sounds like you might be halfway to that family you've been dreaming about."

Ace laughed, shaking her head, but it felt forced. "One step at a time, Misty. But yes, I'm hopeful." Could she have everything she wanted with Shane?

Emma reached across the table, squeezing her hand. "You deserve all the happiness in the world. And if anyone can balance love and life, it's you."

But as they talked, Ace couldn't shake the disheartening memory of her conversation with Shane about kids. She recalled how his focus was more on the hotel and his siblings. The realization had hit her hard; while she yearned to be a mother, he seemed set on a different path. She'd love being an aunt to Shane's nieces and nephews, but she wasn't ready to let go of the dream of being a mom herself.

Would their dreams ever align?

The three women chatted for another hour before they settled the bill and parted ways outside the café, promising to meet again soon. Ace waved goodbye, but a part of her still felt heavy with uncertainty. She hoped that in the coming days, she'd find clarity, not only in her feelings for Shane, but also in the future she so desperately wanted for herself.

# CHAPTER TWENTY-FIVE

ACE SAT ACROSS from Shane in the cozy warmth of her living room, the flicker of candlelight casting soft shadows on the walls. After confiding in Misty and Emma earlier that day, she decided she couldn't keep her feelings bottled up any longer. She'd invited him over for dinner and to talk.

"Shane," Ace began tentatively, her heart racing, "have you ever thought about having children?"

He leaned back in his chair, his expression thoughtful. "Honestly, being a father isn't on my radar. I've never really seen myself in that role. While I know I can find a balance, being a dad isn't my priority right now. Family is, though."

Ace felt a pang in her chest, but she pressed on. "I understand that. But I've always wanted to be a mom. It's been a dream of mine for as long as I can remember." She took a deep breath, trying to steady her nerves. "I know we've been getting closer, and I really care about you, Shane. But I need to know where you stand on this."

Shane shifted in his seat, the warmth in his eyes

replaced with surprise and uncertainty. "Ace, I—I really enjoy our time together, but my focus is on the hotel and my family. They need me, and I can't take on more responsibility right now."

The words hit her like a cold wave. Ace had expected some hesitation, maybe even a discussion about their future, but the finality in his tone felt like a door slamming shut. "So you're saying you don't see a future with kids? Not even down the line?"

He sighed and rubbed the back of his neck, frustration evident in his body language. "I'm just not in that place, Ace. I have enough on my plate already. I…" He hesitated. "It's taken me some time to realize I could be a good husband while running the hotel…but I can't even think about kids when I'm juggling everything else."

She looked down at her hands, the realization settling heavily in her heart. "I get it, I do." She understood what it took to open up your heart to someone. "But I'm worried about where this leaves us. I don't want to hold you back, but I also don't want to miss my chance at becoming a mom."

Shane's eyes softened, but the tension in his shoulders remained. "I care about you deeply. You mean a lot to me, but right now, my family and the hotel come first. Can't we just keep taking it slow and see where this goes?"

Ace swallowed hard, fighting back tears. "I don't want to pressure you, Shane. I just felt it was important to lay my cards on the table. I need to know if our visions for the future align at all."

He looked at her, his expression a mix of regret and determination. "Where is this coming from?" He looked lost for a moment. "Look, I appreciate your honesty, but I can't change how I feel or what my priorities are right now. But we don't need to decide all this right now..."

An uncomfortable silence fell over the room, and Ace's heart ached with the realization that despite their connection, they were standing at a crossroads. She had laid her feelings bare, and now she was left grappling with the uncertainty of what that meant for them.

In that moment, she understood that while Shane was an incredible man who brought joy into her life, their paths might not be destined to converge. And as much as it hurt, she knew she had to consider her own dreams of motherhood—dreams that felt like they were slipping further away with each passing day.

Shane reached out, taking her hand in his. "I hope you understand."

"Of course, I understand," Ace replied, though the words felt hollow.

After Shane left, Ace sat in silence, her mind racing. She knew this was the end of whatever had been blossoming between them. Why pour further into a relationship that couldn't give them both what they wanted? And with that realization came another: she couldn't continue working at the hotel. Being around Shane every day, knowing that their paths were so fundamentally different, would be too painful. She couldn't bear the thought of watching him move on while she remained stuck, her dreams unfulfilled. She'd kept her promise to Angus Jr. by supporting Shane. But the possibility of missing her chance to be a mother…she wasn't willing to give up on that just yet.

With a heavy heart, Ace made her decision. She sat down at her computer and composed a resignation letter. Her fingers trembled as she typed out the words, each keystroke echoing her sorrow. She kept it brief and professional, stating her intention to resign from her position effective immediately.

She thanked Shane and the rest of the team for the opportunities she had been given, but she didn't elaborate on her reasons for leaving. She knew it was better this way.

After sending the email, Ace felt a wave of sadness wash over her. She then sent a text to Misty to let her know that she was going away for the weekend.

Ace went to her bedroom and began packing a small weekender bag. She needed to get away, to clear her head and find some semblance of peace. She packed only the essentials, knowing that she wouldn't be gone for long. With her bag in hand, Ace walked out the house to her SUV and climbed inside.

The island was quiet, the usual bustle of tourists and locals having died down for the evening.

Ace drove away from the island, her mind a whirlwind of thoughts and emotions as she crossed the bridge to the mainland. She had always been strong and independent, but this felt different— like she was losing something precious, something she had hoped would be a lasting part of her life.

SUNDAY MORNING, Shane stared at his computer screen, disbelieving as he read and reread the email from Ace.

Her resignation was effective immediately, with no explanation. He felt blindsided, the words blurring together as he tried to make sense of them.

His first instinct was to call her, his fingers fumbling as he dialed her number. It rang and rang, but there was no answer.

Each attempt brought a growing sense of panic and confusion.

He couldn't just sit here. He needed to see her, to understand what had driven her to this sudden decision. Grabbing his keys, Shane rushed out of the hotel, his mind racing.

The drive to Ace's place felt longer than usual, his thoughts a whirlwind of worry and frustration.

When he pulled up and saw her car was gone, his heart sank. He got out and knocked on the door, peering through the windows, but there was no sign of her.

Standing there on her doorstep, Shane felt utterly lost. He replayed last night in his head, searching for any sign that something was wrong. They had shared a lovely dinner, talked about their days, and enjoyed each other's company. Things got tense when children had come up, but surely tough topics were bound to arise as they started dating? These were things they'd take time to figure out. When he'd left for home, everything had seemed fine.

*What changed?*

Shane knew Ace had been through a difficult marriage and a painful divorce. Maybe this was her way of coping—running away when things got too real. He tried calling her again, but it went straight to voicemail.

He left a message, his voice thick with concern. "Ace, it's Shane. Please call me back when you get this. I'm worried about you."

He sat in his car for a moment, staring at his phone, willing it to ring. But the silence was deafening.

His mind raced through possibilities. Had she changed her mind about their relationship? He knew she had scars from her past, fears that might make her want to flee. But Shane had thought they were making progress, building something real.

His thoughts drifted back to the dinner they had shared. He could still see her sitting across from him, the flickering candlelight casting a warm glow on her face. They had laughed, talked about their future—how they could balance their work at the hotel with their growing relationship. He had felt so hopeful, so certain that they could make it work.

Shane had always prided himself on being able to handle any challenge that came his way, but this—this was different. This was Ace, the woman he was falling for, slipping through his fingers.

Unable to just sit there, Shane decided to drive around the island, hoping to spot her car, to find some clue as to where she might have gone.

As he drove, he thought about all the conversations they'd shared, the moments of vulnerability and connection. Shane remembered how she'd confided in him about her fears, her dreams of being a mother. He had thought they were on the same page about taking things slow, but now he realized he'd been wrong.

He pulled over by the beach, one of his favorite spots.

After getting out of the car, he walked down to the shoreline, the sound of the waves crashing against the rocks soothing yet somehow mocking him with their indifference.

Shane sat down on the sand and stared out at the horizon.

The island had always been his sanctuary, a place where he felt in control. But now, it felt like a labyrinth, with Ace lost somewhere in its twists and turns.

She wanted a family—a life that included children. He had thought they could build something together, but with her dreams of motherhood and his focus on the hotel and his family, he wondered if their paths were meant to cross in this way.

He took a deep breath, trying to steady his racing heart. Shane knew he had to find her, talk to her, make her understand that he was here for her, no matter what. But more than that, he needed to understand what had driven her away. He couldn't lose her, not like this.

As he sat there, Shane made a silent vow. He would find Ace, he would listen to her, and he would do whatever it took to make things right. But if Ace truly wanted children anytime soon, could he be the man she needed? Could he give her the future she dreamed of? And if not, was he willing to risk losing the only person who made him feel this alive?

ACE HAD CHECKED INTO a small bed-and-breakfast just outside of Savannah, Georgia. The warmth and coziness of the place offered little comfort.

She'd spent the last two days exploring the town, trying to distract herself from the pain of her last conversation with Shane. She visited cafés, walked through parks, and spent hours sitting by the river, watching the world go by.

But no matter what she did, the thoughts of him and what could have been haunted her.

Ace replayed their conversation over and over in her mind, wondering if there was something she could have said or done differently. She missed him terribly, missed the way he made her feel, the way he looked at her with such warmth and affection.

In the quiet moments, Ace allowed herself to grieve. She cried for the future she had envisioned with him, for the love she had lost, and for the dreams that now seemed so far out of reach. But she also began to heal. She realized that while this chapter of her life was closing, a new one was just beginning. She didn't know what the future held, but she knew she had the strength to face it. Her phone buzzed, startling Ace from her spot on a bench near the river.

She glanced at the screen and saw Emma's name flashing.

Taking a deep breath, she answered, "Hello?"

"Ace, where are you?" Emma's voice was filled with concern. "Shane is worried sick about you."

Ace felt a lump form in her throat, and tears welled up in her eyes. She took a moment to steady herself before responding. "I resigned from the hotel, Emma. I couldn't stay there anymore."

"What? Why?" Emma's confusion was palpable. "You were so happy working there. What happened?"

Ace bit her lip, trying to hold back the tears. "It's Shane," she said, her voice trembling. "We had a conversation about parenthood, and he told me that being a father isn't on his radar. Emma, I want to be a mother more than anything. I can't give up on that dream."

Emma was silent for a moment. "Oh, Ace," she finally said softly. "I'm so sorry. I didn't know."

"I love him, Emma," Ace continued, her tears now flowing freely. The words struck her and she felt them deeply. She did love him. "But I can't stay at the hotel, working with him every day, knowing that our futures are so different. It would be too painful."

Emma sighed, her empathy clear through the phone. "I understand. But you need to talk to him, Ace. You can't just disappear like this. Shane deserves to know how you feel."

"I know," she admitted, wiping her eyes. It wasn't like her to leave without talking things through, but it was all too much. Falling for him so hard and so fast, then realizing they couldn't be together. "But I couldn't face him. Not after realizing that we want different things. It hurts too much."

"One thing I've learned from the Worthington family is that running away won't solve anything," Emma said gently. "You both need to have an honest conversation. Maybe there's a way to work through this together. You owe it to yourself and to Shane to at least try."

Ace nodded, even though Emma couldn't see

her. "You're right," she said quietly. "I owe him that much."

"Good," Emma replied. "Now, please come back to the island. Let's sort this out together. You have people who care about you, Ace. You don't have to go through this alone."

She took a deep breath, feeling a flicker of hope. "Okay. I'll come back. But I need some time to think first. Please just tell Shane that I'm fine."

"I will," Emma said. "Just promise me you won't shut us out."

"I promise," Ace said, her voice steadier. "I appreciate you calling."

"Of course," she said warmly. "Don't give up on Shane just yet."

After hanging up, Ace sat in silence, reflecting on Emma's words. She knew she couldn't avoid Shane forever, and Emma was right—they needed to have an honest conversation. Although she held no glimmer of hope that they would be able to navigate their differences.

After returning to her room, Ace packed her bag slowly, her mind racing with thoughts of Shane and the life she dreamed of. Whatever happened next, she would face it with courage and an open heart.

# CHAPTER TWENTY-SIX

ACE SAT ON the porch of her cozy cottage. She loved this place; it was her sanctuary, her escape from the chaos that life sometimes threw her way. But tonight, even the peaceful scenery couldn't calm the turmoil in her heart.

Her heart skipped a beat when she heard a car approaching.

Shane had texted earlier, asking if they could talk, and she'd invited him to drop by. She rose, brushing off her jeans when he got out of the vehicle.

He stood there, looking more uncertain than she had ever seen him. His usual confident demeanor was replaced by a vulnerability that made her heart ache. He held a bouquet of wildflowers, their bright colors a stark contrast to the worry etched on his face.

"Hi," he said softly, offering her the flowers.

She took them, a small smile tugging at her lips. "Hi. C'mon in."

They moved into house, settling in the living room, the silence between them heavy.

Ace arranged the flowers in a vase, trying to steady her nerves. Finally, she turned to face him, crossing her arms over her chest, suddenly feeling defensive.

"Ace," Shane began, his voice filled with emotion. "I need to explain. When we talked about children, I didn't mean to give you the impression that I never wanted any."

She frowned. "So what did you mean?"

He took a deep breath. "I want a family someday. But right now, with everything happening at the hotel, I'm stretched thin. I need to focus on stabilizing things there. It's not that I don't want kids, it's just…timing."

Ace felt a tiny flicker of hope as she looked across the room at Shane, but it was quickly overshadowed by her own concerns. "I understand that the hotel is important, but so is my dream of becoming a mother. I'm already in my thirties. I don't want to wait too long."

She took a deep breath, gathering her thoughts as she prepared to reveal the truth that weighed on her heart. "I have polycystic ovary syndrome—PCOS for short. It's a condition that affects my hormones and my ovaries and makes it difficult to get pregnant. My doctor told me that because of my age and my health, I might need fertility treatments if I want to have a baby."

Ace watched as Shane's brow furrowed in concern, and she knew she had to keep going. "Every day, I think about what it would mean to be a mom. I've always dreamed of having children. I can picture it—tiny feet running around, the sound of laughter echoing through the house. But with PCOS, I know that time isn't on my side, and I can't help but feel this pressure to start a family sooner rather than later."

The urgency in her words increased as she continued. "I don't want to risk losing the opportunity to become a mom because we're caught up in the hotel and all the responsibilities here. What if I wait too long, and then it's too late? What if I can't ever conceive?"

Ace studied Shane's face for any sign of understanding, searching for a glimmer of hope that he might share her vision. Varying emotions crossed his face as he took in the news—surprise, concern, and caring. "I get that you're focused on the hotel and your siblings," she pressed on, "but this is my life, too. I don't want to keep waiting and end up in a situation where it's too late for both of us. I want to build a life with you, but I need to know if you're on the same page. Can we make this work?"

The silence between them felt heavy, and Ace's heart raced as she waited for his response. Would he see her not just as a woman caught up in her dreams, but as someone who was ready to fight for a future that included him?

Shane's expression softened as he reached out and took her hands gently in his own. "Honestly, I haven't really considered it before, but I'm starting to realize that we can't just assume that conception will be easy when we're ready. We can talk about this more in depth, make plans, and see how things go with the hotel over the next year." He paused before continuing. "I don't want to lose you, and I didn't realize how much this dream meant to you. But I want to make all your dreams come true, because I'm falling in love with you. And your dreams are my dreams now, too. You'll make a wonderful mother…and with you by my side, fatherhood would be an adventure."

A rush of warmth spread through her as his words sank in. It wasn't just a compromise; it felt like a promise—a willingness to build a future that included both their dreams. Ace nodded, her heart racing with hope. "You really mean that?"

"Absolutely," Shane replied, squeezing her hands gently. "I want to know more about your condition. I'll be there for you every step of the way."

"What if it turns out that I can't get pregnant?"

"Then I'm open to adoption," he responded.

The weight on Ace's chest began to lift as she smiled through her tears. She felt a sense of possibility blooming between them, a shared vision of the future that embraced both their aspirations. It was the beginning of something beautiful.

She leaned in, resting her forehead against his.

"I never thought I'd ever say these words again, but I love you."

He wrapped his arms around her, pulling her close. "I love you, too."

As they stood there, wrapped in each other's embrace, Ace felt a sense of peace. They had taken a step forward, toward a future that was bright and filled with promise. And together, they would make that future a reality.

# EPILOGUE

*Eight months later*

SHANE STOOD IN the center of the living room in his new town house. He glanced around, making sure everything was perfect.

He moved to the dining room.

The table was elegantly set for two, adorned with flickering candles and a bouquet of Ace's favorite flowers—white lilies and roses.

The aroma of a gourmet dinner wafted through the air, mingling with the faint strains of soft jazz playing in the background. Everything was perfect, just as he had envisioned.

He took a deep breath, trying to steady his racing heart.

Tonight was the night.

After weeks of confusion and soul-searching, he was ready to take the next step between him and Ace. He wanted to show her just how much she meant to him, how deeply he loved her. He reached into his pocket, feeling the smooth surface of the ring box, and took another calming breath.

The sound of the door opening pulled him from his thoughts.

Ace walked into the foyer, her eyes widening in surprise as she took in the romantic setting.

She was stunning, her beauty taking his breath away, as always. Her dark hair, now free of braids, fell in soft waves around her shoulders.

"Shane, what's all this?" she asked, a smile playing on her lips.

He walked over to her, taking her hand and leading her to the table. "I wanted to do something special for you," he said softly. "To remind you of how much I love you."

Ace's eyes softened, and she squeezed his hand. "It's beautiful. You're so sweet."

They sat down to eat.

Shane watched Ace, memorizing every detail of her face, every nuance of her expressions. He loved the way she threw her head back when she laughed, the way her eyes lit up when she talked about something she was passionate about. He loved everything about her.

Dinner was a symphony of flavors, each course meticulously prepared to cater to Ace's tastes.

Shane had arranged for some of her favorite dishes from a local restaurant. They had seared scallops for an appetizer, a main course of tender filet mignon accompanied by truffle mashed potatoes, and Kenyon's decadent chocolate-lava cake for dessert.

As he savored each bite, their conversation drifted effortlessly from topic to topic, punctuated by shared glances and soft laughter.

As they finished their dessert, Shane felt the nervous anticipation build up again. He reached across the table, taking both of her hands in his. Ace looked at him, her expression curious and a bit concerned.

"Acc," he began, his voice steady despite the whirlwind of emotions inside him. "This past year has been filled with a lot of changes. Losing my dad...trying to get the hotel back in the black... I couldn't have gotten through any of this without you."

He stood up, moving around the table to kneel in front of her.

Ace's eyes widened, her breath audibly catching in her throat.

"I love you more than anything in this world," Shane continued, his chest filling with emotion. "You are my everything, and I can't imagine my life without you. I know we've talked about the future, and I want you to know that I want that future with you. I want us to build a life together, to have a family, to share every moment."

He pulled the ring box from his pocket, then opened it to reveal a stunning diamond ring. The diamond, a brilliant solitaire, caught the light from the candles, casting tiny rainbows around the room.

She gasped, her hand flying to her mouth as tears filled her eyes.

"Ace, will you marry me?"

For a moment, there was silence. The world seemed to stand still as he waited for her answer, his heart pounding in his chest. Then, she nodded, a radiant smile breaking across her face.

"Yes, Shane," she whispered, her voice choked with emotion. "Yes, I will marry you."

Shane slipped the ring onto her finger, his own eyes misting over. He stood up, pulled her into his arms, and kissed her deeply.

The kiss was filled with all the love and passion he felt for her, a promise of a future together. One that involved a family of their own, which he wanted more the further he'd fallen for her. He loved her and couldn't imagine not having a baby together. Children who would grow up with a second home at the hotel, like he had.

Her lips were soft and warm against his, tasting faintly of the chocolate dessert, and the world melted away, leaving only the two of them in their perfect moment.

When they finally broke apart, Ace rested her forehead against his. "I love you, Shane," she said softly. "I will love you forever."

They stood there for a long moment, holding each other. Everything was perfect. The misunderstandings, the doubts—they all faded away, leaving only the love they shared and the bright future that lay ahead.

Shane knew that there would be challenges, that life would have its ups and downs. But they would build the life they had always dreamed of, one filled with love, laughter, and endless possibilities. This was the beginning of a beautiful new chapter in their lives, one he couldn't wait to start.

* * * * *

*If you enjoyed this story by Jacquelin Thomas Don't miss other stories set on Polk Island Starting with*

**A Family for the Firefighter**

*Available now from Harlequin Heartwarming!*

*Discover more at Harlequin.com*